"Outside"

by Artyom Dereschuk

Yuri - a young man from a backwater Russian town - wakes to find the doors to his crumbling apartment complex welded shut... from the inside.

Before anyone can make sense of it, something not from this world kills a postman stranded on the other side of the door. And when the town's old evacuation sirens begin to blare, Yuri and everyone else in the building realize an impenetrable door could be the least of their worries. In fact, it could be the only thing standing between them and the otherworldly creatures roaming the now deserted streets outside...

Someone in the building knows what's going on. Now, it's up to Yuri to figure out who it is, what they know, how these events are linked to their town's past and how to lead everyone to safety - before the threats lurking outside find their way in.

# Preface

This book wouldn't have happened without the Reddit community of Nosleep.

The original story was a series of posts written from a nameless protagonist's point of view. A story of a young man who one day found the doors to his apartment complex welded shut while strange beasts started roaming the streets outside. A story which became so popular that it seemed only logical to adapt it into a novel format.

When I started writing this novel, I decided to change a few things, so that the old readers could find something new for themselves, and the new readers would enjoy the improved and expanded storyline. It seemed like a great idea on paper.

And, of course, it needed an internal conflict to be a "proper" novel. Internal conflict is, after all, the bread and butter of Russian literature.

But, as I started working on it, I quickly discovered that the old wisdom still held true: "if it ain't broke – don't fix it." As I was searching for ways to expand the plot and add new twists to it, I was getting lost in my own story – and not in a good way. I was starting to think that I would never finish.

It was only due to support of people who had read the original story that I've managed to finally finish it. Each time I saw a message inquiring as to how the novel was doing, I was finding myself back at my desk. So, to all of you who were asking when the book would be finished - thank you. This book wouldn't have happened without you – and now you know that I mean it in more than one way.

I also wanted to thank Galina - for being the only person who stayed with me from the beginning to the end.

# Table of Contents

CHAPTER 1 - The Cricket ............... 1
CHAPTER 2 - The End of an Era ............... 15
CHAPTER 3 - "Stay Where You Are" ............... 31
CHAPTER 4 - Means of Escape ............... 47
CHAPTER 5 - A New Path ............... 71
CHAPTER 6 - Voices ............... 94
CHAPTER 7 - No Sleep ............... 111
CHAPTER 8 - Militia ............... 129
CHAPTER 9 - Rumors ............... 145
CHAPTER 10 - Den ............... 161
CHAPTER 11 - Militia's Finest ............... 175
CHAPTER 12 - Attack ............... 197
CHAPTER 13 - Despair ............... 213
CHAPTER 14 - Believers ............... 228
CHAPTER 15 - A Breach ............... 258
CHAPTER 16 - Eye-to-eye ............... 278
CHAPTER 17 - Gone Girl ............... 293
CHAPTER 18 - The Plan ............... 320
CHAPTER 19 - The Welder ............... 338
CHAPTER 20 - Outside ............... 356

# CHAPTER 1 - The Cricket

The unknown, alien sound came from the forest, beneath my windows.

I woke up in the middle of the night, at that obscure hour where the position of the arrows on a clock doesn't matter - all you know is that it's not a time for you to be awake.

What was that noise that woke me up? I lifted my head from the pillow and tried to look around my room to figure out what it was that got me to open my eyes.

Nothing. Just silence and pitch-black darkness. Not even an echo. I seemed to have a faint memory of what it was, but I wasn't sure if it was a part of my dream or something that originated from the outside.

A distant howl of some animal.

Too sleepy to be concerned with that question for more than a moment, I put my head back on the pillow. Before my mind went blank, I faintly wondered what kind of animal it could have been - the more time passed, the more I was sure that the sound I recalled was unlike anything I'd ever heard. It was strange to even attribute a sound you don't recognize to an animal, yet I was confident that my estimate was correct. But before that thought went anywhere it was swept away by my sleepiness and I was sound asleep, completely forgetting about the entire ordeal.

\*\*\*

I woke up the second time when the alarm went off three times in a row: I had been abusing the "snooze" button too much. As per usual, when I opened my eyes, I was greeted with the familiar pattern of my room's wallpaper - bleak pink roses on the gray background. The flowers had lost their freshness and looked dreary, and perhaps their background had been crisp white in the past, but decades without refurbishing had drained the wallpaper's color palette.

I lazily got out of the creaky bed. The floor covered in linoleum was cold, sucking the heat out of my feet, and my big toe identified a familiar whale-shaped hole in it.

I stretched and headed for the bathroom.

You'd never be able to guess that a young man lived in my apartment. The furniture was older than me - perhaps even older than my parents, based on its design. Through the glass panels of the cupboards, I could see displays of china and rows of books which the previous owners bought just for how they looked and which I knew for sure no one had ever read. Both china and books had been a sign of prosperity and culture in the old days. Both of them were pointless on their own, but mandatory to keep up a façade of success for your guests.

The walls were covered in paintings that matched neither the surroundings nor each other, and in one corner there was a calendar for 2018 - complete with moon cycles for each day.

I couldn't bring myself to replace it, as despite its silliness it reminded me of the last owner of the apartment.

And the smell. The musty, earthy smell of old people. Cozy and familiar, like a pair of boots you've been wearing for the past year. It was everywhere. I got used to it and couldn't sense it anymore, but whenever I returned home after going somewhere for more than a week the scent would greet me again with newfound crispness.

I entered the bathroom - a small room where, between the bathtub and the sink, you barely had any place to stand. The toilet was in a separate, even smaller room. Perhaps the architects had believed that it was more practical that way and gave each other a pat on the back, but I believed such confining design to be a crime against the people. I had just enough space to do everything I needed to do in a bathroom—but not an inch more. The Soviet architects had calculated the living space with inhuman precision to make the building as cheap and affordable as was possible. An honorable goal with a questionable means of achieving it.

I lazily brushed my teeth and stepped outside. While passing through the corridor, I stopped for a second, listened to the sound coming from the guest room, and then shook my head.

The sound of white noise and the chirping of a cricket - interwoven, like milk and coffee in a cup of latte - were idly coming from the guest room. The same sound I'd been hearing for the last 7 months.

"Not today either" - I sighed and headed for the kitchen.

I put an old ceramic kettle with some unidentifiable flowers painted its side onto the stove, and a few minutes later it started whistling, letting me know that the water was boiling.

Perhaps it would be practical to microwave some food in the meantime, but I had conditioned myself to coffee so much that I just couldn't do even the most basic tasks until I had some. Only when I poured the boiling water into my cup did my brain ease up - like a junkie before taking his shot of heroin.

With a cup of coffee in my hand, I approached the window. It was already sealed shut with the duct tape in preparation for winter - an old Russian way of dealing with the cold when you don't have a double-glazed window. I pressed the loose end of the duct tape down to the window frame to put it back in place, grunting when it defiantly popped back up and then looked outside.

Forest. Trees of every size as far as the eye could see. I let out a sigh of relief at the sight of all that boundless nature.

I lived in a small and very old apartment complex on the far outskirts of a small town. Honestly, calling it an apartment complex was a stretch - it was only five stories high, no elevator, and it was built out of concrete panels all the way back in the sixties. It had no attic, so people who lived on the last floor constantly had to worry about rain ruining their ceiling. It had, however, extremely poor sound insulation due to the thin walls so you never felt home alone, and a basement which connected to a sewer system - which smelled horrible in spring.

In Russia, these kinds of buildings are called "Khruschyovka" - named after Khruschev, obviously. I understood the appeal of a low-cost, easy-to-construct building, but I was always confident that there wasn't a single soul in the entire country who'd miss them. In the fifty years since their construction, they should've been demolished and replaced with something better, something newer. As it was, the buildings had long since outlived their usefulness and were no more than a health hazard. Usually, only the old people lived there, since it was the house they received long ago and never moved out.

At least the view from my balcony on the third floor was great - it overlooked the forest, which technically was the border of our town, so no ugly grey boxes of buildings in sight. Just a boundless nature, which, as I had been told, stretched for thousands of kilometers in that direction. An entire ocean of dark wood that curved beyond the horizon.

In a way, I lived on a beach. Pretty sweet if you don't account for the things that sometimes wash ashore.

Even back then, looking at the forest felt like staring into the abyss—the abyss of civilization, the darkness beyond its edges. The greenery had that soothing effect on me, but I also couldn't fathom how much unexplored land was right outside my windows. People had always wondered about what dwelled in unexplored depths of the world's oceans, but few of them had wondered if something could hide in the shadows under tree branches.

There wasn't a day when I didn't want to sell the apartment and move out of town, or maybe even out of the country. But whenever I raised the topic with my mother - whom the apartment belonged to - she'd bulge her eyes at me. "As if someone's waiting for you there, Yuri" - was her most common reply.

She couldn't even fathom how I could reject the apartment that I'd basically received for free.

It once belonged to my grandparents. They received the apartment for free from the government long ago, when the town was founded in the sixties. The higher-ups of the Soviet Union, for whatever secretive reason they had in mind, needed this particular spot of Siberian wilderness conquered and populated, and were more than happy to give out the living space to anyone who'd agree to assist the state with that undertaking.

If I had to guess I'd wager that they'd chosen the location for the town based on how remote it was - deep enough within the biggest forest on the planet that no spy plane would be able to even find its way there. After all, it used to be one of those towns that weren't on any maps, a place that held the secrets so great they warranted the construction of the entire new community. Even its name – Novoyarsk[1], used to have a number assigned to it to signify that it was

---
[1] Roughly translates to "New Ravine"

not just another town, but a special facility closed to any outsiders: Novoyark-23.

With the fall of the USSR, however, thousands of people suddenly found out that the secrets their entire lives were built around were deemed a waste of subsidies by the new authorities, and ever since then the town slowly started fading out, with its secondary facilities not sufficient to maintain the town's reason to exist. People started fleeing the town, especially the younger generation, while the older generation remained behind.

My grandparents were among such people. I knew that many older people were bitter about the state of our town—with younger people leaving every day; it was hard to maintain the town's economy, which in turn prompted even more youngsters to leave. But my grandparents didn't care about that. They'd lived a good life, they'd built our town, and they saw it as somewhat symbolic that its time was running out just as they were getting old. They'd spent their last years trying to cultivate kindness in people, and I remembered that as a kid I liked spending my time with them.

Unfortunately, my grandfather had passed away five years ago. My grandma didn't stay around for too long after that, and passed away two years later. Since I was too young to inherit anything, the apartment was given to my custodian - my mother. Many of my relatives weren't pleased when they had seen the will, as they believed that since they were around for a longer time than me they had more rights to the apartment. But my mother didn't object to such a gift of fate and allowed me to move in once I turned eighteen - even though at that point the apartment was already mine, anyway.

Get an apartment at eighteen, get a job at a local radio shack a year later. Many people would kill to be in my position. Yet as I was thinking about the day ahead, about the leaking pipes in my toilet, about the 4-hour drive to the nearest town, I wasn't feeling very grateful for it.

They say gratitude is a perfect counter-measure to depression…

It seemed to be cold and windy outside: the wind was shaking the trees across my window, tearing off the yellow leaves. In a few more weeks, they'd all fall and rot, transforming the forest into a sea of dead grasping fingers, desperately reaching for the grey sky in a silent and pointless prayer for the sun. With that thought, my mood only got worse. I was not looking forward to the day ahead.

So, at first when I heard the sounds reaching my ear from the guestroom I thought that I was making it up. That it was actually my daydream getting all too real.

But then I listened and my eyes went wide. I was not imagining it. It was not wishful thinking.

The sounds of white noise and cricket singing had gone silent. Instead of it, I could hear a repeating buzzing sound - loud and obnoxious, meant to wake you up if you fell asleep on your post. Meant to warn you that in ten seconds, there was going to be a message, so you better get your pen ready and listen close.

The radio in the guest room was receiving a transmission - and I happened to be home just in time to hear it.

I knew the frequency it was set to by heart. I was sure that I'd be able to remember it even on my deathbed. 4625 kHz. The frequency of a local number station. The station which the military used to transmit encrypted messages. Codenamed "Cricket" for the sound it had been broadcasting for the past fifty years.

The last transmission was 7 months and five days ago, at 13:47. Just a usual set of numbers and letters, spelled by a monotone, bored voice. I didn't manage to crack the code they'd broadcasted - even if I managed to pinpoint the exact encryption method by using grandpa's numerous books on the topic, I'd still need to know the encryption key which only the people the transmission was meant for had. But it didn't matter to me: learning the government's secrets was not the end goal. It was about the thrill of discovery, about being on the right frequency at the right time. About reliving the good old times when me and grandpa were scanning the radio noise, teasing my childish imagination with images of the unknown.

And after 7 months of silence, the radio station came back to life. Only, where earlier it was whispering its secrets, now it was basically screaming. The buzzing sound was over -

sooner than usual, and somewhere, on a base hidden in the endless forest around our town, a man started speaking.

I threw the cup into the sink, heard it reproachfully crack and spill its caffeinated blood. I didn't care about it - I had to make it in time.

I burst into my guestroom and there it was - my grandpa's radio. A giant wooden box with dials yellowed from time and the chrome letters of its name losing their gloss.

In front of the radio lay an old notebook. Its pages had turned yellow thirty years ago, but aside from my recently started log of transmissions, its pages were clean. Just like the radio, it stood the test of time and succeeded.

I didn't catch the beginning of the transmission and was now kicking myself for lowering my guard. The buzzing noise I had heard before was a warning to the listeners that something was about to be transmitted, letting the receiving end prepare for the transmission. My only hope was that they'd repeat it one more time.

"...One! Seven! Eight! A-P-F! Four! Seven! Sunset-Sixty-Five! Zero-Zero-Zero!" - the man on the radio was shouting the numbers and letters into the mic. His voice, usually calm and withdrawn during the earlier transmissions, was now tense, almost on the verge of hysteria. He was shouting as if hoping that the sound waves of his voice would strengthen the radio wave, make it pick up the haste and break the speed of light, arriving at its destination before it even departed.

"Wait a sec!" - I desperately cried out to him as if he could hear me. With a trembling hand, I swung the journal open on a random page, not caring about the consistency of my notes, and started desperately looking for a pen. "One-Seven-Eight, A-P-F..." - I was whispering the cryptic code to myself, trying to remember it while I was looking for a pen, but the damned thing was nowhere to be found.

In desperation, I flung the drawer out of the table and onto the ground. Still no pen, but at least I spotted a pencil flying out of it along with other bits of grandpa's stuff. It was old, and its wood had black spots where it soaked in the oil decades ago. But the good thing about pencils was, as long as they were at least a few centimeters long, they could write.

I started scribbling, writing down the code the man kept spelling out for me. Half of my brain focused on writing down what I had already remembered, while the other half was trying to memorize what the man was saying. When I finally caught up to him without missing a single number or a letter, I let out an audible laugh.

"...Five! Three! S-H-G-T-U! Thirteen Hundred!" - he finished the code. I could hear someone shout something in the back, but I could not make out what was said.

"That's it, pizdets![2]" - the unusual sound of swearing on a government channel jolted through me like a lightning bolt and made me squeal with excitement.

"He said 'pizdets!'" - I whispered to myself, giggling like a preschooler who heard a swear in his favorite morning cartoon while his parents were still asleep, completely oblivious to their child's revelation.

I heard the sounds of ruckus in the background, and then the transmission was over.

I couldn't believe it, yet the sound, familiar to every Russian, was indeed coming out of my radio. The number station which usually transmitted only encrypted messages once a year was now broadcasting "Swan Lake" ballet by Tchaikovsky.

Most people from my generation wouldn't pick up on the significance of it if they hadn't heard about it from someone - mostly because we were born after the fall of the USSR. But everyone who'd lived through those times knew Tchaikovsky's creation as a harbinger of change and turmoil. Russian TV stations were airing "Swan Lake" as a subtle way to alert the people that the secretary of the USSR was dead - the only way Russian leaders left their post since the dawn of the country's history. The last time it had been used in 1991: when the USSR had collapsed, "Swan Lake" was the only thing on for three days in a row.

---

[2] Pizdets – a Russian swear word with many applications and meanings, the most popular one is "a very bad situation".

So, for everyone over thirty, that serene melody meant only one thing. "The end of an era."

I was not intimidated by the implication, though. On the contrary, I was beyond excited.

On late nights, I'd sometimes sit in grandpa's chair and open a sci-fi book - either Heinlein or Belyaev - and read it while listening to the monotone buzz of the radio, dreaming of catching a signal from open space or a passing UFO. Often my imagination would start to go wild - conspiracies, men in black, green men sending me the coordinates of their next landing site - and the author's written fantasy in my hands would take a backseat until my own daydreams would subside.

And now, after hundreds of hours, I had this.

It was unreal. It was my "WOW!" signal. And just like the original, it was just as cryptic.

At that moment, I didn't care what it was. The declaration of war, the warning of a nuclear holocaust, the countdown for a gamma-ray burst - such trivial, minuscule things didn't matter for me. At that moment I felt like some personal mission of mine was finally complete. I felt like my grandpa was proudly smiling at me from heaven, his blessings reaching me through radio waves. I did it. I finally managed to catch something noteworthy. Across these unseen waves, I finally spotted my Moby Dick.

When the initial rush of emotion passed, I sat down and tried to analyze what I had just heard. A military radio station just broadcast a worried, encrypted message. A message which I couldn't yet grasp, yet which made the broadcaster agitated enough that he lost track of his words. I doubted that it was part of the code. For a second, a living, breathing human had peeked through his strict military overcoat. And, after a moment of silence - the universal signal that every Russian could understand. Swan Lake. "We're done here."

I glanced at the clock to check when the message was received. 8:19 AM. I was late for work. I jumped to my feet and rushed for the exit.

# CHAPTER 2 - The End of an Era

I spent a brief minute putting on some clothes - whatever I had lying around - and two minutes looking for gloves and a scarf. The window panes were shaking under the wind's assault, and it would be wise to seek protection from it as I'll be waiting for my bus at a bus stop.

I hopped outside onto the stairwell, closed the door almost identical to the three other doors on the same floor - an iron sheet, covered in puce foam rubber for sound isolation, and rushed downstairs.

Coming down to the first floor, I prepared to hop down the last flight of stairs like usual but slowed down at the last second. There were people on the stairwell - lots of people. Old and scruffy, and with faces that bore a constant mark of dissatisfaction with everyone and everything. My neighbors.

They seemed to be more unhappy than usual - unhappy enough to be voicing their concerns. But everyone was talking at the same time, and I had a hard time figuring out what any of them were saying. All I could tell was that they were complaining about something.

Coming down to them, I realized why they were standing on the stairs - the rest of the space up to the very door was occupied with people. The air was hot and damp from their collective breathing, and I could also feel the heavy atmosphere that lingered there.

I knew that the majority of people who lived in my building were pensioners. Those who came to our town long ago and got stuck here once the town started withering away without the funds from Moscow.

Pensioners always seem to be going somewhere at the oddest hours. Sometimes the reason for it could be to buy groceries on the other side of town where they cost a ruble less, and sometimes, as I suspected, it was to escape the walls of their home. I wouldn't mind it in the slightest if it didn't mean that every bus wasn't filled to the brim with them. Since I was raised to respect my elders, that meant that they always denied me my sitting place. It was at those early hours when I'd look at a seventy-year old woman and start to wonder where she was taking that enormous bag of hers at 7 AM, and whether there really was a good reason for it or if she was just doing it all on autopilot.

So, I wasn't surprised to see so many of them in the morning - unlike me, most of the old people were early birds. What I was surprised about, however, was that they had gathered in one place - the bottom of the stairwell, of all places. Was this some tenants' meeting that I was not informed about? Did the town hall raise the cost of utilities again and they had gathered to vent about it?

I decided not to ask any questions. It was clear that they were already worked up. Why talk to them and face the risk of becoming a scapegoat for their ire?

The tenants didn't like me and were always suspicious of me. I understood that it was not personal. That they were distrustful towards me because after the fall of the USSR, when the country was in disarray, young men like me preyed on the weak like them. That their paranoia that I was after their measly pension check and an outdated TV was a natural state of mind for them. But there was a limit toward how much hostility I was willing to tolerate. And the best way to avoid it was to pretend that it was not there.

I slipped past one person, then another. Mentally congratulated myself for not touching them and alerting them to my presence. But things were getting more difficult fast. I asked someone's shoulder for a permission to pass, received no reply, and tried to gently push past it. The shoulder violently jerked me as I was trying to walk by, and from somewhere attached to it came a grunt of dissatisfaction.

The situation repeated again, and then one more time. Each time the grunts were getting more aggressive, and I was getting more annoyed.

Finally, on the fourth time, somebody voiced their displeasure. "What the hell are shoving me for? Do you need to get somewhere more than everyone here?" - the man in his sixties asked me when I pushed past him.

He growled it into my ear, and I almost lost my footing. I was still on the stairs, and my feet were on different steps. The man was a few steps above me, looming over me, which made me feel a bit uncomfortable. I didn't want to argue with someone who could send me tumbling down with one push.

"I'm late for my job, sir. Sorry for pushing you," - I explained to him.

That, however, didn't defuse the situation. Instead, I incited him even more.

"What job? Hello?" - the man aggressively inquired, bulging his eyes at me as if I was missing the most obvious thing in the world, and my politeness quickly ran dry.

"The one you don't have anymore," - I grunted. "Let me through, I can't be late because you all decided to have an alumni meeting here."

The man shook his head, smirked and gave a look to the man on his side that said - "look at this fantastic imbecile" - before looking back at me and pointing towards the door.

"The door is welded shut! You think you can get through that? Well, good luck," - he pointed towards it with his chin.

I shook my head. I heard him loud and clear, but I just couldn't process it.

"What?" - I muttered.

"I'm telling you, the door is locked! Somebody welded us shut in here!" - the man shouted at me. But I still couldn't understand what he was saying.

The door was welded shut? As in, the entrance to our apartment complex? Somebody would do that?

"But… why?" - I wondered aloud. I was asking no one in particular, just voicing my surprise, but the man thought that the question was aimed at him.

"How would I know?" - the man grunted. "They didn't leave a note with explanations. They did their dirty deed and left."

"And nobody saw or heard anything?" - I wondered.

"Heh! Young man, if we knew who did that we wouldn't be standing here. If I knew what asshole and from what apartment did that, I'd go straight to them and show them why messing with people is a bad idea."

I paused for a moment. Something about what he said made me tick. Then I realized what it was.

"You're thinking that it's someone from this block?" - I asked him.

"I don't think that, I know that. Mikitich from 25th had a look at those welding seams. It was welded from our side. He's a welder with experience, so if he says so it is so," - the man explained.

"And who the hell are you?" - some old woman aggressively asked me, all of a sudden. She was a full head lower than me, so when she grabbed and pulled my sleeve I had to try to maintain my balance. "I've never seen you here."

"I've lived here for the past year" - I explained to her, not hiding my irritation.

"Don't lie!" - she shouted into my face. I stayed silent. "Don't lie!" - she repeated after a short pause. "I've known everyone who ever lived here since '68! Is this some kind of prank you and your friends pulled? Why did you come here? To film the honest people in peril and upload it to your internets?" - she patted my chest, as if hoping to find a hidden camera on me. I forcefully yanked her hand away and locked my eyes with her, but deep within I wasn't feeling so confident.

I knew that she had seen me before. I knew that I had held the door for her at least two times in the past, getting only irritated glances in return.

Seeing that my help was not welcome, I decided not to do so on the third time, and she exploded into an angry rant as the door was closing in front of her. So, it could be that it wasn't that she didn't know who I was. It could be that she was just getting back at me for inconveniencing her in the past. Not from my lack of manners - I suspected that there was some deeper frustration underneath all that.

But it didn't matter at the time. She was aiming the crowd's frustration at me, giving it an easy target in the face of an outsider and an easy suspect. People didn't need her suspicions to be justified - they just needed to vent, to funnel their tempered-by-decades-of-hardship hate into someone, and I felt uneasy when I increasingly found myself under their judgmental gazes. Poking, drilling at me from every direction. Even if they wouldn't resort to violence, even if a cane to the back of my head wouldn't hurt that much if it was wielded by a weak from old age hand, I still felt like an ant under the magnifying glass. Like their gazes could set me on fire at any moment.

"Leave the kid alone!" - someone suddenly intervened. "I know the lad, he's Tamara's grandson. Helped with my bags more than once. He's good people" - a man in the back of the crowd said. I turned to him to express my gratitude, but all I saw was rows of scolding faces. The crowd denied me the opportunity to take a look at my savior.

The old woman gave me another skeptical look, grunted and turned around. There weren't any friends of hers behind her. It was just to rub into my face how unpleasant my presence was. I couldn't resist rolling my eyes.

"Okay, I've had enough! Open up!" - someone shouted from the stairwell. I heard buzzing of a doorbell, muffled by a door, and heavy thumps on the door - it seemed that just one thing wasn't enough. They needed this particular tenant's full attention immediately.

"What are you doing?" - someone wondered aloud.

"I have places to be, I can't stay here, alright? I'll ask these people to let me crawl out through their window," - the man explained while continuing to buzz and knock on the door. "Open up! We have an emergency here!"

"Mitya, the windows on the first floor are all grated, what are you thinking?" - somebody exclaimed. The man paused for a second, breathed out through his nose, and then headed upstairs.

"I'll go to the next stairwell then. I'll get there through the roof," - he shouted to the crowd below as he was leaving.

"Good riddance" - someone quietly said.

"So, what are we going to do?" - someone else asked the crowd. The answers started pouring in immediately. The elders seemingly forgot that they were in distress for a moment and were now eagerly trying to make up for a moment of silence.

"Call the police!"

"Call the firefighters!"

"Can somebody just pry this door open? I need to be somewhere, too..."

"Can you not push? The door won't open, stop pushing me against it!"

"Hello?" - we suddenly heard a male voice coming from the outside. "Anyone in there?"

"Postman..." - one of the women in front of the door sighed. "Petya, is that you?" - she asked through the door.

"Yes! Varvara, is that you? What's with the door?" - the voice from the other side of the door inquired.

"We're stuck here, Petya! Somebody broke the door. It won't open! Call the police or go get someone!" - she shouted.

There was a short pause as the man processed what he'd just heard. I didn't blame him. The whole thing felt surreal.

"I don't know about that, but I'll do my best!" - the man promised. "Oh, where to go?.. I think I'll..." - the man suddenly paused. Then, a few seconds later, the door suddenly shook. The man was trying to pry it open.

"Petya, what are you doing?" - the woman who had been talking to him earlier wondered. "You can't open it on your own."

The door shook again, and the postman said something. The entire stairwell went silent to listen to what he was saying, and I found myself straining my hearing together with everyone else.

In a sudden and complete silence, where I couldn't hear neither rustling of clothes nor anyone's breath, we all heard the postman's quiet words.

"Open this door, please. Open this door."

"Petya, we can't open it" - the woman patiently explained, but the door kept slightly shaking as the man was trying to open it.

"Please, open this door. If you all push it, maybe you can break it," - he quietly pleaded. It was clear he was trying to keep his voice down as much as he could. "Please. There's something out here."

"What's out there?" - Varvara asked again, but the postman just started yanking the door with more strength.

"Shhh. Please, keep your voice down. Just… please help me. Please! I can't outrun it, I can't..."

His last whispers were drowned out by a sound, a sound which alone spoke louder than a thousand words, that painted the full picture for everyone who'd heard it. In an instant, the panic and irrationality of the postman's actions became clear to us.

There was a low growl coming from outside. A deep, rumbling sound - unlike anything I'd ever heard, yet somehow so recognizable for what it was. I didn't know the animal it belonged to, but just from its pitch and volume I could tell - its lungs were at least five times the size of my own.

"Open it, please!" - postman loudly whispered. "Open it! Why won't you open it?"

"Come on, push the door!" - someone from the back of the crowd shouted. "Maybe the seams are weak!"

"We've tried that!" - someone answered from the door. "It's no use! Petya, run!"

"Come on, shove the door! Everyone, push!"

"Don't shove! There's no more space here!"

"Just push the door, don't complain!"

"Somebody call the police!"

"Let me out of here! I don't want to be near this cursed door!"

"I said don't push me! What are you, deaf or stupid?"

"Open this door, please... Don't shout, please, you're making it nervous, just open this door! Open it! Open!"

All the voices were silenced, pushed out of relevance by a loud roar coming from outside. Whatever it was, it seemed that our shouting had aggravated it. The sound's origin was very close - closer than it had been a few moments ago, when the creature was growling. With the roar being so clear it almost seemed as if it was right outside the door, as if the door didn't separate us. As if it couldn't keep it out.

"Open it!" - the postman screamed, his voice breaking through the roar, and the creature growled once more - it did not appreciate being interrupted and now wanted to punish the man for speaking out of line.

It rushed towards the door, each step announcing the creature's massive weight. The metal door that the old man on the outside couldn't get through rang like a gong when his skull collided with it. Everyone inside froze in place. The postman gasped and moaned, tried to say something - but then the door shook again when his body was slammed against it once more.

I heard the sound of tearing cloth, heard the flesh underneath being separated from the bone in the most crude, primal way, and the man gasped in pain. For some reason, he couldn't take a full breath to scream louder - broken ribs? A massive paw pushing him down into the ground?

The door shook again and again: the man's body seemed to be thrashed around like a rag doll, as if it was trying to get a better hold of him. The people standing closest to the door started pushing back at the crowd behind them. Someone screamed after a particularly loud strike.

"Can you see anything?"– I heard someone above me shout. The welded door had no windows next to it, but there was a window on the flight of stairs between the first and second floor facing that direction.

"I can't see a thing!"—someone above replied. "The concrete visor above the door obscures the view!"

Then the creature went silent: its barrage was over. The crowd stopped, froze in anticipation of what was coming next.

Bang! The final strike was louder than before. The force of the blow was such that, in defiance of common sense, the bones of the man's skull made a dent in hard steel. The loud, violent cracking sound, which couldn't be silenced even by the ringing of metal, indicated that the man didn't survive that.

Somebody screamed in fear again. The beast sniffed. I heard its footsteps, followed by a dragging sound.

It was at that moment that we heard them. The sirens. Old and rusty, they were coming back to life after decades of sleep to fulfill their purpose – to warn people of an incoming catastrophe.

The years of slumber did not do them any good – they started out sounding low, but with each second, as their mechanical voice chords were stretching and warming up, they were getting louder and higher, until the familiar sound that everyone had hoped to never hear in their lifetime was drowning out everything else.

The sirens were getting louder, and in the pauses between its pulses, I could hear that the town in the background was getting noisier. The quiet morning suddenly blew up with distant screams, shouts of panic and urgency. Bags full of most valuable things were falling to the ground and were abandoned there, and engines of multiple cars were starting and racing off on screeching tires without even properly warming up.

My neighbors were wordlessly soaking in what was going on. I knew they wanted to scream, to run along with the rest of the people, to escape from where they were – but the final screams of the postman were still ringing in our ears louder than any sirens.

"What the hell?" - I heard the man next to me whisper. His eyes were glued to a dent on the door. "What the hell are we supposed to do?"

Some people outside started screaming. We heard their cries of terror and pain as the unseen forces were preying on them. It was clear that the evacuation was not going smoothly. Perhaps the creature that attacked the postman was targeting them as well.

"My god"—the man that stood near the window whispered in terror. "What the hell are those things?"

"What is there?"—someone called out to him. "What do you see?"

"I... I don't know,"—he answered. "I don't know how to describe it."

"Step aside"—someone pushed him away from the window. I expected the new observer to tell us what it was that he was seeing there, but he remained just as silent as the man before.

"My god"—was all that he whispered before he, too, stepped away from the window. Stretching my neck out to catch a glimpse of him, I saw his face for a moment. The man was in utter shock. It was clear that we wouldn't get any concrete answers from him, either. Both of them simply didn't know how to describe what they'd experienced.

"For God's sake, kick that window out! Break the glass!" – someone from the crowd shouted. "What are you waiting for? We need to get out before it's too late!"

"It's no use – it has grates on it, too" – someone else from the crowd commented. "It's already too late. We'll have to wait for the rescue party."

After what seemed like five minutes, the commotion outside was gone. Everyone had left. We were left alone - probably the only people in the entire district, and maybe even the whole town. Standing together on the staircase in front of the welded door, which separated us from both salvation and our doom.

And when the sirens finally went silent, something in the distance called out to them in challenge. The creature was victoriously howling in the distance, announcing itself to be the sole ruler of the town.

The people started panicking. Our state suddenly became clear to us. In fear of challenging the creature, we ended up being left behind, being stuck, and everyone started panicking at once. The crowd started rushing in all directions—some wanted to get closer to the door, others wanted to get home as soon as possible. I had to grab the railing to avoid being trampled. I didn't approve of their panic, but I also didn't know what to do. Even though I maintained composure it was because I didn't know what to do, and I was listening to the crowd around me. Perhaps some of them had some valuable suggestions about what to do in such a situation?

But as I was listening to them, trying to get a hint or a direction from someone, I realized that I couldn't hear them, as only two sounds were playing out in my mind.

The first one was the howling of the beast. I realized that I had heard it before - back then, during the night. Back when it woke me up the first time at that obscure hour where you know that the position of the arrows on a clock doesn't matter - all you know is that it's not a time for you to be awake.

And the second sound was the one that I'd heard less than half an hour before. The sound that I was reminded of by the dreadful howling of sirens, the harbingers of hardships and catastrophe. The sound which, in a way, carried the same message as them.

The playful tune of Tchaikovsky's "Swan Lake" from the morning transmission. The melody that signaled the end of an era.

# CHAPTER 3 - "Stay Where You Are"

I entered my apartment and slammed the door behind me. I listened. Bickering old people outside, shouting, complaining, bartering with fate. Deciding what to do and where to go. Every fifth word was a "Hello!" - most of them rushed to the phones to call the police or their loved ones.

I took a deep breath and listened to what was on my mind.

Confusion. Conflict. Fear.

What was that thing outside? The only thing so big and strong could be a bear, yet it didn't sound like one. It didn't behave like one, either: I haven't heard of any bears pummeling their victims like that.

Besides, the postman didn't say: "there's a bear out here", he described it simply as…"something." Something he didn't have a word for. Save for his possible extreme short-sightedness, I didn't have any explanations for that.

Could it get inside? I doubted that. Despite its monstrous strength, it couldn't break through the metal door, and as someone had noted the windows on the first floor had grates on them - a simple counter-measure against the burglars which ended up turning our building into a fortress.

I felt a sudden rush of gratitude toward the mysterious welder who shut us all in. There is no doubt, he had made sure we were all stuck in here, but the creature showed up just as I was trying to leave the building. If I had been outside, perhaps it would be my skull cracking under its strikes and not the postman's. Could it be that it had been his intention to protect us all?

But then I remembered what that man who was trying to get out said - "I'll get to the next stairwell through the roof." I realized what he meant - there was a door to the roof at the top of every stairwell in the building, and thus we could exit through the next-door apartment block.

Did it mean that the creature could find its way inside our stairwell through the neighboring one? Of course, that was quite a route, and I doubted that an animal could navigate the building so well, but that wasn't out of the realm of possibility anymore. I looked outside through the peephole to see if the creature was already outside my door, but all I saw were the panicking pensioners, rushing up and down the stairs and actively discussing what had happened.

Had all the doors in our Khruschyovka been sealed the same way, or was it only ours? And if another door was open, what would be the best course of action? To make a break for it, try to outrun the thing in a race across the entire town toward the presumed evacuation point? Or to stay put inside and await rescue?

The latter option seemed more reasonable to me. The siren coincided with the beast's appearance, so it could mean that the crisis we were facing was not just a local event. Perhaps its appearance was just a harbinger of something greater, like the Beast from the Bible rising from the sea to signal the coming apocalypse. The sirens wouldn't be used to warn everyone about the danger that only our apartment complex on the outskirts of town was facing. Which meant that the authorities knew what was going on.

So, the reasonable thing to do was to stay where I was, warn the authorities that we were left behind, and wait for them to come to rescue us.

I slid down my door and looked around. I looked at the old walls. At the paintings that didn't match the wallpapers. At the old furniture that surrounded me. I elbowed the door behind me in frustration. Fate sure had a way to rub its intentions in your face.

When I first received my own place to live, I was ecstatic - to have your own place at 18 years old was amazing, and these old walls had borne witness to many parties I threw with my friends. But as time went on, I was slowly starting to realize that the apartment didn't come for free, after all. It came with a dangerous curse, and I first realized what it was when I caught myself thinking about tearing down the hate inducing grey wallpapers to replace them with something else.

The apartment was an anchor. A cozy harbor that protected me from the hardships of the outside world, but at the same time corroded my hull, covered my engines with rust. Sure, I was starting to call it home, but at the same time, I knew that my attachment to it would not bring me anything good. I knew that if I started sinking money into refurbishing the place and give into that desire to sell the moth-eaten sofa in the guestroom and replace it with that newer one I saw on Avito[3], if I focused on making a better place to live instead of setting my gaze on getting out of town for good, then in some ten years I'd be left here forever. I'd marry some neighboring girl - not out of love, but because there wouldn't be many other options, and, perhaps, out of a hurry to secure her before she chose some tractor driver instead of me, and these walls would once again be filled with the laughter of children - children I wouldn't be able to leave anything save for this old decrepit home. And maybe a few bruises if by that time I had accumulated enough misery to share with them.

I feared becoming the same thing as my neighbors. Old, bitter, and forsaken people, living out their days in a town which would eventually, once again, disappear from the maps.

And now that apartment wasn't just an anchor. It became my prison. That entire building, that ship in my quiet harbor - it sank down, leaving its crew stranded.

My heartbeat was picking up the pace, not letting my brain slow down and focus. I squeezed my fists and held my breath. I kept holding it until I started seeing dark spots in front of my eyes. Until my panicking mind didn't have enough strength to keep struggling.

---

[3] Avito – a popular Russian website with sections devoted to general goods for sale, jobs, real estate, personals, cars for sale, and services.

"It is temporary," - I told myself. "Once this is over, I'll tell my mother that I don't want to live here anymore and that I want to move out of town. I'll tell her that it left me shaken and traumatized. Something along those lines. I just need to endure for now."

That was a lie, I knew that. I had always been too much of a wuss to stand up to her. Had that not been the case I would have already been studying in some University in Moscow or Saint Petersburg - not rotting away in this town.

But even though it was a lie, it gave me strength. I clung to it, clung to the silver lining I'd found in that grey haze of the situation around me. I wanted to believe that I could use the situation to further my own goals. To finally get my shot at freedom.

I got up to my feet and listened again. A new sound was humming in the background. The sound of rushing water.

"They're filling their bathtubs with water" - I realized. After all, we didn't know for how long we'd be stranded and whether the water was going to be supplied. At that moment I couldn't help but feel some sort of respect towards these people, bubbling up from within me. The moment things started going south, they started preparing for the worst. It was perhaps this kind of experience for which the elders had been valued since the dawn of time, where a minute knowledge could save the entire tribe.

Of course, nothing less could be expected of them. They had survived through the Soviet Union and the tumultuous times after its fall. They may have not looked the part, but they were the ultimate survivors.

I headed for the bathroom and opened the valve so that it could join the quiet choir of its brethren. The water pressure was weaker than usual, but I was sure that it was because everyone lit up with the same idea to fill the bathtub. As if the entire building was having a bath day.

I stepped back and took a look. The water kept coming. I congratulated myself on successfully doing something.

"What next?" - I wondered to myself. "I have to do something else. What are you supposed to do in such cases?"

I remembered the sound of people talking on the phone and nodded. The police. You call the police once things go south. That was the appropriate reaction of civilized people.

I knew that at this point it was pointless. At this point, the phone of the local police station was probably bursting from calls of seventy-nine other tenants of our building, and who knew how many more from other parts of town. At this point, they already had the perfect picture of what was going on at our end of town, complete with a thousand details that may have been unnecessary.

They probably weren't even in town anymore. Those sirens were meant for the entire town, police included.

But even with that in mind, I still wanted to give them a call. I just wanted to have a first-hand account of what they would say in case they were still there to get my call and hear me say: "Hello, someone welded the doors to my building shut and there's a monster outside that kills people."

My curiosity, which had already been teased by the morning transmission, was pushing me to learn more - even the most unimportant details.

I pulled out my phone and raised an eyebrow in surprise when I looked at the screen: there was no signal.

I guess I had to use the landline.

I walked up to the old rotary phone mounted on a shelf near the main door, picked it up, and listened. The long humming sound of the dial was in there. The phones were still working.

I dialed 02[4] on the rotary disk and listened.

I expected the silence to be followed by short beeping sounds, but instead, I heard a long beep. Despite the insane number of people trying to reach out to the police, I was the one who cut in the line and succeeded.

An unimaginable, downright impossible luck.

After another beep, someone picked up the phone. "Novoyarsk police department, I'm listening" - a calm voice inquired. There was no urgency, no panic in it. No usual swagger inherent to our police inspectors. Just a quiet, dutiful expectation.

---

[4] An emergency phone number of the Russian police

I was so taken aback by that, that at first, I thought the siren was some sort of mistake, and we all foolishly misunderstood something, blowing a chain of random events out of proportion. The voice didn't sound like its owner was under any stress. Which would be weird even under the normal circumstances. There wasn't anything our local police hated more than being bothered by phone calls.

Then I heard it. Dozens of voices talking in the background on the other side of the line. Calm and monotone, they were colliding with each other and against the spacious walls they resided in, humming at the frequency of a bee nest.

I tried to remember how big our police department was.

Clearing my throat, I started. "Hello, I'm calling from Krayevaya Street" - I started talking, carefully picking my words. "Someone has welded our doors shut, and we're stuck here, we can't evacuate with everyone else. And…" - I paused, trying to come up with a better way to describe what I'd heard. Suddenly it was much harder to put it into words than I'd expected. "There is something lurking outside on the streets, so we can't leave" - I mumbled under my breath. "Please send someone in. There are a lot of elders here" - I said, faking concern.

Once I finished talking he stayed silent for a few seconds. I expected the man to burst into anger, to tell me that he had no time for my pranks, but all I heard was the pitter-patter of a keyboard as he was typing something in.

"Have you seen it?" - he demanded to know with a sudden strictness in his voice once he finished typing. I was taken aback by his question: out of everything I'd told him that would be the last thing I expected him to verify.

"No, but I..."

I heard a loud tap of a keyboard key - so loud and definitive it stopped me from talking. As if the man put a stamp on something or checked a box.

"Stay where you are, the situation is under control," - he coldly instructed me and hung up.

I looked at the phone, as if hoping to see a note with further explanations crawl out of it, but the only thing coming out of it were short beeps.

The weird phone conversation defied all of my expectations. I had had a faint hope of getting answers - reading our local papers I knew that our police was police in name only. What I hadn't expected was getting more questions.

Somehow, even though the conversation turned out to be just as useless, it didn't feel like I had a conversation with our town's finest. The commanding, indifferent tone, their lack of surprise when I described our situation, the strange question…

The more I thought about it, the more I came to the conclusion that I never reached our police department. That the man on the other side of the line was from a different line of duty altogether.

I then dialed my mother – she lived on the other side of town, not far from the road leading out of it. I was calling to make sure that no one would pick up the phone, that she had evacuated, but instead I heard only short beeps. The line wasn't working.

She was probably also trying to reach out to me, too, I realized. Also, desperately trying to reach out to her only child, her only future crutch. The only one who, according to her, would be bringing her a glass of water when she'd turn old.

I quickly dialed my relatives who lived out of town. The result didn't change - short beeps and nothing else. The mysterious police department was the only place I could reach.

Seeing as I had exhausted all possibilities, I hung up the phone and headed for the kitchen - I needed to make sure that I had enough food.

Luckily, I had picked up some groceries the day before - not a lot, but better than nothing. Perishable foods would have to go first - that included things like eggs, bread, and milk. After that, if I was still locked up, I'd have to switch to potatoes and rice.

While in the kitchen, I searched through my bottom drawers until I found what I was looking for. A hatchet for meat. It wasn't very big and impressive and remembering the postman's final hours I doubted it would help me against the beast lurking outside. But feeling it rest in my hand, feeling the weight of its steel and carefully thumbing its blade, I felt a bit calmer. The hatchet was not for self-defense as much as it was for making me feel in control.

I thought about doing a quick check online - perhaps I'd see something on the news that would shed some light on what was going on? But when I turned on my old PC, I immediately noticed that there was no Wi-Fi signal. Restarting the router did nothing - just like the landline, the internet didn't work.

Which meant that my only contact with the outside world was my radio. At that moment, I thought that I was probably the only person in the entire town who had that kind of power.

Seeing as there was nothing else I could do, I went toward the guest room, where my radio was. Perhaps I'd be able to filter some news out of the radio noise.

The radio wasn't playing "Swan Lake" anymore - the transmission was over, and not even the usual song of the cricket was there - for the first time in many years. The unusual silence made me a bit anxious: I could understand the internet and the landline not working, but if even the numbering station went silent, then things really were serious. I checked the frequency to see if perhaps I had changed it before leaving, but it was correct.

"The Cricket" was dead. It had outlived its usefulness and was now abandoned. The object of my infatuation, the thing that I had been stalking for the past year, was now gone, and I had little doubt that it wouldn't return.

At least I was there during its final moment. Held its hand and recorded its will as it was sending out its final message to the world.

Of course, there were other numbering stations across Russia, but "The Cricket" was not only the closest one - it held a special place in my heart. It was the station that my grandpa used to introduce me to what became my hobby, and in doing so unveiled the mysterious world of cryptography, with its rich history, with stories from war times which could easily rival the epicness of any Ian Fleming novel, and, of course, with the numbering stations. The mysterious metal monoliths that were erected long before I was even born.

Numbering stations first appeared after WW2, and they are still used to this day. Their main purpose was to transmit encrypted data. Since there is no real way to "hide" radio transmissions the military decided that it was more practical to encrypt the message instead. And so, throughout the state, numerous stations sprang up, filling the broadcast with noises.

Normal people - pretty much anyone with a radio - could still listen to the numbering stations. It wasn't even prosecuted - the military was confident in their encryption abilities. Most of the time the stations were idly transmitting some dedicated sound - like the squeaking of a wheel or water dripping. And only sometimes, their monotone sound would break up for the actual transmission. It wasn't anything like in the movie, no convoluted coded phrases. More like a string of numbers and letters.

A completely dry, boring, and uncrackable code. Yet still, there were those who were intrigued by it.

Which was how the entire new hobby emerged. "Radio stalking." Something my grandpa had gotten me into. The hobby of patiently waiting for your game. Waiting for months for an opening that lasts only 30 seconds - and if you were lucky to score, to write it down, you can try to dissect it. Break its code if your mind is sharp enough to crack its purposefully uncrackable shell of encryption and feast on the secrets the mortals like you were not supposed to know. Eat the fruit of knowledge and get away with it.

Which was what I had been doing for the past year with my crude tools. An old radio and a notebook.

Many radio stalkers would scoff at me for being so backward, and some would tell me that digital radio, which could automatically record the message which could then be further analyzed on the PC, would be better and easier to use. In a way, I agreed with them - in the same way, smokers agree with non-smokers that their habit is deadly. But for me, it wasn't about the efficiency. It was about nostalgia. It was about being authentic, keeping it real.

For my humble needs, the machine did the trick. Yes, it was way past its prime, and yet just like in the old times, it could pick up the transmissions all the way from the other side of the globe. Grandpa said that in his youth, before he got into radio stalking, he was using it to get some help from Louis Armstrong to give his dates some class.

I sat down in front of the table and opened my logbook. The string of code, written in my shaky hand diagonally across the page, was staring at me. Teasing me with its secrets.

Without the encryption key, special equipment, and internet access I wouldn't be able to crack the code, I knew it. I could only dream of learning about what was hidden behind the encryption wall.

But even though its contents would forever remain a mystery, there were a few things I could piece together. First of all, the fact that the numbering station went silent after the transmission was leading me to think that the station had served its purpose - whatever that was. Second, I was confident that the transmission taking place some ten minutes before the sirens went off was not a coincidence. Perhaps it was even meant to alert the military higher-ups to sound the alarm, as well as everyone else beyond the town's borders.

Which, in turn, could mean only one thing: whatever had transpired that morning, the military was expecting it. Expecting it for decades, perhaps even since the town's inception… or perhaps, considering that the town's purpose was an enigma, even since before that.

The only mystery that I had absolutely no clue for was the identity and, even above that, the reasons of the unknown welder who had sealed us in. What could possibly drive someone to do such a thing, and why did it happen on the same day as two of the most important events in the town's history? Was he trying to protect us from the dangers outside or condemn us to a horrible hungry death? Did he know something about what was going to happen as well?

I saw no other explanation, and the fact that he held a secret I couldn't crack was driving me crazy.

I knew only one thing: he was probably still with us. There was no reason to weld the doors shut from within if he didn't intend to stay. Even if he planned to get out of the building after doing his deed, it would be more practical to seal the door from the outside. One of the nineteen other apartments was holding the answer to my questions - or at least some of them. I just needed to find out which door to knock on.

*"Well, eighteen other apartments"* - I thought, remembering my neighbors from the fifth floor. They definitely weren't the ones behind it - I simply knew them too well to know that for a fact.

And if I found him, if I learned why he did it, then... Perhaps I would get an insight into what was going on around us. It wasn't like it was some important information, but...

I looked at the radio, which was quietly buzzing with white noise next to me. "The Cricket" was still dead.

My previous hobby which I poured a year of effort into turned up to be a dead-end, so it wasn't like I had anything better to do anyway to spare some time.

The pensioners outside got quieter: the original shock of being stranded had passed, and their voices got a bit calmer. They seemed to be discussing something with each other.

It was no use staying alone, I decided. I got up and headed for the door outside.

It was time to pay a visit to Nikita and Natasha.

# CHAPTER 4 - Means of Escape

As I left my apartment an old man charged past me. He threw me an annoyed glance before proceeding downstairs. I shook my shoulders and headed upwards.

Almost all of the doors were open, and the tenants were outside their apartments, discussing the events. Every now and then someone would hurriedly leave their apartment to immediately enter the next one, where their voice would join the others that were already arguing about something in the kitchen.

Even though all means of communication were down the news about our situation was spreading fast, through the old-fashioned, sometimes unreliable but always inextinguishable method - the word of mouth. The old people were reliable gossipers, so in the twenty minutes, I'd spent inside my apartment they had alerted everyone in the building on every little detail they knew - and, as I was sure, a dozen details they had made up.

As I was passing the talking crowd, I slowed down to catch their conversation. Perhaps they'd learned something new about our situation.

"The phones are down" - the old man conspiratorially whispered, looking around. His hands were trembling to the beat of agitation in his voice. I noted a faint smell of alcohol coming from him. When his gaze passed through me I pretended I didn't even see him. I didn't want to make him think I was eavesdropping.

"I tried calling my brother who lives out of town but there was no connection" - he continued after a small pause. "I called the police but those shmucks are of no use. They just asked me what I'd seen and then told me to await rescue. Now they're not even picking up the phone."

"They must be already out of town by now" - the other man said with authority, rubbing his beard.

"I tell you, the police are not what they used to be when I was young. They only care about meeting the quota now, that's all - and they can't even do that. They don't care about people" - the first man said.

I remembered that the outdated practice of setting a quota of solved cases for the police was established back in the USSR, and to that day there was a rare chance of "winning a lottery" - by being blamed for a crime you haven't committed. But I decided to keep my thoughts to myself.

"Well, maybe it's not their job at this point" - the woman in her fifties defended them. "If the air horn sirens are being used it's not the police's job to protect the people anymore - it's up to the army then."

"Army isn't what it used to be, either" - the trembling man argued.

"Why did they sign the sirens, by the way?" - the second man wondered aloud.

"Isn't it obvious?" - the first man seemed to have all the answers. "The Americans must've attacked our town because of the strategic importance it holds! That thing outside that ate the postman - it was their mountain lion, I'll tell you that."

"Don't give me that" - the bearded man made a face like he ate something sour. "Our town *used* to be deemed important" - he reminded everyone present.

"Don't you think that what happens now could be because of...?" - the woman started before the man glared at her to shut up. When she raised an eyebrow in surprise he nodded at me. Immediately the three of them turned to me. The trembling man crossed his arms and puffed out his chest in a weak attempt at displaying strength.

"What apartment are you from?" - he inquired with suspicion.

I sighed and proceeded upstairs. It was clear that they wouldn't share their theories with me - no matter how outlandish they were, and I wasn't in the mood for another interrogation.

"Don't walk away when I'm talking to you!" - I heard the man shout at me, but he didn't follow me: his indignation could only push him so far.

I reached the fifth, final floor. Since there wasn't another flight of stairs leading upward, space there was less cramped. But there was still an opportunity to ascend – if you had the desire and the bravery to do so: going above the railings there was a metal ladder, leading to the hatch in the ceiling – an entrance to the roof. The ladder looked old and rickety, and for some reason the architects decided to put the hatch not near the wall but right above the stairwell, scaling it would require some serious bravery.

There was no one at the stairwell, but two doors were open, and I could hear the sound of a heated discussion coming from within. The tenants, usually secretive and protective of their property, must've decided that at that point the door would only serve as an obstacle on their way down, where they could pick up some new rumors.

The door I needed was the one on the right - it was the apartment where my only friends in the entire building, Nikita and Natasha, lived. A boyfriend and a girlfriend, both of them were around my age, and we'd spent a lot of hours playing board games or simply talking. In the situation I was facing, it was the best course of action to stick to my people. Climb up to the highest point of elevation and regroup with my tribe - which technically was exactly what I was doing.

I walked up to their door and rang the bell.

No one opened. I rang the bell again and again. Were they even home? Was I all alone, left to my own devices?

After two more minutes, I heard the sound of someone's feet lazily shuffling against the carpet, and I breathed out in relief. Somebody was home, after all. I wasn't alone.

Immediately I felt a poke of guilt that I was hoping some other familiar face was stranded in there with me, but when the door opened I forgot all about that.

It was Natasha who opened the door. She was wearing her improvised pajamas - an oversized t-shirt and a pair of boxers that looked male - and her hair was an unkempt mess. She could barely keep her eyes open and was stretching and yawning all the time.

"Were you sleeping?" - I wondered, genuinely surprised. I knew she and Nikita were sleepyheads, but I was surprised that they managed to sleep through even the literal end of the world.

"I went to bed very late today" - she explained.

"And you…didn't hear anything?" - I carefully asked her.

"Earplugs" - she explained, patting her left earlobe. I saw an orange piece of foam still sticking out of her ear above it. "I barely heard you ringing. Was it you earlier? I thought I heard someone ring the doorbell but I'm not sure if it was a dream or something."

"No" - I said. Her words confirmed my earlier suspicions about her: it seemed that not even the end of the world could wake her up.

"I see" - she yawned and stretched, lifting herself on her toes. A little bit more and I'd expect her to take off and float to the ceiling. "So why the early visit?" - she wondered, rubbing her eyes. "I thought you had work today."

I sighed and bit my lip. There she was, so carefree and chipper, so refreshed despite not having enough sleep. Probably the last blip of happiness on our town's misery radar. There was just no right way to break such news to her. I didn't have it in me to pull her out of her blissful ignorance.

But before I said anything, I realized that something was wrong. We were standing at her door for a full minute…Yet still, there were only two of us.

No one else joined us, no one else came out of the apartment to see what the early visit was about.

"Where's Nikita?" - I wondered.

"I don't know, what hour is it?" - she asked me.

"It's about nine in the morning, give or take" - I quickly said, wanting to get back to the topic. "So where is he? Is he inside?"

"He stayed at his friend's place. He'll come back later today. We wanted to go to the park to feed the ducks one last time before they left" - she explained, rubbing her eyes.

"You mean he's not here?" - I asked, raising my hand to my mouth in shock. Terror spilled through my guts. It felt like I swallowed a cup of ice - everything went numb.

"Yeah, but we agreed that he'd come to wake me up at noon" - she explained. "Why?" - she suddenly asked. It seemed that she finally recognized from my expression that something was wrong. "Did something happen?"

\*\*\*

Five minutes later, we were sitting in her kitchen - similar to mine, only you could tell that they took more care after it. No dirty plates in the kitchen sink, no towels clustered around. Everything was clean and tidy, and I knew if I opened one of the shelves all the cutlery would be organized.

"You can't be serious" - Natasha told me as she was holding the phone up to her ear. She was calling Nikita - again and again. The girl I saw five minutes ago was gone. That last blip of happiness I admired had gone silent.

"The phones aren't working, give it a rest" - I told her. "And neither does the landline."

"Damn it" - she whispered anxiously, carelessly throwing the phone onto the table. "Why would they do that? Don't they understand that people will want to know if their close ones are safe? What is it, 1986?" - she wondered aloud.

She was biting her thumbnail as she started pacing back and forth across the room - similar to a tiger in a cage I once saw in a zoo. Her gaze, cute and sleepy just some minutes ago, now had a razor-sharp focus in it.

"I'm not sure" - I answered her question. "Maybe they're trying to keep it all under the lid. Maybe they don't want the panic to spread."

"So they're hiding something" - she said, nodding her head in agreement. "Right. What, like a catastrophe of some sort? Like Chernobyl? Like Kyshtym[5]?"

I just shook my shoulders: "I don't know, but I doubt it's anything as dangerous as that. There are no nuclear stations or anything like that nearby."

"Yura[6], you don't use the sirens to evacuate the city and you don't cut off all means of communications unless it's something VERY dangerous and they want people to shut up about it" - she argued. "This is bad. This is very, very bad. We need to get out of here!"

"Natasha, I've told you already, haven't I?" – I told her patiently. She was very worked up, and I didn't want to argue with the last close person I had left. "There's something outside, and-"

"Something outside? Yura, do you hear yourself?" – she questioned me. "What can possibly be there that we have to stay inside? You make it sound like there's some bigger-than-life monster out there!"

"I don't know what it is," – I explained to her patiently. "But let's face the facts: it's dangerous outside, there's been a town-wide evacuation, and the doors are locked anyway. Why risk everything and go out there?"

---

[5] Kyshtym – the second worst nuclear incident after Chernobyl, which took place in 1957. The information about it was kept secret by both the USSR and the USA, as the CIA was concerned the panic would harm the emerging American nuclear industry.
[6] Yura – a petting form of the name "Yuri"

"Because Nikita's out there and I can't even reach him!" - she exclaimed, grabbing her head. There it was. The true reason for her being so worked up. She didn't care about her own safety – she just wanted to know if her closest person was still safe. As someone who also had a relative somewhere out there – the only close relative I had left – I felt a sting of shame: why wasn't I so worked up about her safety? Why wasn't I ready to go out there, risking my life, to make sure that my own mother was safe?

"Listen, I'm sure Nikita is fine" - I told her. In a way, it felt like I was talking both of us down. "That siren was a signal to evacuate the town, the *whole* town," – I stressed the word. "He probably got out of town along with the rest of the people" - I paused for a moment and thought about the implications of those words. "And he probably thought you'd done the same" - I added.

She stopped for a moment, and I saw a glimpse of relief in her eyes.

"Yeah…Yeah, you're probably right" - she said. She walked up to her kitchen window which, unlike mine, was facing the town. "I don't see anyone in any windows."

I got up and stood next to her. It was the first time I'd seen the town since the sirens, and also the first time I'd ever seen it so empty.

There was no movement on the streets. Even during our night parties, when me and Nikita, craving some smoking, would lock the kitchen door, open the window to let the fresh air in, and silently observe the town during its most serene hour, it wasn't as motionless. There was always some person getting home at an odd hour, or a rare stray cat running across the street, hoping not to be seen. Or even a branch shaking in the wind.

Nothing. None of that could be observed outside, and not even a single leaf was shaking - it seemed that even the wind which I'd been dreading so much in the morning seemed to escape along with the rest of the townsfolk. It was like looking at an apocalyptic glass painting. Like the town stopped breathing - and you weren't sure that it was just holding its breath.

There were traces of panic and commotion on the streets: open suitcases, abandoned in panic, with long tongues of clothes sticking out of them. An occasional scarf or a handkerchief, waiting for the wind - or at least someone - to pick them up.

It felt odd thinking that people abandoned those things less than an hour ago. It felt like we were the ones who missed the train - or maybe we were the discarded things as well.

"We need to get out of here, too" - Natasha said. I didn't look at her, but I could hear the determination in her voice. The same kind of determination people show before taking their first jump with a parachute.

"I don't think that's wise" - I argued. "I've called the police and let them know that we're stuck here - as did probably every other tenant in this building. They said that the rescue's coming."

"I don't know if we can believe them" - she sighed. "Remember Kursk? Remember Chernobyl? The first thing they do is try to hide it, to save their face. I bet they're ready to leave us to die here and make it look like an accident."

"We don't know if it's that serious. Maybe it's just a wild animal attack. And by the way, at least one such animal is still outside, and it's very violent" - I argued. "It murdered a man in less than 30 seconds!"

"So, we stay together and take our chances!" - she exclaimed. "There are many of us and only one wild animal there, if we group up it won't even think to attack us, we won't even have to fight it!"

"Well, the doors are still closed, so..."

"All of them?" - she interrupted me. I hesitated to answer: I didn't know for sure.

"I don't know" – I answered. "I didn't hear anything from the other staircases, but I guess it makes sense."

Natasha was quiet for a few moments before answering: "We better make sure. If the other doors are still open, it's a big deal. Give me two minutes to get dressed – I want to go and take a look."

\*\*\*

Climbing onto the roof turned out to be scarier than I imagined: the iron ladder, while seemingly sturdy, was welded to the unstable railings of the stairwell, and thus was shaking every time I put my foot down on it.

"Well?" - I heard Natasha ask me. "Are you going up or not?"

I realized that I froze halfway up and spent a good thirty seconds looking down at the distance I'd have to fall.

"I am" - I said. "It's just a bit scary."

"Yeah, it always is the first time. When me and Nikita climbed it last summer to look at the stars I thought I'd rather die than take another step. But it's rather sturdy, so don't worry - it even held both of us" - she said.

Her reassuring words, coming from below, echoed across the walls down the stairwell, once again reminding me how high above the stairs I was.

"Well, that's good to know" - I said, taking another step. I was still just as scared as before, but after her reassurance, I didn't want to look like a wimp.

I climbed up to the hatch in the ceiling which led to the roof and gave it a push, but it didn't budge. I pushed again harder and had to instantly grab the ladder when it started shaking under my legs.

"Push harder" - I heard Natasha's advice and sighed. I was starting to suspect that she secretly wanted me dead.

"If I push even harder it's either going to open or the ladder will disconnect from the ceiling and I'll fall down three flights worth of height" - I considered my options and then pushed the hatch open. The ladder shook violently but didn't fall. Sighing in relief, I quickly scaled the rest of the path and climbed all the way up.

Natasha followed just a few moments after - it seemed that she really wasn't scared of scaling the ladder.

The hatch led to a tiny room on the roof - a concrete shed, maybe five by five feet, and barely tall enough to stand up in it. One of the walls had a small door with a high threshold - the door to the roof itself. So small you wouldn't walk through it - more like crawl through, keeping your head low. I opened it and for the first time since I woke up, I finally stepped outside.

The view that opened from the roof wasn't much different than the one from Natasha's kitchen - just broader. The clouds above were grey and heavy - another roof over our heads. Another ceiling, only much higher.

We headed towards the far side of the building, where the lonely concrete cube - the same one as the one we've climbed out of - was overlooking the town's border from the roof's edge. As we walked, I couldn't stop thinking about how surreal it felt to hear nothing but our footsteps. We had a forest on the right and a town on the left - yet not a single sound was coming from them. Without the familiar hum in the background, I felt naked to the world, like I was on its central stage and every set of eyes on the planet were aimed at me, waiting for my next move. I felt exposed to the very skies above. I felt like at any moment the sounds of footsteps would vanish as well and we'd float upward, to the vacuum of space.

It was putting me into a strange feeling of unease and anxiety. Like the rest of the world had stopped existing.

"Yuri?" - Natasha called for me.

"Yes?" - I turned around to face her. Did she notice something in the distance?

"Nothing" - she shook her head. "I just wanted to say something. This silence was giving me the creeps."

"Yeah, I get it" - I nodded. "I feel the same way."

Even though our conversation had no point it felt right to speak up. The sounds of our voices made the world feel a bit less lonely, and the trip through the "outside world" with its unknown evacuation-warranting dangers - a little less scary.

We were approaching the door when a single sound from the outside world broke the silence. It started low, and for a moment I thought that the sirens started again - but it was something else. A low, rumbling howl that lasted a good ten seconds and made us stop in our tracks for its entire duration. We felt like we had to bear witness to it. To soak in every moment of it. To feel its presence out there so that there wasn't any doubt left that it was dangerous out there. Like it was only proper etiquette to hear the new owner of our town announce itself.

In the eerie silence after the howl, Natasha turned around to face me. Her eyes were wide from shock.

"Is that…?" - she didn't finish the question, but I knew what she wanted to say.

"Yes" - I confirmed her suspicions. "That is *it*."

She was silent for a few moments, and then said: "I've never heard anything like that. What is it?"

"I don't know" - I said. "I didn't see it - only heard it."

Once more she took a moment to think it over, before saying: "I thought you made it up that it sounds like that."

I could relate to her disbelief – it was only reasonable to doubt my words, but still I decided to inquire: "Why did you think I made it up?"

"I don't know" - she shook her shoulders. "I thought maybe you were in shock from that postman's death. Something like this…It's hard to believe."

I felt sorry for her. I could see that she had been trying her hardest to rationalize what was going on. She went to sleep in her old apartment, located on the edge of her old town, and woke up in a new world where unseen and unheard-of threats roamed the abandoned streets.

We opened the door and climbed inside the shed. I made sure to check the door behind closed tight - it felt right under the given circumstances.

Natasha pulled the hatch, and the sounds of people talking flushed out of it - it felt like opening a can of noise. The world returned to how it was supposed to be.

"Never thought I'd be so glad to hear those old-timers" - I joked.

"Don't be mean" - Natasha said before quickly climbing down the ladder. I winced when I heard the metal shake and ring under her feet.

"Natasha!" - I called for her. "I think since we can hear them down there then it means they haven't left and their door is welded shut as well?"

"Yeah, you're right" - she said after a small pause. "But I want to see for myself. Are you coming down?"

"Yes, give me a moment" - I told her, carefully lowering my foot through the hatch. The ladder trembled when I put my weight on it, and so did my calves, though for a different reason.

"You sure take your time with these" - she noted when I climbed all the way down.

"Easy for you to say" - I grunted. "I'm 20 kilograms heavier than you."

We headed downstairs toward the first floor, past the small groups of people. The faces were different, but they behaved the same: most of them were out of their apartments, talking to each other about our situation.

We didn't stop to listen - instead, we were carefully and silently walking down the stairs, trying to avoid drawing anyone's attention. I didn't want to repeat the earlier confrontation. It seemed that Natasha was also not in the mood to talk with anyone.

I did, however, catch bits of conversations here and there. On each floor, the people were discussing something new. Sometimes it was hard to piece together without context what those people were talking about, but what I heard was interesting.

"They say someone died in the 3rd Entrance. They say it was the postman. He couldn't get inside and something got to him. Gnarly stuff."

"Yes, I heard that beast's howl. It had a mighty pack of lungs, I'll tell you that."

"The police won't help. I asked to talk to my nephew - he works there, you may remember him from last Easter - but they told me he was too busy and just hung up. This is what I get for hosting him so many times..."

"Wasn't your nephew out of town on a vacation? I thought he went somewhere abroad with his wife."

"This is how they're trying to get to us. They've been waiting for 30 years, and when they finally saw that our country was rising from its knees they decided to attack. They are threatened by our presence on the world map."

"Vasya says that they've finally answered. They should start any day now, so stay tuned - you can't miss a single one. You still have it, don't you? Good, keep it on at all times..."

"Do you have enough drugs at home? I was going to go to the pharmacy this morning when this happened. I'll borrow some from you, can I? My heart isn't what it used to be..."

"Hey there" – a man in his late thirties called us over. Unlike the other tenants, he wasn't wearing his home clothes: on the contrary, he was dressed as if he was planning on spending the next few days outdoors, with layers upon layers of clothes on him. A large duffel bag was hanging from his shoulder, and my eyes were instantly glued to a walkie-talkie that was hanging from his belt – I could instantly tell that thing had a lot of coverage. "Where are you from? I haven't seen you here before."

I felt defensive: I did not feel like being questioned again and tried to walk past him without acknowledging him. But before I made another step Natasha answered the man's question: "We're from the next stairwell. We wanted to see if everything has been welded shut here as well."

"So it's true. It's not just us who've had our doors welded shut" – the man eased up. "You're stuck in here as well. Sorry for snapping at you – I'm all tense since the morning and I thought… Never mind" – he shook his head. He stretched out his hand to greet me and I reluctantly shook it. Natasha got only a nod from him. "I guess you're looking for a way out, too?"

"Yes, we are" – Natasha quickly answered. "Is there any way out of this building?"

"Well, you kids came just to the right place" – the man smiled. "Me and a couple of my pals here are thinking about making a break for the military base in the forest – or some other evacuation point if we find it on our way there."

"You can break the door?" – I wondered.

"Well, no, but we've thought of a different way out" – the man answered, getting flustered. "We'll make a rope out of bedsheets and climb down from the second-floor window. It's unreliable and sounds silly, but it's the only way out we've come up with at the moment, and we can't be losing time thinking about anything else. We leave in about ten minutes and there's going to be about a dozen of us, so if you want out you better hurry up and pack your things" – he told us.

Instantly, I knew that Natasha wanted to agree to it. She did not like being stuck in the building, and she did not believe that the authorities were going to rescue us any time soon. On top of that, she was worried about Nikita. He was out there somewhere, possibly all on his own. Perhaps he was going through crowds of other evacuees trying to find her, or maybe he was even risking his life trying to get to her through the abandoned town.

Perhaps he was hiding somewhere in the streets, wounded and in need of help, with no way to get out on his own. Perhaps he needed her as he had never needed her before.

I knew it wasn't my place to make that decision for her. I was so unsure of what was going on that I wasn't sure if I could decide for myself. Yet at the same time, I remembered the howl of the beast, the screams of the postman. The panic in the military officer's voice during the morning transmission which ended the Cricket's broadcast.

"We're good, thanks" – I said, grabbing Natasha's hand and squeezing it. She gave me a confused look. The man noticed my gesture and furrowed his eyebrows, drilling our locked hands with his gaze: "You don't believe in those rumors about some creature outside, do you?"

"I do" – I told him, looking him in the eye. I could tell that the man was displeased about me defying him, and I started to feel nervous, but I didn't want to show it. "I've heard him die with my own ears. I was just on the other side of that door when it'd gotten to him."

"Well I didn't hear anything, and neither did any of us here" – the man puffed out his chest and crossed his hands. "Listen, I don't know what you've heard but there's nothing out there. Maybe it was a stray bear from the forest, but that's about it. I've seen plenty of those in my life and I know how to scare them away."

"It was not a bear" – I told him with confidence. "It didn't sound like a bear. Tell him, Natasha" – I asked her to confirm my words.

I could see that she felt conflicted. She knew that what she'd heard was real, that the unknown feral animal was stalking our town… But at the same time, there was a very real chance to get out of town right in front of her.

I remembered how easily she scaled that ladder just minutes before while I was scared to set foot onto it. She had it in her to overcome her fears. She could take such a risk.

"Do you have any weapons?" – I asked the man. "Do you have anything to scare it away?"

"I have a hunting rifle, but I doubt I'll need it" – he said with confidence. "No animal will attack a large group of people."

"No animal is dangerous enough to warrant an evacuation of the entire town" – I told him bluntly. "This morning, the radio transmission of the nearby numbering station stopped transmitting for the first time since it had been established. It can't be a coincidence. Something dangerous is going on outside."

Each sentence was a challenge for me: I was finding it hard to argue with someone so blunt and confident. While I was sure that I was right I was not much of a speaker. I knew very well that the arguments were usually won not by being reasonable, but by representing your argument better. And from what I could see, he was not sold on what I was telling him.

I could see by his face that he wasn't convinced, but I didn't care about him anymore. I saw that I couldn't change his mind. What mattered was changing Natasha's opinion. As a friend, I had that responsibility on me.

"Listen, if you want to cower here in fear along with the rest of the elders – that's on you" – he poked my chest with his finger, pushing me back a little. "We don't need to continue this conversation, so keep your mouth shut around my people."

"These are not your people" – I reminded him, rubbing my chest where he poked me. "And this is not about being right or wrong – it's about the safety of the people."

"Whatever" – he frowned and dismissively waved his hand at me. "Have it your way. I'm done with you. Are you with us, girl?" – he asked Natasha.

She looked at me then at the man, keeping quiet. I could see that she was considering her options.

"You'll let them know that we're stuck here, right?" – she asked him. I sighed in relief. It seemed that my words had an effect on her, after all.

He clicked his tongue and shook his head: "Have it your way. If you want to stay here – don't let me stop you. I don't have time to break it down to you why you're making a mistake, but in any case, you'll see it for yourself soon."

"Don't do this" – I warned him. "You'll be needlessly risking your lives."

He rolled his eyes and turned around: "Ot'yebis[7]".

He turned around to leave, but I stopped him: 'Wait! That walkie on your belt – you're going to use it to contact the military, right?"

"Yes, I will" – he told me. "I've tried it already, but they aren't picking up. Guess I'm out of range here..."

"What frequency are you going to use?" – I inquired.

"What is it to you?" – he wondered.

"I'll be listening. I have a radio of my own" – I explained to him. "If you get there safely we'll know that we can follow. And if anything happens to you on your way there... We might get you some help" – I suggested.

"We won't. Need. Help." – he told me through his teeth. "I can take care of myself, and I don't need anyone to rescue me."

"Please" – Natasha interfered, putting her hand on his shoulder. The man leaned back from her touch as if it burned him, but eased up a moment later when he saw the begging look in her eyes. "We just want to know what's going on out there. We're scared."

He gave her a condescending look – no doubt the anger he felt toward me was still affecting him. But then his features eased up and looked away: "You'd be wiser to go with us – that way you won't waste any time with this coward. Fine"

---

[7] Ot'jebis – Russian swear word, means "f*ck off"

– he sighed. "I'll tell you the frequency. When we clear the town we'll let you know."

"Thank you" – Natasha said. The gratitude in her voice was sincere. The man reluctantly told me the frequency, asked me twice if I got it – no doubt just to gloat and rub it in my face that I'll be just a listener to his heroics - and then headed inside his apartment.

"Why didn't you go with him?" – I asked her. She shook her shoulders: "He doesn't seem like the kind of person who thinks before acting. He's more bent on having it his way. Out there, I'd have to be dependent on him, and I don't think that it's a good idea."

I nodded in understanding. As much as I wanted her to say that I sounded more reasonable it was not the time to be vain.

"Come on" – I urged her to hurry up. "Let's finish what we've come here for and head back. We have ten minutes, tops, before he leaves."

# CHAPTER 5 - A New Path

When we reached the first floor there were only three men - all of them in their late forties or early fifties. One of them had an open can of beer in his hands. They seemed to have a friendly chat and did not share the mood of the rest of the people upstairs.

"...so I am not sure, but since this is an emergency I think our salaries will be covered by the government" - one of them said.

"So it's like a vacation?" - the one with the beer can asked.

"Yes, yes, I guess you can put it that way" - the other one laughed.

"Oh, look at these lovebirds" - the third one pointed at us. "Looking for a way out of the building? This door is sealed as well, don't try it" - he laughed.

"We guessed as much" - Natasha said, seemingly irritated by the man's description. "We're just looking around."

The men whispered and snickered to each other but Natasha passed them without giving them any more attention. I grunted and followed her.

"Bunch of idiots" - I heard Natasha whisper when I got closer to her. "They think this is all is very fun."

"Don't pay them any attention" - I told her. "I think they're just dying from boredom."

"I know" - she said, coming closer to the door. "I'm just not in the mood to crack jokes with them." She traced the welding seam with her finger and then gave the door a slight push.

"Look" - she told me. "The welding seams are on our side. You've said that our doors have been welded shut from within as well?"

"Yes" - I nodded in agreement.

For some reason, the mysterious welder had gone through the extra effort of welding all the doors from within. Even if he wanted to seal himself in along with the rest of the tenants, it would be much easier to walk from door to door with a welding stick in hand, before coming inside and welding the last door after him. But instead, he made sure to weld all of the doors shut from within. Taking extra time to get from one door to the next through the roof instead of through the street.

I could see only one possible explanation for such behavior: the welder was aware of the dangers outside. And he feared them to such a degree he didn't risk going outside even for a few seconds it would take to walk from one door to the next. Perhaps the beasts were already outside our walls during the night? Or maybe the threat outside was even bigger than we'd thought before?

"Hey, don't push yourself too hard, girl, you'll hurt yourself" - one of the men told us. I was ready to tell him to mind his own business but it didn't seem like he was teasing her: he seemed genuinely concerned. "We've tried that already; the door won't budge. Whoever welded these doors did a lousy job, but it'll do the trick."

"How do you know that?" - I asked the man. "Did any of you see or hear him?"

The man straightened out and puffed his chest out. His eyes lit up with pride and excitement at a chance to gloat about himself: "Son, I've been working as a welder for over twenty years. I can read those seams as if they were a book. The man who welded those doors had a steady hand, but he did make a few mistakes here and there - mistakes someone with experience wouldn't have made."

"So, if you're a welder, don't you have any tools at home?" - Natasha asked him. "Perhaps something we can use to weld these doors open?"

"You don't weld things apart, you weld them together" - the man snickered and gave his friends a look. They smiled back at him, rolling their eyes. "You need a gas torch or a metal saw to cut it open now."

"Alright, do you have any of those tools?" - Natasha patiently asked again. I could tell that, considering how much she wanted to get out, she was already at her limit.

"No. What for? They are heavy, they smell…I keep them in my garage, where I do my work" - the man explained. "Besides, why would I unseal the door? You've heard what's going on out there. We should stay put until the army has it all under their control. They have a base nearby, somewhere in the forest. So they should swoop in soon."

"Right" - Natasha said with thinly disguised sarcasm. "Leave it to the army."

"Exactly" - the man either didn't notice her sarcasm or didn't bother to dignify it. "We're not just any town, remember? We used to hold great strategic importance. Whatever it is going on out there, they're going to get it back under their control very soon - they don't like it any other way."

Natasha crossed her hands and turned around to examine the door again.

"And no one heard anything?" - I looked at the other two men to let them know that I was talking to them.

The one with the beer can shook his shoulders: "I didn't hear nothing. It might be because of my pills."

"Hey, Yuri" - I heard Natasha call for me. "Take a look at this."

She showed me something she'd picked up from the floor - an orange cigarette butt. It was burned right up to the filter, but luckily the flame had stopped just in time to spare the name of the brand at the base of the filter: "Soyuz-Apollo."

"I know these" - I said, leaning back from it: even though I was an occasional smoker the smell of that brand always made me retch. Despite its fancy name, that brand of cigarettes was among the cheapest, most vile cigarettes there were on the market. If there was hell then the Devil himself must've been smoking those to torture his victims some more.

"Is this one yours?" - Natasha asked the men, lifting her finding so that they could see it.

"What, are you going to scold us for littering now?" - one of them asked before the one with the can interrupted him: "Ain't nobody littering here, alright? We have a paint can the flight above for cigarettes, all the butts go there. We're keeping it clean here, alright?"

"I've found it near the door" - Natasha explained. "It seems it was left there recently - it's not dirty yet. I think it was left by the one who welded these doors shut. Do you know anyone who smokes these?"

"What brand is it?" - one of the men asked.

"Soyuz-Apollo" - I said, almost gagging just from the associations I had with that name. The man mirrored my behavior, frowning in disgust: "God, no. They are awful."

"I see" - Natasha said, curling her fist around it. "I'll throw it out on our way back."

"Much obliged" - the man with the beer can saluted her with his drink and then finished it in one go.

"Do you really think it was left by the welder?" - I asked her. "It could be a coincidence, you know."

"I know," - she nodded. "But we can't dismiss that possibility, either. At least it's something."

I didn't want to argue - it wasn't an argument I saw fit to be arguing over. Even if it was an unlikely clue, it could theoretically turn out to be correct. Either way, it yielded us nothing.

"Let's go" - I told her. Those people are going to leave soon. I want to listen to how it goes… And I hope I'm wrong about this."

\*\*\*

We didn't talk until we got all the way back to our stairwell. The disturbing silence that had haunted us there before was now set aside by the sounds of a car alarm going off - something must've set it off in the short time we were inside the building, and I had a few guesses as to what that was.

We started our observation from Natasha's apartment - only her windows were facing the town, and we wanted to see the beginning of that small expedition with our own eyes.

We weren't the only ones: somehow, the rest of the people had either found out over the grapevine or heard the people climb down the makeshift rope made out of bedsheets because when I stuck my head out the window I saw many more heads below doing the same. Despite the chilly weather outside, they wanted to see it with their own eyes, and I was sure that many more people were looking through their glass panes.

It felt just like in the primordial times when men hadn't yet shed their fur and couldn't walk upright. The entire tree had gathered to see their tribesmen climb down to the surface and was staying silent so as not to attract the tiger.

No one was talking: though I was sure that many of those people had something to say, none of them made a sound. The people who were climbing down the rope were doing their best to stay silent, too. One of the women coming down grunted when she almost slipped, and the rest of the people shushed her. Even though they were confident that there was no threat outside, they were careful not to make a sound. Just in case.

A few minutes later, all of them had descended. A group of ten people - mostly men, but with a few women as well. Most of them old enough to be my parents. Some of them were puffing out their chests and putting extra effort into standing straight, to show that they weren't afraid, but nobody was buying it.

They were but a small group, venturing into the world that had stopped being familiar just an hour before, and from the height of the fifth floor, they seemed even smaller than usual.

Their leader, the man who organized their great escape, was also silent. His confidence was gone: whether he believed that the creature existed or not didn't matter anymore. The quiet that had descended on the town was unsettling enough to make anyone nervous.

He looked up and stared at us for a few moments. For a moment our eyes met: I didn't know whether he could see me behind the glass pane, but the next moment he lifted his fist in a display of strength. A promise to the rest of us that he wasn't going to perish. That he was going to return to our harbor from his voyage with help.

"Let's go" - he told his group and slowly headed into town. One by one, people started following him. Looking around and trying not to lag behind, they didn't make an impression of people who were confident that their trip was going to be safe. They looked like people who were desperate to get out.

Looking at them, I started having second thoughts: if they were scared to go outside yet still decided to do so, then perhaps it wasn't such a bad idea? Perhaps they weren't as reckless as I'd thought them to be, and wanted to get out before things turned to worse?

Maybe they were right and I was wrong?

"Godspeed" - one of the women looking out the window told them, and some people hushed her.

The man at the front of the procession pulled out his radio and started quietly whispering something into it. No doubt, he had already started trying to contact the military to let them know that they were coming. Perhaps he hoped that they would meet them halfway there, and spare them from having to walk the entirety of their nightmarish path.

After a minute or two, their slow procession disappeared behind the building. We could neither see nor hear them. The tenants, however, stayed where they were, looking into the distance. Some of them were probably second-guessing whether they should've gone with them. Bravery was always a good way of setting an example, even if a bad one.

I didn't have to guess about their fate, though. I had the means to be with them on their path. I just had to do what I'd always done best. I just had to catch the right frequency and listen.

"Come on" - I told Natasha. "Let's hurry."

\*\*\*

We hurried to my apartment, and a minute later, we were already sitting near my radio. I noticed that Natasha was looking at it with great interest - before that, she had only heard about my hobby, and even when I was telling her and Nikita about it, I was keeping the details sparse. I had never wanted them to think that I was a weirdo. I felt flattered: even though she was only interested in it because it ended up being useful, I still felt proud that my hobby drew her attention.

"Here it is" - I said anxiously, tuning to the frequency the man had given me before. There were no voices, no sounds - nothing. For a moment, I felt worried: what if the man gave me the wrong frequency?

"Is the frequency correct?" - Natasha wondered, leaning closer to the radio, her thoughts seemingly mirroring mine. "Say something, maybe he'll answer."

I just impatiently shook my head - to say something over the radio could put them in danger. Those people were doing their best to evade being detected - to have their radio suddenly start spouting questions about whether they could see anything dangerous would negate their efforts at keeping a low profile and put them at risk.

Provided there really was something dangerous outside, of course.

Natasha didn't say anything else. We both listened to the white noise in silence afterward, straining our hearing as if that would help hear something. As one minute followed another one, I started wondering: why were they silent? Did he give me a random frequency, after all? Or there was some other, more sinister reason for the radio silence?

"Military base, come in," - we both jerked when the man's voice suddenly came through the static. He sounded quiet and careful - it seemed that just as I was worrying if there was something outside so did he start to consider such an option. "We're coming from Novoyarsk. There was a siren and we didn't evacuate in time. There are eleven of us. We would appreciate it if someone come to meet us or give us some instructions."

He didn't sound as confident anymore - perhaps he was just doubting that the military would come to save them. Or was there some other reason?

"Military base, come in," - he whispered into the radio again. "There are eleven of us, and we're heading for the main road out of town. We urgently need someone to come pick us up."

"Do you think they've seen or heard something?" - Natasha whispered to me. Even though they couldn't hear us unless I pressed the button down she was still hushing her voice. It was clear that she was concerned for their well-being.

"I don't know," - I told her. "I hope not."

"Military- hold on, I'm talking on the radio" - the man whispered to someone. This time, when he pressed the button, I could hear that people around him were quietly talking to each other and to him. They didn't sound as composed as him - something had agitated them. I was hoping that it was just the town's unusual serenity.

I didn't hear what the person next to him told the man, but I could guess the content of his words from the man's answer: "It's too late to turn back now. We'll be just wasting time." It seemed that he forgot to take his finger off the radio's button.

"How far away do you think they are?" - Natasha asked me.

"Can't be too far," - I told her, furrowing my eyebrows. "Stubborn fool. He just doesn't want to appear weak in front of the people here if they come back."

"You've made the right choice to stay here," - I told Natasha.

She just raised the finger to her lips: "I want to listen. We can talk later."

"Military base, come in!" – the man whispered into the radio quickly. "Come in. We urgently require your assistance. Have someone pick us up. Come in goddamn it!"

Something was going on there - that much was clear. Something's gotten him worried and made him start requesting the military's help. He wasn't thrilled with just walking to the base on his own anymore.

Natasha couldn't just stand by quietly: she rushed to the radio and, before I could stop her, pressed the button down and whispered into the mic: "Come back to the building! It's not worth it!"

I tore her hand off the button and threw her a disapproving glance. She didn't back down and instead glared back at me.

"Don't give me that look! We have to do something!" - she told me. Just as I was about to reply, the radio spoke again.

"Who is this?" - the man asked the radio. People in the background were still restless. It sounded like they were right next to him, banding together into one small group. Personal space wasn't a priority anymore.

"Military base, is that you?" - he asked the radio again. I glared at Natasha again: now the man was thinking that someone from the base could hear him, after all. "Military base, repeat! I didn't get it."

A few seconds later, he came in again: "Please repeat" - he pleaded the radio. "We need an extraction ASAP, I beg you." Just as he let go of the button, I heard it. A short, abrupt sound which was cut off along with the man's transmission. A sound I had never heard before that morning, yet the one I could already recognize as the sign of trouble.

A howl of the beast. With how abruptly the transmission ended it was hard to tell how far away from the radio it was. Maybe fifty meters, maybe a couple hundred.

Too close for comfort either way.

I looked at Natasha: her eyes were wide with terror. I didn't have to ask her whether she'd also heard it- I could tell just by looking at her. She also recognized the sound she'd heard on the roof earlier.

She raised her hand to her mouth. Her breathing got heavy.

"Military base, please" - the man pleaded again. The despair in his voice was almost tangible. "Please, come in" - he begged again, his voice almost breaking into tears. "Screw it, we're coming back. Military base, we're going back. Pick us up at-"

"Oh my god!" - someone screamed in the background, and the transmission was cut off again.

The tone of the exclamation was not just mere surprise. Whoever it was, they didn't seem to expect an answer to their plea. It was a shout of awe, of shock. It was a desperate cry of a mind that couldn't grasp the sight that opened before it.

In other words, the same emotions the postman showed before he was brutally killed at our doorstep.

No more transmissions followed. Natasha and I were sitting in complete silence, listening to the static. We were afraid to say a word, to even let out a loud breath - what if at that moment someone tried to reach out to us and we'd miss what they said?

Aside from that, we were afraid of one more thing. What if there was no one left to send a transmission? As horrible as it was, we were more concerned about the implications of the man's disappearance, rather than his fate. I had been confident in my decision not to go with him - but now when I had received the confirmation that I had been right all along, I felt horrible. It was a hollow victory. A victory with no worth to it.

Regardless, we kept on listening. Walking away, saying a word - those things would mean that we admitted that he was dead and that we couldn't walk outside. Without sharing a glance, we kept doing the same thing - clinging to blind hope that the man was going to turn out alright and that it was just a misunderstanding.

The radio kept teasing us with static. It was the only sound in my apartment on the edge of the world. The sound of abandonment. The sound of radio silence.

"Hello?" - the familiar voice suddenly spoke to us through the radio, startling us. I breathed out loudly when the tension created by the radio silence finally dissipated, and Natasha let out a short, sobbing laugh. But it seemed that we were premature in our cheering.

"Anyone there?" - the man asked his radio. He didn't ask for the military base - this time, he was trying to reach out to anyone listening. While he didn't sound very confident before, now his voice was noticeably shaky, trembling. He was quietly whispering into the mic, and it was clear: he wanted to make sure he wasn't heard by anything that could be lurking nearby.

"If you can hear me - please send help. Please, I beg you" - he whispered again. "We tried walking to the base, and… Well, we didn't make it" - his voice almost broke into tears when he uttered that sentence. "I thought we'd make it there safely, but…I was acting rationally. We needed to get out. They've all agreed to it. We were all volunteers. I didn't know what… what was out there."

Natasha raised her hand to her mouth again.

"We have been attacked by- something. I've never seen such an animal before. I thought the people were talking about a bear, but it's…it's…it's much worse than that. We didn't know how to react, and we ran. If it was a bear…we need a strike squad to deal with it. We can't deal with it on our own."

My suspicions were true: the strange creature was indeed something unknown, something alien to our town. The man wasn't giving us any details on what it was, but he didn't need to. It was perfectly clear that he'd never seen anything like it before, and thus had no words to describe it. The best description he could provide for it was to say nothing.

"I hid inside one of the buildings. It's on that street…Oh, I can't remember the name now. I don't know where the rest of the people are. We all split when it attacked the crowd.

Maybe they escaped or hid, just like me. I don't know. I've only heard their screams, but I don't know how many it caught."

The man started sobbing: the emotions overwhelmed him. He spent around thirty seconds crying into his walkie, as if he wanted someone to bear witness to his misery, to have some sympathy for him, before finally letting go of the button.

I glanced at Natasha. Both of us were thinking the same thing: we were trapped in that town, after all. Our building was a cage, but the thing about cages, they could also keep things out.

"I can't go back," - the man came back from radio silence, still sobbing. "I can't come back and tell those people that I'd gotten their close ones killed. If anyone's listening," - he suddenly got serious, overcoming his grievance. "If anyone else has been stuck inside or didn't evacuate in time, do not go outside no matter what. Don't follow our mistake."

I felt pity for him. To think that less than an hour ago me and that man were locking gazes and arguing about the best course of action. If only I'd been confident enough to stop him! I now knew that back there, I hadn't been confident to decide the fate of those people. Had I convinced them to stay, I'd be ridden with guilt whether I'd made the right decision - and I knew I hadn't been ready for that burden. I'd decided to let things run their course, to let those people call their own shots - and now I was witnessing the aftermath of that.

Even though that man didn't even know that I was listening to him, I was sharing his guilt.

I looked at Natasha: "Should we talk to him?" - I asked her.

She shook her head: "Don't. If we talk to him, we might attract that creature."

She sounded shaken when she said that. I looked at her just to check if she was alright. It was clear that the chain of events that had been unraveling in front of us had stressed her out, but it almost seemed like she was overreacting. She was taking the drama happening somewhere on the streets way too personally. Was she perhaps concerned that Nikita had faced the same fate?

It was a poor time to discuss it - there were more pressing issues at a hand. But nevertheless, I still tried it: "Natasha, are you alright? You don't have to listen to it if you don't want to."

She crossed her hands on her chest and shook her head - so quick as if she was having a seizure: "Let's not talk right now. I need to know how it ends," - she pointed at the radio with her chin to let me know what she was talking about. I nodded and turned back to the machine.

"Military base, come in" - the radio buzzed again. The man was even quieter than before. "Please, someone, come in. Please."

"Screw it" - I said both to Natasha and to no one particular. The man's life was already at risk. The least I could do was give him some closure, keep him some company. So that he knew that he wasn't there alone and that people could hear him.

But before I pressed the button, the radio came back to life once more: "Please, send someone to Gornaya Street. I've hidden inside one of the-" - his words were interrupted by a strange clicking sound in the background. An animalistic, curious sound which, judging by its volume, couldn't originate more than a dozen meters away from the man.

A sound which, no doubt belonged to some animal - but once again, I couldn't recognize what kind of animal it was. It was not anything I could've heard on a Discovery Channel, nor was it a mighty roar of the creature that had slain the postman and attacked their group.

It was something new. Something that had been stalking inside the building where the man had hidden and had been attracted by him talking.

"Oh, God" - was all the man managed to say - a shocked, exasperated, and tired exclamation - before ending the transmission. Just before the transmission ended, the creature screeched once more, louder than before - no doubt a declaration of its attack. With everything that'd been going on, I had no reason to believe that it was not hostile.

There were no further transmissions from him. His last words and their tone made me think that he didn't even try to run. Whatever he'd seen outside had left him too shocked to try to escape.

We'd spent a few more minutes waiting - just to make sure. But the radio just kept on spewing white noise.

"I don't think we'll hear from him again" - I quietly said, feeling the need to break the silence. I felt that if I'd spent a few more seconds listening to nothing but white noise, I'd puke my guts out.

Natasha quietly nodded, then shifted around uncomfortably. I could see that she wanted to say something.

"Do you think that animal attacked them because… it heard me speaking through the radio?" - she quietly asked.

"Oh God, of course not" - I quickly assured her. It finally dawned on me what had been gnawing at her, and I couldn't even imagine how tough it must've been for her - thinking that the death of those people was her fault.

I also wanted to calm her down because I myself could relate to that feeling of guilt. I could relate to what it was like – feeling like you could've prevented it from happening.

"Those people were doomed the moment they set their feet outside," - I said, feeling my own feeling of guilt grow stronger as the words were leaving my mouth. I disregarded that. I could take it. I had to calm down Natasha first. "I'm sure that creature had already been following them for some time. There was a dozen of them, after all. They'd be hard to miss."

"Yeah… I guess you're right" - she hugged herself and nodded, turning around to leave. I noticed her hand rise up to her eye for a moment as if to wipe off a tear. "I'm going back home" - she told me without turning around. "I'd like to spend some time alone."

"Of course," - I nodded, though I was feeling a bit disappointed that she was leaving. I didn't want to be alone again. "If you want to talk - my door is always open."

"Thanks" - she said and headed for the exit.

I could see that she was still distraught, and as she was putting on her shoes, still looking away from me, I felt that I had to say something to calm her down or cheer her up.

"Listen, if you're worried about Nikita then I'm sure he's alright" - I told her.

"Thanks" - she nodded quietly. "It helps that you think that" - she added, though nothing in her behavior showed that she really thought that.

"And I'm sure he'd come back for you if he had such a chance" - I added for some reason. Immediately I felt a rush of embarrassment for what I'd said: if she'd been having such thoughts it would be a bad idea to remind her about them.

But to my surprise, she turned around and sent me a sad smile: "It's nice of you to think that. Thanks, Yura. I'm sure you'd do that if you were him."

"Ha-ha, no, I'm too much of a wuss for something like that" - I laughed off her suggestion before realizing how I made it sound. "I didn't mean to say that I'd abandon you" - I quickly tried to explain, but Natasha just raised her hand in a stopping gesture and smiled again: "It's alright. I understand what you mean. I know you wouldn't."

"Alright. Then… See ya around?" - I asked her.

"Yes. See ya" - she told me and opened the door.

The sound of people going up and down the stairwell and talking to each other had already become background noise - something new, but something we'd already grown accustomed to. And yet despite that the moment those sounds entered my apartment and reached our ears we realized that something was wrong. We could hear that, once again, the voices of our neighbors had grown restless. Something had agitated them.

We walked outside together, without sharing a word - she was already wearing her sneakers, while I stepped onto the cold concrete floor in nothing but my socks. Not the most comfortable sensation, not to mention that they'd instantly gotten dirty, but it didn't matter at that moment. I needed to know what was going on.

Everyone had gathered near the windows between the floors - the ones leading to the town outside. They were eagerly discussing something, and some of the people were pointing at something outside. It was hard to tell what exactly they were talking about, but just from the sheer number of people, it was clear that they've spotted something noteworthy.

We came closer and although no one wanted to surrender their spot and let us closer to the window I've managed to catch a glimpse of what they'd been looking at.

My blood ran cold.

The asphalt in front of our building had a huge pool of blood on it - no further than thirty meters away from our walls. Still bright red, and possibly still warm to the touch - had anyone dared to come out and check. It was surrounded by splatters of blood, indicating that whoever that blood belonged to had suffered a heavy blow. We were all thinking the same thing: we knew of only one creature that could deal such damage.

There was no body - the pool had bloody drag marks on one side of it, indicating that the stranger had been pulled away after the creature had killed them. From what I could gather, no one had seen or heard anything - they only noticed the blood after the deed had already been done. Yet not a single person had any doubts about where that blood had come from. Considering how close it was to our building and how abandoned the town was, there was only one possible explanation.

That blood was telling a story so clear it could as well be written across the pavement.

That pool of blood was the only thing that remained of the expedition that had tried to brave the outside and reach the military base. The last survivor from it had been slain just mere meters away from their home after they had realized their mistake and tried to come back.

# CHAPTER 6 - Voices

Once Natasha went home I looked at the clock. Just a little bit past twelve. The day had just begun and yet so many things had happened.

I had no more places to go to. I had no more things to do. The food supplies were checked, and the bathtub was full of water. Perhaps Natasha would come over in the evening, but until then I had to kill some time.

I walked over to the guest room and sat in front of the radio, sliding the microphone closer. The best thing to do was to keep doing what I'd always known to do best - to surf the radio.

Before I started, I checked "The Cricket." Still nothing. Just the background noise. The background radiation, the leftovers from the primordial times when the Universe first expanded, as well as the radio noise produced by our sun and distant stars. While the sentient part of the Universe - humans - remained silent, the rest of it kept on endlessly whispering.

It felt mind-blowing the first time I learned what the white noise is - to listen to the celestial bodies and the echoes of the Universe's birth itself while sitting in my small old apartment. It was like eavesdropping on God himself while he was busy in his heavenly workshop. But after some time, the novelty of it wore off. I certainly wasn't so bored as to keep listening to the white noise now.

I sighed and started searching the radio waves. The movements of my hand were precise as never before - I was turning the dial so slowly it seemed like it wasn't moving at all. Like a skilled, patient hunter, I was combing through my domain, looking for a prey, careful not to scare it away... or, in my case, not to walk past it.

I became so focused on my task I didn't even notice the passage of time. The search for a radio transmission completely engrossed me, so I didn't even know what time it was when I finally heard the whispers of radio chatter.

"...Moving in at 1700. Yeah, I don't know about that. I didn't know that he knew all of our hiding places. Yeah, probably."

The voice belonged to a young man - my peer. He was talking to someone I couldn't hear - someone not on the other end of the line, but rather on the other side of the room, with his radio on. His voice was quiet and barely heard through the radio static.

I carefully turned the dial to hone in on the signal, feeling sudden anxiety. Other survivors! Other people nearby, talking on the radio! I had to make sure to zoom in on the frequency perfectly. If only I had one of those digital radios! It would easily take care of that for me, tuning in on the frequency automatically to provide the best signal.

After a bit of playing around with the dial, I managed to clear up the signal to the best of my ability, yet the voice didn't get any louder. It seemed that just as I suspected: the unknown speaker was talking to someone else in the room, while his radio was on.

"Hello?" - I said into the microphone to attract their attention.

There was a moment of silence on the other end, and then the sounds of commotion. "Military base Novokureevo speaking" - the man said quickly.

The sudden seriousness in his voice made me hesitate a bit before introducing myself, but then I realized: he was probably thinking that I was from another military base.

"Hi" - I repeated, thinking over my words. I didn't want to scare him away: he probably was not supposed to talk to the civilians. "I'm from the nearby town, Novoyarsk. You've heard about it, right?" - I tried to remember the map of the nearby villages and locations: Novokureevo sounded familiar.

"We're not supposed to talk" - the young man said, and I heard hints of panic in his voice.

"I understand, trust me" - I quickly said before he switched his radio off. "It's just that we've been locked down here and couldn't evacuate in time. Someone welded our doors shut."

There was a pause - a far much longer one than I was comfortable with. I thought that he had already walked away from the radio when I finally heard his voice: "What do you mean, 'somebody welded your doors shut'?"

"It's exactly what it sounds like - all the doors in our apartment complex are welded shut, and we have no clue why or who had done that" - I explained breathing out in relief that he didn't end the transmission. His curiosity got the best of him.

If it was some officer or even a professional soldier then I'd have nothing to hope for - he would not break the protocol so easily. But Novokureevo was a small village, and most of the military personnel there, aside from the high-ranking officers who were in charge of the place, were just conscripts. The man was probably younger than me, and he was there only because he was told to serve there.

"Wow, that's…That's pretty bad timing. So, you're locked up right there, in Novoyarsk? What is even going on down there?" - he asked me.

It seemed strange that he was asking me about that and not the other way around. But then again, perhaps he thought I'd already seen something and wanted a first-hand witness report?

"Honestly, I have no clue," - I told him. "Everyone just left when the sirens rang. Everyone but us. And now there's some animal outside that attacks people, so we can't leave."

"Huh, I see," - the man grunted. "I expected the end of the world, judging by how worked up the superiors at our base have become. How many of you are there?"

"Eighty apartments" - I said. "Maybe some other buildings are locked up as well" - I was sure that wasn't the case, as the doors had been sealed from the inside, but I decided that ramping up the civilian count would get us help sooner. "When we heard the sirens, we couldn't leave anymore."

"Oh" - he said. "That's quite a lot of people. Hang tight in there, bro."

"Bro." Such a short yet reassuring word. In an instant, I felt some sort of camaraderie established between us - a bridge he set up between us. It felt good to know that I had some allies somewhere in the world.

But his last sentence made me suspicious, so I asked him: "Haven't you received any orders to help people still in the town?"

"Sorry, mate" - he said. The regret in his voice was sincere. "No such orders have been received. We were told to stay put until the reinforcements arrive."

"No such orders." I felt gutted and betrayed. A part of me wanted to misinterpret the man's words - perhaps he meant that there were no such orders yet? Maybe they didn't know that we're here?

"But they will come, right?" - I asked, trying to bargain with fate. "Now that you know that we're here the army will come for us, won't you?"

"Ehh, sure, I'll report your message" - he was seemingly confused by something. "But if you're saying it's clear down there why don't you just climb out the windows?" - he asked me. "I'm not sure how serious this is or what is even going on, but you should be alright. Just head down the Western road out of town and you'll hit the roadblock."

"We CAN'T leave" - I stressed the word. "Because of the animal."

"What animal?" - he asked me after a short pause. I could tell from his voice that he really didn't know.

"The animal" - I repeated. "There's an animal outside our building, I don't know which one, it appeared at the same time the sirens were sounded and killed a man outside. Some of us have tried walking to your base, but they didn't make it far" - I patiently explained to him. I was starting to feel frustrated: here I was hoping to learn something, to hear that we were going to be rescued soon – but it seemed that I was the one doing all the talking.

"Haven't they told you anything about it?" - I cried out in frustration.

"Bro, they don't tell us nihuya[8]" - the young man was getting more and more comfortable while talking to me. "You know how the old school officers are - we are not meant to know anything, we just need to follow the orders. I'm not even aware of what's going on out there. Now, you telling me that there's some creature out there - that's the first thing I've learned about what is going on outside of the base."

"So, they keep you in the dark?" - I asked. I was glad that Natasha wasn't around to hear that: knowing that the military

---

[8] nihuya – a Russian swear word, means "absolutely nothing"

kept it all under the lid even from the lower ranks would send her into a fit of panic. While she would be de facto right, I didn't want her to be bothered about that. Yet.

"I'll tell you more: they are not just keeping us in the dark, they've taken away our phones as well. All of them! There was no reception anyway, so why take away our phones?"

*"So that you couldn't take the pictures"* - I thought, thinking back to what Natasha said: the first priority was not the people - it was keeping everything under wraps.

The man on the other side continued rambling in the meantime: "They swooped the barracks not long after the morning transmission and took away everything, even things we had stashed away. They knew where to look. They left the cigarettes though, so thanks for that."

"Hold up! When you're talking about the morning transmission, are you talking about 'The Cricket'?" - I asked him, bewildered. I was surprised that it didn't dawn on me sooner: "The Cricket" was a military numbering station, after all, and I was talking to a soldier over the radio. If anyone could know something about it that would be him.

"Yes, The Cricket! How do you know about it?" - he asked me.

I thought about dodging the question but then decided that it would be dishonest: the man was giving me the answers, after all.

"I am a radio stalker" - I said, trying to keep my voice even. Suddenly I was ashamed to admit that my hobby was listening to the radio for days. "I was listening to it for a long time, and this morning it sent out a transmission and then went silent."

"Yeah, that's what I heard as well" - he said. "My shift has just started, so I wasn't the one who received it, but the guy who did says that… it was just wild. The base has been fully mobilized since the moment we've received it."

Oh yes. I could clearly imagine the effect such a transmission would have on the soldiers. It was one thing when you're just a radio amateur who eavesdrops on transmissions for fun, and completely different - when the message you receive sounds like the declaration of a war you're going to participate in.

"Do you have the encryption keys?" - I asked him, with a bubble of hope rising in my chest.

'Nah, we aren't allowed anywhere near them" - the man burst in instantly. "We just write the message down and deliver it to the higher-ups. If anyone has the encryption keys, it's them." He thought about something for a moment and then added: "Plus, I wouldn't give them to you, anyway. Sorry, bro, but you're asking for a little bit too much."

"I wouldn't ask about that" - I quickly lied. I felt a bit disappointed, but then again it was silly to expect any other outcome.

"I mean, I'm sure you understand" - the man suddenly started to sound apologetic. "It's confidential information and all that. Everyone here is jumpy as it is. I'm not sure if I'm not going to be court-marshaled just for talking to you. All contact with the outside world has been cut off. Right now, we're on a lockdown, standing by for further orders."

"So, your base wasn't involved in the evacuation? Well then, where are they taking the evacuated people?" - I wondered. "I thought since the sirens are a big deal they'd be taken somewhere where the military can take care of them?"

"They are not here, I can tell you that," - the man told me. "Our major took fifty soldiers and took off somewhere - I guess they are wherever your people are. I've also heard over the grape wine that reinforcements are coming - I think they'll be setting up a camp for the refugees."

I tried to remember how many people lived in our town - three thousand, four? Where could you comfortably locate all of them? Sure, some of them probably had relatives living in the nearby villages, but most of them were like me - one apartment, with no other options.

"Got it," - I said. "But you will let them know that we're still here, right?"

"Yes, of course," - he said. A moment later he added: "But I'll have to omit some parts of our conversation. I'm sure you understand, right? They are all really jumpy here since it all started, and I don't know what I was and wasn't supposed to say to a civilian, so don't shill me out, okay?"

"I won't say a thing" - I assured him. Then, after thinking for a moment, I asked him: "Isn't this a military channel? Is anyone else listening to us?"

"I doubt it," - he said. "I switched the frequency randomly after I sent the message I was told to send. How did you even find it? Were you just combing through them?"

"Yes, I was searching for someone else in town," - I admitted.

"Any luck?" - he asked me.

I shook my head as if he could see me. "Not yet."

"To be fair, not a lot of people use the radio nowadays to chat with each other" - he said. I wasn't sure if it was meant to be a jab at me or not, but I decided to let it pass. The guy seemed to be too sincere and straight-forward for that.

"Will you let me know if you receive any new orders?" - I asked him.

"Ummm..." - he thought for a moment, no doubt considering the fallout of his superiors learning about his conversations with someone from the outside of the base. "Sure" - he finally agreed. "We can use this channel. But don't contact me first - I'll be the one to contact you, okay? Somewhere between 10 and 12 AM tomorrow, so stay tuned."

"Got it, thanks!" - I was pretty happy with myself: despite being stuck in an evacuated town, I'd already found the informant on the outside.

"I gotta go, talk to you later. Stay safe out there," - the man told me.

"Okay" - I said. "My name's Yuri" - I suddenly remembered that we haven't even introduced ourselves to each other.

"Leonid" - he introduced himself. "Signing off."

I leaned back in the chair and stared into the ceiling. There was just too much information to digest.

First of all, it seemed that Natasha's suspicions were proving to be real: the military was not in a rush to help us out - at least not yet. Sure, they were organizing a camp for those who evacuated in time, but what kind of camp would it be? How can you keep an entire town in a camp without it devolving into a den of misery and infection? And why even set up a refugee camp when the citizens could be moved to another town? Sure, it was far away, but still, wouldn't it be easier than keeping them in camps?

Second, the military was keeping it under wraps even within their ranks - although that much wasn't surprising. The soldiers were never supposed to think; they were supposed to follow orders. I couldn't help but feel sorry for those boys at the base: had it happened a year earlier or later they'd be civilians - some of them in their late teens, having fun with their peers.

Draw the short stick, be born just in time to serve during the war - and you're not a civilian anymore. You're a soldier, and the lowest grade of a soldier at that - a conscript. A toy soldier who had played with toy soldiers himself just a few years before. Someone whose only value on the battlefield is to serve as a distraction for the main forces. The line between being a civilian and a meat shield of the country seemed to be too thin.

And most importantly, despite gathering a handful of clues, I haven't managed to come closer to solving the mystery of what was going on. I saw that the most drastic measures were being taken, and yet I hadn't a clue why. It felt frustrating, almost maddening. It felt like being locked up for committing a crime without being told what it was.

I could do only one thing. The same thing I had been doing for days before it all even started. I could only keep on listening, hoping to hear something else.

\*\*\*

It was four hours later when I stumbled on a transmission by accident - as was usually the case with radio stalking. Fishing across the radio waves until you pick up a faint signal, your ears perk up when you catch a bit of some conversation. It was akin to seeing your reel tremble a bit while fishing.

Carefully turning the dial, I tried to home in on the signal. Slowly, without a rush - as if afraid that I could scare it away if I tuned in immediately. By that moment I had spent so much time trying to pick up something that I had already lost hope of hearing anything and was doing it just on autopilot, not hoping to find anything. So, when I thought I'd heard a voice, I thought that I was imagining it. Only when I realized that it wasn't the case did I rejoice: my quest hadn't been in vain, after all.

Besides, I was really curious to hear what somebody could be broadcasting at such a critical hour for our town.

Little by little, the voice on my radio started to gain clarity until it finally became clear enough to understand it.

"...and the child will love the parent and the parent shall love their child, and your house will be full of harmony and respect once more.

And forward will come his beasts - his spears and shields. And they will pave the way for the king in rags - both the true king and the king in name only. And he'll bring the judgment to those who write laws, and he'll share with those who have none, and those who partake his blood and flesh shall be made of his blood and flesh, too."

I raised my eyebrow - I suspected that I wasn't the only one with the radio who had been stranded in the town, but I didn't expect the church of all places to start transmitting their messages. But, on the other hand, if there were any safe havens where people could find shelter from the horrors going on outside, it would be a church. Built centuries ago, they had always doubled as small fortresses during the wars and conflicts of the past. Their thick stone walls could endure a direct hit of an artillery shell, and their cold basements were rumored to be always stocked to the brim just in case of a war or another cataclysm.

I had also stumbled across the religious radio messages in the past, though I'd never bothered to remember the frequency, so I couldn't confirm if it was the same one I was listening to at that moment.

And, of course, with what had been going on outside, there was no way they wouldn't interpret it as the judgment day finally coming. If anything, it was their prime time - their best moment to start drawing in new followers.

The man on the radio continued talking:

"And the great wave shall cometh from below, sweeping across this land and giving the power to those who built this world, tearing it out of their masters' hands along with their nails. And the worker shall be the man, and the masters shall be his cattle, and the Earth shall be the earth of his, a blooming paradise filled with awe and colors no human eye has ever seen.

And each and every man and woman shall be made the king in rags, for there will be no kings and no rags anymore, and the meaning of those words will become forgotten and meaningless, and everyone will have just as much as they need and not an ounce more. The men shall bear the fruits of their labor, and each will give as much as they can and take as much as they need.

He is coming. He's in the ground. He's in the air. He's in the water. He is the fire to unbelievers – and the light to his followers.

We have been waiting for this day for a very long time, and the day has been laborious indeed. I know some of you are displeased with how things have turned out, but fret not – His glory is well within our reach. Rest. Gather your strength. In three days, at noon, you will hear from us again. You know what's coming. Make sure you're ready when the time comes. Not even your faith can keep you safe when those beasts roam our lands."

With that, the transmission ended. I expected the man to continue his religious tirade, but it seemed that he was done talking - no further messages followed. I leaned back in the chair and contemplated what I'd just heard.

Something about that message was bothering me. It started as a typical Christian end-of-times message - although I'd never heard of them referring to Jesus as "The King in Rags." But somehow, that description was making sense, so I didn't mind. The talks about scorched earth and the beasts rising to cull the unbelievers also matched the church's narrative.

What didn't make sense was that at the end, it started to sound more like communist propaganda - with the talking points like "the workers should seize the land", "end the bourgeoisie", "to each according to his need" and etc. From what I knew, the church and the Soviet State had never gotten along, with the latter actively preying on the former at the dawn of the Communist era. And yet the influence of the Soviet rhetoric was evident in that message.

"Then again," - I reminded myself, - "I'm living in a country where there are religious icons of Stalin and the current Communist Party celebrates religious holidays. It's not out of the realm of possibility that somewhere on the backwater edges of our country there could be a Christian Communist Church. I wouldn't be surprised if their King in Rags they keep talking about is actually Lenin."

\*\*\*

The rest of the day was uneventful: I was searching the radio waves for more people, yet I wasn't successful. Nothing was being broadcast. All I could hear was the white noise.

Natasha didn't come over, and I decided not to bother her - if she wanted some company she would've come.

The elders outside got calmer over time: I couldn't make out the words, but I sensed that the tone of their conversations had shifted, becoming less anxious and more mellow. I could hear the clanking of their plates and cups, whistling of kettles, and chitter of the tenants as they were gathering into groups. I could understand them: even the soldiers on the front lines of World War 2 had reported how unbearable the boredom was when nothing was happening.

It was pleasant background noise - it allowed me to forget that we were the only people in that entire dead town. That there wasn't a soul for kilometers around and the only life outside was wild and hostile. We resided in a small, cozy pocket of life, protected from the terrors outside by sturdy walls that allowed us to feel safe even in such tumultuous times.

While I was sitting in grandpa's chair, reading a book that took me far away out of town, I was almost enjoying the quiet outside, allowing myself to forget its context. It wasn't the pressing silence of an abandoned town anymore.

But no matter how hard I tried to focus on the story in my hands, I couldn't bring myself get lost in it, to forget about my situation. My gaze was constantly falling into spaces between words, and instead of roaming imaginary worlds, my mind was navigating the memories of the streets outside. I was thinking about the park, the alleys, the central street which could be reached by foot from any corner of the town in less than thirty minutes, the playgrounds where I'd been playing as a kid…All of those things now housed elusive nightmares that stalked the places from my childhood memories at that very moment. The town that I had grown up in was gone - what was left was some twisted reflection of it that had been hastily abandoned by its inhabitants.

Only the beast's roars were pulling me back into reality. It would announce itself every few hours, reminding us that we were its prisoners. When its roar echoed through the streets and forests, the entire building would fall silent, listening to the voice of their captor. Listening and trying to determine how far away it was.

# CHAPTER 7 – No Sleep

I woke up to the sound of someone knocking on my door. Raising my head from the pillow, I glanced at the clock - it was half-past nine. People outside were already chatting, and I could hear that once again their tone was worried.

Getting out of bed I went to open the door. I didn't know what the commotion was about, but I was hoping that it was the news about our liberation: perhaps the military finally decided to rescue us and everyone was getting in the line.

But when I opened the door and took a look at the face outside, I immediately realized that it wasn't the case. The man outside was old - somewhere in his sixties, and his face did not indicate that he brought me good news. On the contrary - his apologetic look was telling me that he needed something from me.

"Good morning, young man," - he said, tugging at his hat, which he held in his hands. "I'm sorry for disturbing you at such an hour..."

"Yes, how can I help you?" - I asked him, trying to get him to finish his sentence already. While the old man did nothing to deserve my irritation, I was disappointed that the old man was not the bearer of good news I expected him to be.

A couple of old men rushed downstairs past the old man, almost knocking him down. He had to grab the doorframe to regain balance.

"I'm just wondering, do you perhaps have some insulin to spare? I'm out of my own," - he said quietly, averting his eyes.

"Oh" - was all I could say. I felt like a dick for feeling irritated before. I could see that he wasn't comfortable going around asking people for help, but in his situation, it was a matter of life or death. "No, I'm afraid I can't help you" - I told him, looking away. While it was the truth, I felt bad for not being able to help.

"Are you sure?" - he trying to look me in the eye. "I understand that everybody who has it needs it, but I'm all out of it," - he explained to me.

"Sorry, but I don't have it," - I told him again.

The old man deflated: "Do you perhaps know someone who has it?"

"No, I'm not exactly... close with my neighbors" - I told him, feeling uneasy. If only I was more involved, more talkative! Perhaps then I'd be able to point the old man in the right direction.

"I see..." - the old man deflated even more. "No one has it - or nobody admits they have it," - he told me. I sympathetically nodded. "This is the second stairwell I'm checking - I came all the way from the first one. I was going to grab it from the pharmacy yesterday," - he started to awkwardly explain it to me as if feeling guilty for not being prepared for the events that had happened. "They were out of stock the whole week and were supposed to bring it in from another town yesterday morning. I even got out of bed earlier than usual to go to take a place in a line but when I came down the doors were already locked..."

"Excuse me," - I interrupted him. "When did you say you saw that the doors had been welded?"

Up until that point, I was listening to him, letting him pour his heart out, but when he mentioned that he had tried to go out early my curiosity was peaked.

"Oh, I think it was around 6 AM," - the old man tried to remember. "Yes, I think it was around that time," - he confirmed. "They usually bring in insulin early but there's not always enough for everyone, which is why I try to come as early as possible - to have a good spot in the line," - he explained.

"I see..." - I nodded to him, rubbing my chin.

If the doors had already been welded shut at 6 AM then it meant that the mysterious welder was already finished by then. Which meant that he had done it somewhere between 11 PM - the latest it could be done - and 6 AM - when the doors had already been found welded. An odd hour to do that - but perhaps that was the intention?

While I was thinking, another old woman walked downstairs past us. She seemed in a hurry, and she was visibly worried about something. I could already hear the commotion downstairs growing.

"Excuse me, do you know what is going on down there?" - I asked the old man, pointing at the woman's back. "Where is everyone heading?"

"Oh, you know how they say, 'the misfortune never comes alone'" - he told me, rubbing his temple. "Someone found one of the tenants downstairs dead. I think her heart gave out from all the stress. What a horrible time we're living in..."

The events of the previous day had already taught me that nothing was a coincidence. So, excusing myself to the old man I went to my room, quickly changed my clothes, and headed outside my apartment. I found it too suspicious that someone had already died in our building.

As I was approaching the first floor, I could already hear the lamentations of the people downstairs. Some woman was crying. When I came to the first floor, there were so many people on it that they occupied the whole flight of stairs. From where I stopped I couldn't see inside the apartment, but I could hear what the people were saying pretty well.

"What's going on?" - the old man who arrived just a few seconds before me asked.

"A woman was found dead in her apartment," - a man standing a few steps lower than him answered. "Galina from 22nd - do you know her?"

"Galina? Oh, dear… What happened, heart attack? Aneurism?"

"Hard to determine, they say" - the man mused. "Her neighbor wanted to borrow some tea from her and noticed that the door was open. She came inside and found Galina dead on the floor, right next to the door."

"Oh, lord. Dreadful, dreadful. Why do you think the door was open?" - the man wondered.

"I don't know, but..." - the man talking switched to a sinister, conspiratorial whisper: "But they say that her eyes bulged and her tongue is sticking out. I haven't seen it myself, but it sounds like someone had strangled her."

"Oh, dear. Just one day in isolation and people start to rob each other again. It's the nineties all over again..." - his interlocutor complained.

The old man's guess was a good one, but I doubted that it was the case. Robbed on the first day? By whom - the neighbors she'd lived with for decades? And on the first day after the isolation had started, with the culprit having nowhere to run? It seemed far too reckless and spontaneous to be the case.

No, if what the old man had said was right, then I saw the clues pointing to a different motive. The woman was strangled right in her hallway, next to the open door, and, most importantly, she lived on the first floor. These clues were lining up into an arrow, pointing towards a particular culprit - the same person who had welded our doors shut.

The more I thought about it, the more it made sense: the one who had killed the woman was the same person who had shut us all in. He had been working at night, hoping to avoid being seen, but welding was without a doubt a noisy affair. Despite that person's precautions, it must've attracted unwanted attention - the attention of an elderly woman, living right next to the door leading outside, who decided to come out and see what the commotion was about. Many old people are light sleepers, after all. Old age makes one wary of dangers lurking in the night.

The welder must've had serious reasons to remain unknown - so much so that when the woman came out and saw him, he realized that he had to keep her silent. By whatever means necessary.

And if he was so afraid that she'd recognize him later, then perhaps the last face she'd seen before she tried to draw her last breath was a familiar one. The face of one of her neighbors. While I had little doubts that the welder was one of the tenants - he did go through the effort of sealing the doors from the inside - that last piece of the puzzle finalized the deal.

Which meant that one of our eighty apartments housed not just the person who had jailed us - it housed a murderer. An individual who'd go to great risks to keep his identity and reasons hidden. The benevolent motive I had considered earlier - to seal the doors to keep us protected - was now out of the question. Whoever did that, and for whatever reason, they were not driven by the care for their neighbors. If anything, it was rather the opposite.

"Hey, what are you doing? Have you no shame?" - I heard someone downstairs lament.

"Stand back!" - an old female voice replied. "I'm not taking anything valuable - it's just food. She won't be needing it anyway, and I want to live some more! You'd be wise to take something for yourself while there's something left to take!"

The crowd became agitated: there was reason in the woman's words. In just a few moments, the people who had been condemning her a second before started arguing about their spot in the line and who needed the food the most.

I thought about grabbing some food for myself, but I had seen the extent to which these people can get violent over the last discounted chicken in a store, and I could only imagine what would happen when they were presented with "everything you can carry" deal - especially during the food shortage. With me being at the very end of the line, there wouldn't be anything left for me. The most I could count on was a backhand insult being thrown my way.

From the depths of the apartment, where people were already arguing about how much each of them should get, came a sound of a bag tearing, followed by the clatter of rice hitting the floor as if to confirm my suspicions. I turned around and headed upstairs. Leonid was supposed to contact me soon. Perhaps I would get some good news from him at least.

\*\*\*

A few hours later I was still waiting for him to contact me. It was almost noon, but he hadn't shown up. I wanted to make some coffee. To cook breakfast. To brush my teeth. My bladder hadn't been relieved once since the start of the day.

But I was too afraid to step away from the radio even for one moment. I felt that his absence was due to other, urgent matters going on at the base. And if he contacted me and I wasn't there to get his message he wouldn't wait for me.

The wait felt like he was drawing the bow's string. Like he was deliberately drawing out the suspense. Like he was teasing me. It was exhilarating, but I knew the payoff would be worth it.

At half-past noon I allowed myself a quick break to relieve myself – only because I couldn't hold it in anymore.

An hour later I went to the kitchen to prepare breakfast - a couple of eggs. Whenever they didn't require my immediate attention I'd go to the guestroom to sit near the radio. Without me around to control the process, the eggs turned out to be a bit burned, and I forgot to add salt.

At two minutes past noon, while standing near the window, I realized that I spoiled my breakfast for nothing. He was not going to contact me anymore.

Perhaps his superiors weren't very keen on him talking to the civilians during the emergency, after all. Or he simply changed his mind and decided not to stick his neck out for someone he didn't know.

*"Or maybe,"* - I thought - *"The base doesn't even exist anymore. Perhaps whatever has caused this all is much more serious than it seems, and this has gotten to them."*

My thoughts were interrupted by the bell ringing. Someone was at my door.

It turned out to be Natasha. She seemed calmer than the day before, but at the same time more exhausted. I could see bags under her eyes. She didn't calm down – she just didn't have the strength to worry anymore.

"Hey" - she quietly greeted me, looking at her feet. "May I come in?"

"Sure" - I welcomed her in. "How are you today?"

"Horrible," - she said. "I didn't get an ounce of sleep last night. Couldn't stop thinking about Nikita."

"I get it," - I told her.

"I think I'm going crazy from this isolation," - she complained to me. "This constant howling is driving me crazy. Yesterday I think I heard someone walking on the roof."

"Maybe it was just one of the tenants" - I suggested, trying to sway away from the alternative. It was too horrifying to think that something could get up on our roof.

"I thought so as well," - she sighed. "But it didn't help me get to sleep. I was thinking that maybe it was him, and one time I woke up during the night because I dreamed that he was looking through my window."

"You're just tired," – I assured her, trying not to think about the implications of her words. My skin started crawling when I imagined what it was like – looking out the window on the fifth floor and seeing someone peeking in.

"Yeah, I guess," – she threw a concerned glance at the door leading to my guest room. "Say, have you heard anything new on your radio?" – she wondered, trying to sound as casual as possible. Only her nervous gesture of putting her hair behind her ear betrayed the fact that she was worried. She was blindly hoping to find out something about her boyfriend's fate, but it seemed she was ashamed to come off as desperate.

"Nothing" – I shook my head. I decided not to tell her about my new acquaintance – why give her false hope? I had already been disillusioned myself, and I didn't want her to share my fate.

"Ah… I see. Let me know if you hear anything. About our situation," – she added quickly, worried that I would misinterpret her words, before turning around and heading for the door.

"Do you perhaps want to stay? I was just going to put on some tea," – I suggested. Natasha froze. I already knew her answer – she was just picking her words to excuse herself.

"No… Sorry, I can't. I have… things to attend to back home," – she awkwardly explained. I knew that it was a bald-faced lie – there was nothing she could possibly be doing back home at such a time. She just didn't want to say that she wanted to be alone. And I didn't have it in me to call her out on that.

"Sure," – I nodded and smiled, even though she wasn't looking at me. "I get it. Go get it done. If you want to talk – you know where to find me," – I joked.

"Yeah, okay," – she answered. Her mind was already elsewhere. "Bye, Yura."

With that, she left. I spent the rest of the day waiting for either her or Leonid to show up, but neither did. In the evening, I went to bed feeling more lonely than usual.

\*\*\*

I woke up during the night from another roar. It seemed much closer this time than before, and even through the haze of sleep, I recognized the fact that it sounded different.

I searched for my phone in the darkness and looked at what time it was. 3 AM. It was the dead of the night.

I wanted to think that I made it all up in my sleep. It almost sounded reasonable, too: I had been listening to that beast's roars throughout the previous two days. So, of course it would haunt my dreams as well.

But I had already made such a mistake before. The last time I was woken up by the beast during the night it wasn't just a dream - it was very much real as the creature was announcing its presence to us.

Plus, I couldn't forget Natasha's words - that she heard something in the dead of the night. Her account wasn't the only one I could rely on - I knew all too well by now that the night indeed hosted something terrible. The time of our ancestors when they were scared of things in the dark, coming up with names for their new fears, was again upon us.

I stood up and walked out onto my balcony. The air was chilly, and I could see my breath, but I didn't feel like going back inside to put on clothes - I didn't intend to stay outside for long. I just wanted to find out what the source of those howls was.

Just as the day before, it was dead quiet outside, only now I also could hardly see anything. My eyes, not yet accustomed to the dark, could only make out a few grey shapes of the forest, but aside from it - nothing else.

"You heard it too, Yuri?" - consumed in my thoughts about things in the night, I jumped when a familiar voice reached out to me from the dark. "Heh! Sorry, didn't mean to spook you," - the voice laughed.

"I almost had a heart attack, Maxim" - I replied, taking a deep breath. Still, I was relieved when I realized that the voice was just my neighbor and not something else. "These past few days made me jumpy."

"Yes, I can relate. Only an insane person would stay calm in such a situation," - Maxim replied, leaning onto his balcony.

Maxim was my neighbor - I've met him on that very same balcony when I first came out to smoke. Our balconies were close to each other - not close enough to climb from one to another, but close enough that we could chat during the night without being worried about waking up other neighbors, and we often chatted before going off to sleep.

We weren't close friends - more like acquaintances. Someone you could vent to without bothering to listen to the other side. I didn't know too much about him, but from what I could gather, he was a widower who lived alone. A lonely soul just like me, although for different reasons.

I patted my pockets, looking for my cigarettes, and realized that I forgot them back in my room.

"I'll be right back" - I told Maxim, but before I could leave he stopped me: "No need. Catch!"

He threw me a pack of cigarettes and I caught it mid-air. Through the thin carton, I felt that the box was full - a surprising generosity. Even though I wasn't sure he could see me, I gave Maxim a puzzled look.

"I've got a full block of these back in my room," - either Maxim saw my surprised face or he simply decided to explain himself. "More than enough to last me a few weeks…Though, I hope we won't be staying here for so long."

I looked at the brand of the box, and in the dim light of the moon, I saw the brand.

"Soyuz-Apollo."

My guts sank when the terrible suspicion crossed my mind.

Before that thought went anywhere, I suppressed it: I could look into that later. For now, I could continue chatting as if nothing had happened. If Maxim really had something to do with the state of our doors, he wouldn't just tell me - not after what had happened to the neighbor downstairs. But he could carelessly drop some hint in a casual conversation.

"We've got ourselves quite a pickle, Yuri" - Maxim thoughtfully said, looking into the distance. "We're all locked up here, and the police aren't coming. Soon there are going to be food shortages. And then that woman from the first floor… Soon it's going to be complete and total chaos."

I nodded in agreement. The situation seemed grim.

"We've got to do something about it" - he said, taking another puff from his cigarette. "I've already talked to some able-bodied men - they agree to help me out. I'm thinking about organizing a militia to keep everything under control."

"A militia?" - I raised my eyebrows.

"Yes, you know, to keep everything in check. We need to bring order back within these walls. I think people need to feel safe these days, and we can give it to them. And if they feel safe, then they will act properly. Unrest is the product of fear, Yuri. In the nineties, when crime was rampant, everyone was afraid. Everyone was ready to be stabbed in the back, so they did it first. Look at where it brought the country - it almost collapsed. It's up to us men to have it all under strict control. We need to show people that they have nothing to fear."

His words made sense: I remembered how vicious the people had gotten when they started fighting over that woman's food. If there was a group of individuals who'd be around to keep everything in control, to flex their muscles at an unruly crowd, then perhaps we'd really all benefit from it.

And most importantly, it meant bringing life back under my control. I wouldn't be a passive observer anymore. I'd be doing something about the situation. Even if it was a pointless or silly endeavor - to play the police - it was something to keep me busy with.

"So, what do you think?" - Maxim asked me. "Do you think it's a good idea? Would you join me?"

I took a full breath to say: "yes." But I never exhaled.

Instead, I froze, trying to not make any noise. I froze and held my breath so that the air rushing out of my nostrils wouldn't hinder my hearing so that I could strain my hearing to its fullest and confirm what I had just heard.

The sound of branches snapping under someone's foot. The sound that came directly from beneath my balcony.

Maxim froze as well. In the silence that ensued, we clearly heard the confirmation of our earlier suspicion: something was moving beneath us. Rustling the grass under its feet as it was heading towards the forest.

I leaned over my balcony's rails to see it, and Maxim did the same. "There!" - Maxim screamed and pointed, although I didn't need any help to see a massive grey shadow enter the forest.

My blood ran cold. It was standing there throughout our entire conversation, and neither I nor Maxim noticed it. We were merrily chatting as the beast below was biding its time, listening to our voices.

"Holy! Have you seen it?" - Maxim loudly whispered. The disbelief in his voice was almost palpable, confirming my scariest suspicions about the beast's nature.

"I- I didn't" - I stuttered, still shocked that the creature we'd been hiding from for the last few days, the one that had killed several people over the last couple of days, was mere meters away from me. "Hold on, I'll light it up."

I searched my pockets for a phone, pulled it out, turned on the flashlight, and pointed it at the forest.

At the very next moment, I shuddered and dropped it, catching it at the very last moment. I was not ready to see something like that.

The phone's flashlight was not particularly powerful, so the cone of light quickly dissipated. And yet some of the photons had found their way between the branches deep into the forest to reflect from the beast's lone giant eye - the size of a small platter - and travel back to me.

At that short moment, I was unwillingly participating in a staring contest with it. Something told me that I was the first man to do so and walk away to tell about it.

There was no doubt about it now: the creature was not a bear, or a mountain lion - or anything I'd ever heard of. No land creature I knew of had an eye of such size. Despite common sense, despite how impossible it seemed, I had to admit an undeniable fact: the creature that haunted our town, the strange newcomer that fell onto our heads from seemingly nowhere, was not a mere animal, native to our world.

It was one thing to suspect it, to build strange theories based on what I'd heard myself, and on the radio, and completely different to bear witness to the facts with my own eyes.

"What's the commotion? Go to sleep already!" - I heard one of the neighbors speak. Our shouts must've woken them up, and one by one, the neighbors were waking up, turning on the lights, opening their windows, and coming out to their balconies to see what the commotion was about.

"What's all this noise?"

"Did the military arrive?"

"Pasha, good night. Do you know what this is all about?"

"I think someone saw something."

"Look! There, under the branches!"

As people were waking up and turning on their lights they started flooding the forest with it. Like tiny dim projectors, their windows illuminated the forest, casting long, dark shadows - yet also making the creature easier to spot. In a few seconds, the alarmed screams of the witnesses woke up the rest of the building and made those who were reluctant to wake up get out of their beds to see what was going on. In a few moments, half of the building was watching the creature.

I saw someone on the first-floor turn on the lights and then turn them off a moment later. I doubted they could see much beyond the bushes - even from my height I could barely make out the details. But seeing something unknown outside your house's window, knowing that it could also spot you, was probably terrifying beyond reason.

Seeing that it had attracted the unwanted attention, the creature turned around and ran deeper into the forest - into the shadows, away from the light.

"Yuri... Have you ever seen such a creature?" - I heard Maxim ask me in bewilderment. His alarmed whisper barely registered with all the noise the neighbors were raising.

"No" - I shook my head, gazing into the forest's depths. For the first time in my life, I saw it like my ancestors had seen it: a domain of darkness and unknown. A wooden ocean where the monsters out of the fairy tales dwelled. "I haven't."

# CHAPTER 8 – Militia

That night, I barely managed to close my eyes for some sleep. For the first time since I was ten, I was afraid of the dark and was rather thankful that we still had electricity. I didn't risk turning on the lights, but the cheap night-light that reeked of plastic and could probably leave a chemical burn if kept in hands for too long was turned on for the first time since I'd bought it. The green light was not my favorite, and it didn't make me feel cozy, making the scenery more sinister instead, but it was better than nothing.

Our town didn't have a power station, and all the electricity was provided from the outside, yet I knew that the military could shut it down at any moment. They should've known by now that we were still there - they just couldn't be in the dark about that. Somewhere at the power station far away the meters were still spinning, counting electricity for our bills and letting the world know that we were still there. Still burning energy. The mere fact that they hadn't turned it off meant that someone out there still gave a damn about us. And if they cared, it meant that they were planning to save us… eventually.

But if they knew that the civilians were stuck in the town, if they knew what we were up against… what was taking them so long?

I woke up in the morning from the noise of a helicopter. In all of my life in that town, I hadn't ever heard one.

I knew that one of the military bases nearby had a long stretch of road, meant to accommodate the cargo planes as an improvised landing strip, but I had never heard of them using a helicopter. Which meant that the military had already started pulling in more personnel to our town from other parts of the country. And the flyby they were doing was no doubt an exploration of the territory.

Perhaps even to see if there were any survivors left?

I jumped out of bed and rushed to the balcony. I was hoping that the helicopter was flying on the side my windows were facing - that way, I could signal them that I was still there, that we were here.

And if they spotted us and decided to land on our roof to pick up a few survivors - what then? Would I find it in me to push the others aside, to rush toward the helicopter and ask them to pick me?

The helicopter was slowly circling over the forest in the distance as if searching for something in the woods. Immediately I understood that its mission was not to find the civilians - it was something else.

But still, it was someone who could get us out, and I'd gotten hopeful. The planes flying over the uninhabited islands do not aim to find anyone stranded there, yet they pick them up if they have such a chance.

"We're here!" - someone above shouted. Looking there, I saw that other tenants were starting to come out to attract their attention. "Help!"

More and more people were coming out to shout, to wave. To attract the pilot's attention by any means necessary. I could hear both hope and despair in their voices. Hope that they were going to be rescued... and despair that they wouldn't be noticed.

I joined the rest of the people.

The helicopter didn't change its course to fly closer to us, stopping to hover over one spot instead. I didn't know what was going on, but I wanted to think that the pilot was contacting the base, letting them know that he'd spotted the survivors and requesting the instructions.

Whether it was the case or not, after a minute or two the helicopter gained speed and flew away.

People were still begging for it to come back, but I turned around and entered my apartment. It was clear that they weren't going to rescue us - at least not that particular helicopter. I had to face the music: we were on our own. No one was going to come and rescue us.

"Fly away," - I whispered. "We don't need you."

The words felt alien, not my own. It wasn't common for me to think like that. Deep inside, I knew I wanted a group of happy, polite people to land on our roof and rescue us from that hell. Take that burden away from us and make our lives easy again. Make all the decisions for us.

I went to bed and tried to get a few more hours of sleep. At least the sun was up, so I didn't have to fear the dark anymore.

\*\*\*

I woke up the second time when someone knocked on my door. I looked at the phone: it was 10 AM. Quickly putting on some clothes, I went to answer the door.

"Good morning, Yura" - Maxim greeted me. His face was sunken: it was clear that he was not happy that the helicopter hadn't picked anyone up.

"Hello, Maxim" - I greeted him, looking over his shoulder. Behind him stood three more men - all of them in their forties. All of them just as serious as Maxim.

"Have you thought about joining the militia?" - Maxim asked me. I understood that the men behind him were people he'd already gathered.

I felt a bit intimidated by them. All of them were grown men, with families and responsibilities, all of them had had their own share of salt in life. Them coming to my apartment felt like a group of high-schoolers coming to a kindergartener to ask him to join them for a party. I felt out of place among them.

But at the same time, it told me that they were willing to accept anyone. That Maxim had put his trust in me and vouched for me. That my childish misconceptions about my worth were just that, and to them, I was another pair of capable hands. It felt good to have someone have trust in me.

And besides, it was a way to get my life under control. It was much better than to wait for men in the sky to decide our fate. The old world had crumbled, and I needed to settle in the new one.

"Yes" - I told him. "I want in."

"That's the spirit," - Maxim nodded. One of the men behind him came closer, almost shoving Maxim to the side, and pointed his finger at me: "Just take this seriously, alright? This isn't going to be a game, and no one's going to wipe your ass. You have to be capable to handle things, alright?"

"He's good, Pasha" - Maxim said with annoyance.

"I need him to understand what he's signing up for," - the man named Pasha grunted. "He'll join now, and then what? When the push comes to shove, will he do what's necessary or is he going to cower behind our backs?"

Maxim opened his mouth to tell Pasha something. I could see that it wasn't going to be pretty.

"I can handle it," – I said before Maxim said anything. "I have grit, and I understand that we're locked in here. No helicopters are coming to rescue us. We have to handle it ourselves," - I looked the man in the eye. "So please back off."

For a moment the man froze, letting what I'd said sink in. I didn't know how he was going to react, and I couldn't tell anything from his face, either. But then he leaned back and grunted: "Good. Just don't disappoint me."

Seeing that the situation was resolved, Maxim took time to introduce us to each other. The man I'd argued with was Pasha - a former policeman who was now on a pension. Despite him being in his early fifties, his face was covered in wrinkles that stayed the same no matter what his expression was - as if someone carved them in the stone of his weathered face. He carried a pistol in a holster on his chest, and when he reached out for a handshake, I found out that he had a stone grip as well. It felt like underneath his skin and blistered palm he was packing a few bolts.

The man next to him was much older, in his middle sixties - almost a full head shorter than me and not too strong from the looks of it. He looked serious, but when I reached out for a handshake, he beamed me quite a genuine smile. He introduced himself as Mikhail.

The third one was Maxim's age. He did not smile or emote in any way, and he was wearing attire more fitting to a hunter or a fisherman than to a member of the militia - a camo jacket which was so loved by hunters in Russia, thick pants and rubber galoshes reaching all the way up to his knees. The footwear of someone who had spent their fair share in forest swamps. He either forgot to introduce himself or decided that it wasn't important. I decided to ignore it.

"Is this it?" - I asked Maxim. "Is this the whole militia or did you want to ask someone else?"

"You think we aren't enough?" - Pasha asked me, scowling.

"I'm just asking," - I told him. "Is this it?"

"Yes" - Maxim answered. He obviously wanted to squeeze in a word before Pasha started talking again. "You're the last one we've asked. The rest of the men, they... they didn't appreciate the idea."

I didn't know what was more disheartening: the fact that they asked me the last or the fact that I was now in a band of misfits. Whether we believed it to be a good idea or not, the fact that the rest of the tenants didn't approve of it made it difficult to sign up for it. Perhaps if the others didn't agree, then it really was a stupid idea?

No. I needed to take control of the situation, I reminded myself.

"Then we don't need more," - I told Maxim.

"I wish it were so" - Pasha grunted. "It's going to be tough to keep control of the situation if people don't want our help. Trust me, I know" - he assured me with an obnoxious know-it-all look. I sighed and pursed my lips but didn't answer. I didn't want to start another argument.

"More will join if we do our job right" - Maxim said with confidence, though his body language did not carry the same message.

"So, what are we doing?" - I asked Maxim.

"We need to make sure that the building is secure and let everyone know that we're taking the charge here," - Maxim said, sighing. It seemed that he did not look forward to that part, and I could see why. Few people would appreciate a group of people walking around with guns. "I think we should start with the basement - there is a manhole cover leading to the sewers there. I wanted to see if it is accessible."

Maxim looked at me from top to toe, and after a short consideration said: "And put on something…more appropriate. If we walk around wearing our house clothes, people won't take us seriously."

Five minutes later we were on the first floor, trying to find the way into the basement past the door locked on a hanging padlock. After asking the tenants who had lived on the first floor, it turned out that only a janitor had the key.

"Maybe we should abandon this idea?" - I suggested. "I don't think it's a good idea to break the door."

"We need to be sure whether the manhole is welded shut or not" - Maxim insisted. "It may be our only way out of here."

*"Or maybe you'd forgotten about the sewers and you want to have a door there broken so that you could finish the job at night,"* - I thought, making sure that my face didn't betray my thoughts.

"The basement has small windows leading into it - what if something finds its way in?" - I argued again.

"You've seen that thing yourself, Yuri - it simply won't fit in," - Maxim said. But after a bit of consideration, he agreed with me: "Perhaps we can be careful in how we remove the lock… If we do it carefully, we might be able to repair the damages to the door afterward."

After five more minutes of looking for appropriate tools, Mikhail brought a crowbar from his apartment, and we pried off the lock. He tried to be careful, yet a piece of the door came off with it, the bolts tearing through old wood. It seemed we wouldn't be able to hold the door locked again.

"I'll nail it back" - the man promised, giving everyone present a guilty look.

"What is going on there?" - a woman came out of one of the apartments on the first floor. Her tone reflected that she did not approve of our actions, and the volume of her voice was no doubt meant to attract other neighbors. I couldn't blame her. Her neighbor had been killed on the threshold of her home just a day before, so she had to be careful.

And yet, I couldn't wince when the echo of her voice boomed in my ears. We were just a few meters away from her, after all.

"Don't worry, babushka" - Pasha said, taking a step forward. He meant to calm her down, yet the woman took a step back when she saw an armed man approach her. "We're the militia. We're just investigating a few things."

"A militia? Who appointed you?" - she asked him with distrust. It was clear as the day that she did not appreciate the initiative. "We somehow lived without a militia until now."

"Until now, things were different" - Pasha said, doing his best to stay calm, though everyone could hear the strain in his voice. "Until now, we've had the police to take care of such things."

"As if they were good for anything," - the woman grunted.

"As if you'd know anything about that!" - Pasha loudly argued. "The police have been doing a good job, so don't talk about things you don't understand!"

The woman must've struck a chord with the former policeman. The woman, taking another step back, got defensive, and didn't answer. Pasha's outburst intimidated her. I've decided that I should interfere: perhaps my less than intimidating build was just what could be used for negotiation.

"Have you seen or heard anything after the night of the murder?" - I asked the woman. Throwing a careful glance at Pasha, she turned to me and started speaking: "I didn't hear anything. And I didn't hear anything before that, either. If you want my opinion, Galina was just too trusting. She must've let in some hooligans who wanted to rob an old woman..." - she sighed. I noticed that she gave me a mean, suspicious look and sighed, too. Even if I wanted to help these people, they would still see me as an outsider and a danger.

"By the way, since you're here, can you help me move her? The people yesterday helped me move her to her bathroom - I couldn't leave her lying on the floor in those same clothes, you see, and I thought it'd be a decent thing to wash her body," - she explained. I had to struggle to avoid imagining that picture. "But now everyone's gone, and I can't move her to the guestroom."

"Why the guestroom?" - I asked. The woman rolled her eyes at me: "What, do you think I should just leave her lying in a bathtub? Have some decency. Besides, it is common for the recently deceased to spend some time in their house while their relatives pray for their soul," - she told me with such a look as if I was supposed to know that. As if I was burying friends every other day.

But I remembered when I was little I had attended a funeral of one of my distant relatives who lived in some village. I had expected it to be like in the movies I'd seen - a nice, well-lit church, a pastor giving a speech about how the deceased will be missed. Instead, I found out that the coffin with the dead man was put right in the middle of his living room so that all who attended could come closer to say their final words. Some people were grieving, others were just casually chatting with the relatives they hadn't seen in years - and in the middle of all of that stood an open casket. With a dead man inside. To the six year old me it seemed as if in that short time span between your death and your burial you had to play the role of some ritualistic furniture.

"Who's going to pray for her if we're on a lockdown?" - I wondered.

"I will," - the woman declared, raising her nose and puffing out her chest. "I know how to pray. If no one else will - I'll do it. She was my neighbor, after all."

"Yura, you go help Maxim and ask someone to help me out here. I want someone strong to help me carry her" - Pasha said. He didn't mean it as an insult, so I didn't say anything, yet being dismissed like that still hurt a bit. I nodded and headed to the basement where the rest of the men were.

The basement consisted of a long, cold, and dusty corridor stretching underneath the entire building that was connected to numerous empty rooms – "concrete sweat-boxes" as I liked to call them. Its bare concrete walls were covered in pipes and cables. Yellow pieces of paper, empty packs of cartons, and wet, old cigarette butts were unevenly scattered across the floor - how'd they gotten there, considering that the basement had been locked up for a long time, was a mystery.

The wall next to me had small windows almost at the ceiling – wide, low rectangles that were the only source of light in there. Even if there was a switch somewhere, I doubted that the lightbulbs above still worked. Most likely, they hadn't been replaced since the moment the building had been built and now were no more than dusty globes with dead flies inside.

I followed the voices of men, navigating the cold, dark rooms and corridors, and soon I found them, squatting next to the manhole leading to the sewers.

I barely managed to contain myself when I noticed that the manhole wasn't welded shut. The welder must have forgotten about it.

The men had already pried it open prior to my arrival and were now staring into the dark depths below them. Even though it smelled horrible, I couldn't help but associate that smell with freedom, with the outdoors.

I looked at Maxim - the look on the man's face was not a happy one. If anything, the man was distraught, concerned.

"So. we can escape now if we want?" - I wondered aloud. "Escape without any risk?"

"I wouldn't be so sure," - Maxim said. "We don't know where these sewers lead and whether there's enough room for people to walk."

"We better find out, then," - Mikhail said. "This smells horrible, but if we are not evacuated soon, we might have to start looking for a way out."

"I don't know if we're going to be rescued any time soon," - I told him. Maxim gave a confused glance: "What makes you say that?"

I realized that I'd said too much. I didn't know if I could trust Maxim enough to disclose that I'd had access to the information from the outside. In a situation where the welder's motivation was still unknown, it was too dangerous to disclose what I'd learned about our situation.

"Just a hunch," - I said. "This morning the helicopters ignored us. I don't think that rescuing us is a priority."

Maxim silently nodded.

"I think it's a good idea to investigate where it leads, then," - the nameless man said. "I have some hunting equipment and a flashlight - I could go down there and map out the place, see what I could find."

"Good idea," - Maxim nodded in agreement. "And I think we should keep this manhole a secret for a while."

"Why?" - I wondered.

"If people find out about it, they may start going down there before we know if it's safe to do so or whether it leads anywhere. I don't want to crawl around down there looking for the lost elderly, and I think everyone present thinks the same," - he said.

His words made sense, and yet I couldn't shake off the feeling that he had some ulterior motives. That he wanted to keep this manhole a secret since it was a miscalculation in his plan. A literal loophole people could use to escape the building.

But I didn't show it. I just nodded in agreement.

"We better keep a lookout on this place, then" - I said. "If the welder learns about this place, he might want to seal it, too" - I said, looking at Maxim. Was his armor going to crack? Was he going to give himself away when he heard me mention the welder?

Nothing. Either Maxim operated well under pressure, or it wasn't him.

"Well, it's settled then," - the nameless man said, getting up to his feet. "We keep our mouths shut about it until we have some concrete info about what's on the other side. I'll go down there in a couple of hours."

I couldn't help but feel admiration for that man, and at the same time, I felt ashamed that I didn't volunteer instead of him.

"If this turns out to be a dead-end, we might take our chances by leaving the town together over the surface, as a group," - the man added. "The salvation of the drowning men is their own business, as they say."

"Do you think it's a good idea?" - I asked him. "We know nothing about that thing outside."

"Well, if we keep sitting here we'll be out of other options," - the man said.

I nodded in agreement. While I was not looking forward to venturing outside, it was nice that we had a plan to fall back to. Everything was slowly starting to come together.

"What now?" - I asked Maxim.

"Now… I've had an idea when I saw you talking to that old woman. We should visit all the apartments and ask the tenants if they'd seen or heard anything suspicious. That way we'll gather some information and inform everyone that we're here to protect them," - Maxim said.

"We might get more people to join us if they see us in action" - the nameless man chimed in.

"Will we cover all the staircases or just ours?" - I wondered.

"I think we should do all of them," - Maxim said, thinking it over. "And we should pay extra attention to the first floors. If the tenants there had seen anything, we could learn a thing or two about this… welder."

"Makes sense" - I nodded. It wouldn't make sense for Maxim to make such a suggestion if he was the one who'd locked us in there - if there had been witnesses, they could recognize him. Then again, maybe he was confident that he remained unseen.

As we were leaving the manhole, I couldn't help but feel a bubble of hope rise in my chest. It was a good start, no matter how I looked at it.

# CHAPTER 9 - Rumors

We headed upstairs - while we could just break the locks on the doors which led to the other staircases we'd decided against it. It wouldn't be wise to break the doors without any means to fix them, and besides, we wouldn't make a good first impression on the tenants if we started by breaking their property.

Pasha was already standing outside the apartment of the deceased woman. He bent over and was heavily panting, but when he saw us approach he straightened out to hide that he was tired.

"Where the hell have you been? I could use another pair of hands," - he grunted. "Didn't I ask you to go bring someone?" - he turned to me.

"Sorry" - I apologized, feeling my cheeks blush. While I didn't like the guy, I felt bad that I let him down. The discovery of the unsealed manhole had made me forget about his request altogether.

"Forget it" - he dismissively waved his hand at me. "What are we doing next?"

Maxim told him. Pasha nodded. We headed upstairs.

\*\*\*

On our way above, Anton left us and headed for his apartment. "I want to prepare for my trip to the sewers" - he told us with a scorn on his face. It was clear that he wasn't looking forward to it, even if he volunteered for it.

"What's that?" - Pasha asked him, but Maxim hissed at him: "Not here. We'll explain later."

Pasha grunted with disapproval but didn't say another word. He understood that whatever we wanted to share with him could only be told in privacy, away from unwanted listeners.

We'd started going from one apartment to another to introduce ourselves. The idea was to let people know that we were going to look after them, that we were getting things back under control. But wherever we went, people were looking at us with mistrust. Very few appreciated our initiative: most of them were looking at us with eyes full of suspicion.

It was hard doing that - it felt like we were trying to sell them on the idea, and I was never much of a salesman. Though I tried to act with dignity, with confidence, people were noticing my doubts and it was making them wary. After all, why would they be sold on the idea I, myself, was not very confident in?

Somehow, even though I was the least intimidating one - save for Mikhail, who was way too old to be intimidating - people weren't trusting me in the least. Some of them refused to even open doors to talk to me and told me to get lost while glancing at me through their peephole. I was called a hooligan, a bandit, a misfit, a liar, a fascist, and even a liberal, for some reason.

"It's alright," - Maxim assured me. "People of their age just don't trust the youngsters. Don't take it personally."

"It's hard not to take it personally, especially when you're only trying to help them," - I complained.

Maxim smiled: "These people weren't always like that. The gloomy world of walled-off people you grew up in didn't exist in their youth. People weren't afraid to look each other in the eye or talk to strangers. It's just that after the nineties when people of your age were gathering into gangs, robbing and tricking old people, they have a mistrust for... well, people of your age," - he finished awkwardly.

"I understand, but I wasn't even around during the nineties!" - I told him. "The only people who were around were their generation and the generation of their children, so I'm tired of hearing that excuse."

"True," - Maxim nodded. "They don't trust the youngsters that grew up in the world they've created. I imagine it's a bit tragic - if anyone stopped to think about it, that is," - he nodded toward the next door. "Don't hang your head too low. They'll come around. Come on, we have a lot more ground to cover."

His optimism was contagious, so I decided not to let my gloomy thoughts cloud my judgment.

A few apartments later, people finally started opening up to me. A man in his sixties welcomed me and invited me in for a cup of tea. Even though I was flattered and wanted to accept his invitation and relax a bit, soak in his hospitality, I politely declined and asked him if he'd seen anything.

"Oh, I've seen things alright" - he told me, getting serious. "Heed my words, young man - the old age is a terrible thing. I've been spending these past few days doing nothing but looking out the window. And the things I see there nowadays are not the same as what I'd seen there last week."

He leaned in closer and whispered to me: "You saw that thing last night, didn't you? That horrible one-eyed monster. Well, I've seen it many times since this whole thing had started. It is very secretive and keeps out of sight, but it is always there. I've been telling people about it before, but nobody believed me. But it is out there, and it's not alone. Sometimes, when it howls - something answers."

"You mean there are more of them?" - I asked him with disbelief, and he furiously nodded, excited that he'd finally found somebody willing to listen. "Precisely right, young man. They are everywhere there, hiding in shadows. I saw it enter other buildings, and if our doors hadn't been welded shut, it would no doubt enter our building as well. They've been planning this from the beginning. Why do you think the doors have been welded shut on such a day?"

"Who are they?" – I asked him, noticing that I also switched to a whisper. I wasn't sure if I believed him, but the conversation was taking a rather interesting turn. The old man, whether he knew it or not, was playing on my vulnerability to conspiracy theories. Talking to him was like finding something interesting on the radio, on frequencies where you don't expect anyone to broadcast anything at an odd hour.

He looked around and then leaned even closer, cupping his mouth with a hand. I involuntarily turned my ear to him and whispered straight into it with all the pomposity he could muster. As if he was sharing the meaning of life itself with me.

"The Freemasons."

I couldn't help but roll my eyes and lean back in frustration: the old fool got me worked up for nothing. "Freemasons" was one of those answers some people could insert into any conversation – and they did so with religious fervor. They had been blamed for so many things all over the world I couldn't take such claims seriously anymore.

Here I was hoping to learn something about our situation, find out about more sightings through the word of mouth, but I ended up with nothing more than an old man's flight of fancy.

The old man noticed my reaction and had gotten a bit flustered – that was not what he expected based on how our conversation had been going up to that moment. "Heh, just you wait, young man" – he said, brushing his hair back. He tried to smile to show me that he wasn't hurt by my disbelief, but the smile didn't convince me. "You'll see. They've locked us in here, they're brainwashing us with their 5G towers and they've poisoned our water supply – it's already gone really bad," - he complained.

"What nonsense! It's just a bit stale, is all. No need to imagine new problems when we have plenty on our hands" - another old man, the man's neighbor, interrupted him. He was just talking to Maxim and when he heard our conversation he couldn't resist chiming in. "The pipes are good, I laid them myself back in the day! Just drink it and don't complain. You want to have a taste?" – he suddenly asked me and Maxim. He looked me in the eye and licked his lips: "the water's good, I tell you. Never better."

"You're the same as always! Don't listen to that old fool, young man," - the man I was talking to assured me. "He's always been so stubborn. Just another sheep for the slaughter. I'm telling you - the water's bad! They must've mixed something in to poison all of us."

"Who are 'them'?" - Maxim wondered, raising an eyebrow. I was too late to signal to him not to raise that topic.

"Them!" - he exclaimed, making round eyes. "The freemasons, the ones who have started all of this. Our government has been in their pocket since the fall of the USSR, and they..."

I didn't get to hear the rest: the other man chimed in again, only this time he was practically screaming. The conspiracy theorist I had been talking to answered with the same, and they started loudly arguing in that strange manner only old people had mastered: where they were screaming insults to each other, yet at the same time you couldn't make out a thing. It was like watching the dogs having a barking contest, so seeing that they weren't interested in talking to me anymore I quickly slipped away.

\*\*\*

Once we'd reached the fifth floor, men started climbing to the roof. I hesitated for a moment, eyeing a familiar door.

"Are you coming, Yura?" - Maxim asked me. I nodded: "In a moment. Give me a minute, I want to talk to a friend of mine."

Maxim nodded in understanding and started climbing. I pushed the familiar buzzer and, in a few moments, heard soft footsteps on the other side of the door. I smiled: Natasha seemed to be up early.

"Hey, Yura" - Natasha greeted me. She didn't seem sleepy. "What are you doing here?"

"I've joined the local militia" - I told her, smiling. I wanted to share with her the news about the manhole in the basement, but Maxim and the rest of the militia were still within the earshot, climbing to the roof, and I knew they wouldn't appreciate it if I started sharing that news with other tenants. "We're walking around warning people about us, so" - I tipped the imaginary hat on my head: "I'm at your service."

"That's so weird," - she smiled. "But good for you - I know you've been anxious to do something while we're stuck here."

"Yes, apparently I'm this building's first and last line of defense," - I joked. "I mean, I'm not sure if they know who they've accepted into their ranks but they were really short of hands."

"What do you mean?" - she inquired with genuine curiosity, and I felt a bit awkward: self-deprecating humor only worked when the idea at the center of the joke wasn't challenged.

"Well, you know, I'm just kidding..." - I tried explaining myself. "They're all grown men and I'm really not fit to be among them."

"Aren't you a grown man yourself?" - she asked me innocently. She wasn't judging me or trying to dissuade me, but it was making me feel even more awkward.

"Well, yeah, but-"

"Yura, if they've asked you to join them then they must see your worth," - she told me bluntly. "Don't put yourself down like that."

"Alright. Thanks" - I blurted out. It was uncommon and thus uncomfortable to hear compliments. As such, I didn't know what else to say, and with each moment the silence between us was getting more and more awkward.

"I gotta go, so... Talk to you later?" - I excused myself, pointing at the ladder to the roof.

She nodded: "Sure. Come see me after you're done. I wanna hear how it goes." With that, she closed the door, and I turned around to leave for the roof.

Once on the roof, I spotted the rest of the men: Maxim was explaining something to Pasha. No doubt he was informing him about the manhole in the basement.

"So that means that we can leave through it, without endangering ourselves?" - Pasha wondered, looking to the horizon.

"Not immediately," - the man in the hunting gear told him. "I want to explore it first - we need to know how far it goes. If it's a dead-end, it's going to be pointless to mobilize everyone."

"Not to mention that people aren't going to trust us in the future," - Pasha added, enthusiastically nodding. "Yes, that makes sense. I gotta tell you, you've got some balls on you for agreeing to something like that. What's your name, by the way?"

I barely contained a smirk: it turned out that I wasn't the only one who didn't know the man's name. At the same time, I felt a bit of relief: up until that point I had a small suspicion that I was the only one he didn't bother to introduce himself to, and I'd been thinking that it had something to do with my value in the militia.

"My name is Alexei," - he told us.

"You're the man, Alexei," - Pasha came closer to shake his hand. "When do you plan to go there?"

"Right now. It's best we don't postpone it anymore," - he said, pointing to the entrance to the furthest stairwell - the one me and Natasha explored a day before. "It won't take me more than half an hour to gather everything for the trip."

"Alright, got it," - Maxim said. "We'll be there. I think right now we should split to quickly cover the rest of the stairwells."

"I'll inform my neighbors," - Alexei said. "There's not a lot of them left, anyway, so I can do it alone."

"Mikhail and I will cover the third one," - he pointed at the old man, who nodded in agreement. "Pasha, Yura - why don't the two of you go to the fourth one?"

I wasn't excited to go there with Pasha - out of all the men he was the only one who openly disliked me. But I didn't show it - now was not the time to complain about such trivial things: "Sure. No problem."

"Damn right, no problem," - Pasha grunted. "You're coming with me, after all. I've got it all covered."

I restrained myself from giving him a piece of my mind. We had more pressing issues on hand than to argue and bicker.

"Don't argue with each other" - Maxim told us patronizingly. Neither of us answered, indicating that we'd do our best but wouldn't promise anything, and we headed to the furthest door.

"Listen, Yura, I'm going to need you to follow my lead there, alright?" - Pasha started lecturing me while we were walking. "If I tell you to do something - you do it, alright? Those people don't know us and everyone's very tense, so we need to stick together, alright? Have you served in the army?"

"No" - my answer was short. He offered a reasonable idea - to work as a team, but it didn't feel like he wanted to cooperate with me. More like he wanted a lap dog to follow his every command.

"Well, that's too bad - they would've taught you how to follow orders, as well as some discipline. But, I'll work with what I have..."

I zoned out: listening to his ramblings was pure torture. Out of all the people I could've gone with, I went with the type of person I liked the least. He and my mother would get along just fine.

Trying to distract myself, to mentally escape from the present moment, I looked at the forest. The place that had always calmed my nerves in the morning.

And there, in the distance, something caught my eye.

From the roof, I could see above the tallest branches, so the changes in the forest were easy to spot. The closest trees still had the same bright yellow and red leaves, but that wall of color ended abruptly after a few hundred meters. It was not just a coincidence: while the leaves had already started falling from trees, most of them were still hanging on branches. A hundred meters into the forest, however, something was going on. All the trees beyond that imaginary line were naked, without a single leaf, a single pixel of color. A sudden, stark difference that couldn't be missed or explained by the usual change of seasons. As if the winter came there prematurely and was just taking a rest before proceeding further - toward our town.

I knew that just a few days ago that hadn't been the case. Back then, when I was looking around with Natasha, the trees were all the same - otherwise, I would've noticed the difference. Something had changed since then. Something had happened in that forest beyond our town since the night it had started spawning those horrible creatures. It felt like it was dying out, like the wave of death was slowly rolling across it, coming closer to our walls with each day.

"Hey, are you listening to me?" - Pasha jerked my shoulder to get my attention. The sudden movement irritated me, and I angrily shook off his hand, forgetting about the forest in the process. "This is what I was talking about - you need to pay more attention to what's going on. This is serious, Yuri. If you're not up to it - go back home and spend your days there, okay?"

"I'm up to it" - I told him with irritation and looked him in the eye. Immediately I felt intimidated by him, but at the same time, I felt a strange excitement. It felt thrilling to stand up to him. It wasn't like barking back at annoyed elders with their off-handed remarks about me. The man in front of me could retaliate with more than a few harsh words, and I was nowhere near as strong as him.

And yet there I was. Openly challenging him to establish that I wasn't just a lackey. Trying to let him know, to get it through his thick skull, that I was his equal. I had heard that sometimes, you don't earn respect – you have to claim it, but it was the first time I was checking that theory.

"Well, I don't see it," - Pasha said, crossing his hands.

"You'll see" - I told him, going through the door. No further comments from him followed, and I wanted to think that it was because I'd gotten through to him - not because he's given up on arguing with me.

The room with a hatch was the same as the others I'd seen before. Below us was a part of the building I'd never visited, and everything that was going on around us opening that hatch felt like unsealing a catacomb or a nuclear vault with survivors inside. I knew that it was just a silly game of pretend, that just a few days had passed - but who knew what could've gone down there during that time?

I got the answer to my question the moment I opened the hatch: somewhere in the stairwell below, a chanson song was playing.

Chanson was an old-school Russian musical genre that had formed in the nineties during the time of turmoil when people weren't sure if the next day would come and the mafia ruled the streets. It was the direct product of that environment, and although those times had passed it still persevered to our days through fan-following alone.

I didn't like that genre - and neither did the majority of the population and yet I could sometimes hear it coming from a passing taxi cab or pick it up while radio surfing. It was a genre of music where forty-year-old men were singing about the tough life of a thief, about their loved one marrying someone else while they were in prison for stabbing a snitch to the death, or sometimes simply about how the thugs dealt with those who opposed them.

A genre of music for those who romanticized crime life - or actively dabbled in it.

I looked at Pasha - although we weren't exactly getting along I wanted to see his reaction to that music. Predictably, he made a sour face: he was not looking forward to talking to people downstairs.

"You listen to such music?" - he asked me, giving me a mean eye.

Frankly, it was insulting and even a dumb suggestion. So, I decided to push my luck and humor myself a bit by teasing him.

"No. Do you?" - I asked him, looking him straight in the eye.

I expected him to blow up in anger, but surprisingly, the man laughed instead: "Good one. Come on, you go first."

I smiled and did just like he suggested. Internally, I congratulated myself on defusing the tension between us.

The music seemed to be coming from the fourth floor - not from any apartments, but straight from the staircase, as if someone had set up a camp right there. When I descended down the ladder, old metal squeaked and rumbled under my feet, alerting people downstairs to my presence. I heard hushed voices speaking to each other in a hurry, clanking of glasses being put down, and finally the shambling of feet as those people rushed upstairs to see what the commotion was about.

At first glance, I recognized that those guys were bad news. The men who were coming upstairs to greet us weren't young or particularly buff - in fact, out of five of them only one of them didn't look like a walking skeleton. Their skin was pale, their faces - sunken, and their eyes full of animosity. Despite the fact that it was not exactly warm on the staircase they were wearing nothing but wife beaters and tracksuit pants, and I could see their arms covered in tattoos. Not the colorful or flamboyant ones, meant to attract attention. No, those were rough ink paintings, displaying crosses, barbed wire, churches, and other cryptic words the meaning of which eluded me.

My blood ran cold when I realized who we were dealing with, and I was sure that Pasha recognized them, too - he had been dealing with people like these for the entirety of his career in the police.

The bandits. The thugs. The people who spent the majority of their lives in prison and only left them to commit another crime and go back behind the bars. The people who had spent so much time in imprisonment they had formed an entire prison culture - with its own rituals, symbolism, hierarchy, and even language.

The music made sense now. We were in a thug den.

# CHAPTER 10 – Den

"Who the hell are you?! Got lost!" - one of them screamed at us with surprising volume. His voice echoed from the walls, bombarding me and Pasha with hostility. He reached out behind his back and pulled out a knife from behind his belt. Just one look into his bloodshot eyes told me that he wouldn't hesitate to use it.

"Come here!!" - he shouted, gesturing at us to come at him.

"Goddamn it" - I heard Pavel grunt. His clothes rustled, and I looked at him just in time to see him pull out his gun.

"Stand back!" - he shouted, raising his hand with a gun and getting ready to make a warning shot.

It worked: the people stopped just a few steps from our floor, their eyes glued to the weapon. They understood violence. It was the only thing they submitted to.

"Hold back, Pashtet[9]" - one of them stopped their aggravated friend. Judging by the fact that Pashtet did as told, it was easy to deduce that the man was their gang's leader. "Why are you coming into a house of honest people uninvited?" - he asked us.

"Honest people, right" - Pasha said, gritting his teeth. I could see that he was very worked up. While it was hard to keep my composure, I noticed that, surprisingly, I was doing a

---

[9] Pashtet – "pate." Russian thugs often refer to each other by nicknames rather than by their real names.

better job than him. He was slightly trembling, and his finger was already on the gun's trigger. Even though he should've had the experience of dealing with such people, he was seemingly more nervous than I was. Even if he had such an experience, it was seemingly working against him at that moment.

He didn't have any composure: he was ready to either fight or flee.

"I've seen how honest your kind is," - he told the gang's leader, licking his dried-up lips. "And this ain't your house, either. I've lived here for a long time and I've never seen any of you here."

"Have you heard it, men? Looks like we've got some trash[10] here" - someone from the group in front of us said. The rest snickered.

"Who said that?!" - Pasha screamed, pointing the gun at the crowd. "Come out, say it to my face! Don't cower behind your friends!"

"Like you cower behind that gun?" - the man who was threatening us with a knife smiled; the dry, yellow skin parted to expose black teeth.

"You're a cop, aren't you?" - the gang's leader inquired. His eyes narrowed and the way he shifted around reminded me of how a cat prepares to leap at its target. I wanted Pavel to

---

[10] In Russian language, "trash" is slur used to refer to police officers.

lie, to tell them that he was anyone other than a policeman. But that wasn't meant to be.

"Damn right, I am" - he confirmed, taking a step forward with a trembling leg and pointing the gun at the gang. Not a single one of them showed signs of being intimidated, although the gang leader raised his hands in mocking concern.

"And I know who you all are" - Pasha said, wiping the sweat off of his face. "What the hell are you doing here? Has it been you who has sealed the doors?!" - he shouted, becoming horrified at the prospect that us being stuck here was just a part of their plan.

"Be careful where you point that thing," - the man calmly told him, smirking. "And don't shoot your runt there by accident," - the man carelessly waved his hand in my direction to let us know who he was talking about. "Your hands shake so much you're going to drop it any moment."

"Answer the question," - Pasha hissed.

"Locking people up is what trash like you does - we're just here to pay a visit to a good friend of ours while we're passing through the town," - the gang leader explained. "We were sitting here, protecting the good people who live on this stairwell from those beasts outside, and you just barge in, uninvited? Tell us - did we do something to deserve the police staining the air here with its presence?" - he inquired. The men behind him laughed.

"We're this building's militia," - Pasha told him. "We've come here to check if people need any help so that they don't have to deal with scum like you," - Pavel said. He tried to sound confident, but his heavy breathing was giving away that it was just an act.

"Militia, huh?" - the man raised one eyebrow and rolled the unfamiliar word on his tongue as if tasting it. "So, you play the police here, huh?" - he smiled when he managed to make the connection in his head. "I guess once trash - always trash."

There was that word again - the one that made Pasha reeling before. The man said it with his head held high, his eyes staring straight into Pasha's. He was openly challenging him, openly calling him 'trash' in front of everyone, and he even puffed out his chest to make it easier for the former policeman to find his target… And he was waiting on whether Pasha was going to do something about it.

It was a big risk on the man's part, but it worked: Pasha hesitated to act. He didn't open fire, didn't say anything - he was just standing there, frozen like a deer in headlights.

Seeing Pasha became unresponsive, the man shifted his bloodthirsty gaze toward me. I tried to keep a straight face, but I wasn't sure if I managed to pull it off when the man asked me: "And who are you, boy? Are you also playing the police here?"

"So young and already trash" - somebody snickered in the crowd.

The man came closer to me, and I had to do my best to keep staring at him. I knew that if I looked away, it would be recognized as a sign of weakness, an invitation to attack. He was like some mythical creature, a Zeno paradox in action - he could only strike me, only change his state and position when I wasn't looking at him.

"You know, you can stay with us, if you want to," - he told me quietly, but just loud enough that the rest of the gang behind him could still hear him. "You've already stained your reputation by associating yourself with this trash, but we've got a nice spot for you. Right near the toilet."

The rest of the thugs started laughing again, and my eyes went wide from horror. I had never listened to any of the chanson songs, never met a person who had ever gone to prison - but some things about the prison culture, some most shocking aspects of it had inevitably become known to the general public, me included.

"What?! You think we won't mess you up?!" - Pavel suddenly woke up from his stasis, taking a step closer to the man. Surprisingly, his bravery came back when the man decided to threaten me instead of him. I could clearly see why: his intense, reckless gaze was freezing you on the spot, hypnotizing you like a snake mesmerizes a mouse before lunging at it. The man didn't fear death to such an extent that when he was facing you, it was easy to believe that he was indeed immortal.

"Stand back!" - Pasha shot a warning shot at the ceiling. I'd heard it in the past that the gunshots were loud, but I'd never really experienced just how loud they were. Pestered by the Hollywood movies and Russian flicks where the action heroes were spraying the bullets by the dozen, I had never realized just how loud and terrifying the gunshots were. It was one thing to observe a tense situation on the screen, and completely different to get a first-hand experience of it. To know that the deafening sound that was echoing from the walls and bombarding my ears was a real deal. A weapon – a thing made to kill – going off just mere meters away from me.

I was getting concerned that Pasha was going to shoot them - from the beginning, he wasn't taking the pressure very well, and their constant mocking wasn't helping either. The man was taking himself way too seriously to endure that. Perhaps if he shot one of them, if he showed that he wasn't scared of a confrontation, they'd back away. But what if they wouldn't? After all, they weren't strangers to danger, not to mention that to them, backing away from the confrontation with the police was considered to be a disgrace. Once the fight broke out, they wouldn't stop until one side was annihilated.

I had a faint hope that, if I let things run their course, they'd let me go. That if I kept my head low, or rushed for the ladder while they swarmed him, I'd be able to get out. But I knew that it was unlikely, and besides, the man had already protected me from the thug, even though he was obviously scared of them. It would be dishonest not to return the favor.

They had asked me to join the militia because they knew they could count on me. Because I had value. Because I could be brave.

"We're leaving" - I announced to everyone present and took a step toward the ladder while still looking at the crowd. Pasha threw me a confused glance, but I ignored it – I wasn't interested in playing along with his bravado and try to prove something to those men. At that moment, I was the one thinking straight, and so it was on me to call the shots.

"Why? Stay a bit longer" - the head thug said, standing closer to the wall. The rest of the men took it as a signal to advance and started coming closer. Covering maybe an inch per second, drawing closer to that moment when they'd be able to leap at us and pry the gun from Pavel's hands before he had a chance to shoot.

I had to act fast. I had to make it known that I wouldn't stand for it. That I was armed, too.

"Stand back!" - I shouted, raising the hatchet over my head. My voice didn't sound impressive or intimidating - it squeaked, betraying me at the most important moment. Luckily, the hatchet did its job for it - the crowd froze, looking at the blade made to cut the meat. A bullet could deal more damage, but it wasn't as brutal as a cut from an ax. There was something primal about the lacerated flesh – something that made it a more tangible, more real of a threat.

Gunshot wounds were a relatively new concept, but living creatures had been associating cuts and slashes with predators, with being chased and devoured to sate someone's hunger for millions of years, so that fear had been deeply rooted in the human psyche ever since we'd inherited it from our ancestors. And those men knew it too well.

"Your hand trembles, you little puppy" - the thug teased me, eyeing the blade in my hand, but nevertheless keeping his distance. "You sure you're not going to piss yourself?"

"I'll piss myself from happiness when I carve your mug open with this" - I hissed at him, raising my hatchet higher. I knew what he was doing: he was trying to intimidate me, to make me doubt that I'd be able to defend myself against him. Perhaps that could've worked in some other situation, but I was too high on adrenaline to succumb to his words. I was so scared for my life, so desperate to get out alive that, ironically, that fear was giving me the courage to stand up to him.

"Tough words for such a runt" - the man smiled, seemingly not intimidated by my reply. Still, he wasn't coming any closer. I took it as a sign to act and, still having my eyes locked with him, gave Pavel a slight nudge.

"You go first" - I told him, keeping my eyes on the crowd in front of me.

"Don't be stupid, go up, kid. I'll cover you" - Pasha told me, irritating me. Why was he so dense? Why did he decide to act all strong now, when I needed him to just get out of there?

"Just go!" - I shouted at him in frustration. In truth, I wasn't staying behind just because I wanted to prove something to myself or to him. It wasn't the time for playing the hero. But I knew that Pavel had to go first because then he'd be able to cover me with his gun from above while I was climbing the ladder. If I went up first, I wouldn't be able to protect him - my hatchet could only reach so far. So, him going first was the surest way we'd both get out of there unharmed.

Only I couldn't tell him that. Not with them within the earshot.

Luckily, Pasha decided to listen to me - something in my voice had made it clear that I wasn't going to surrender my post. Perhaps it was the desperation, or maybe determination - I wasn't sure, but the man started climbing the ladder, awkwardly keeping his pistol pointing at the people in front of me. I saw them getting restless as Pasha was climbing higher and higher. Their prey was getting away.

I raised my hatchet even higher, to show that I wouldn't hesitate to put it down on their heads if they made their move.

Would I really do it? Possibly - I was so scared that I barely saw them as human beings - to me, they were not too different from the beasts that roamed the streets outside. Ugly, horrifying, inhuman - just with different origins. And unlike those monsters, they were already inside the building. They were much closer, and thus much more dangerous.

"If any of you move I'm going to shoot!" - I heard Pasha's voice behind and above me. "You're all sitting ducks from here, so don't even think about it! Yura, start climbing."

I took another step back, grabbed the ladder, and started ascending, still watching the crowd and having the hatchet ready to strike.

"Yura, huh?" - one of the thugs purred. "Such a nice name. When we get our hands on you you're going to be Yulia[11], you get what I'm saying?"

"Yeah, is that what they call you here?" - I snapped back at him: the adrenaline in my blood was still making me act boldly, and it was making great use of my sass that was usually reserved for my irritable but harmless neighbors.

"Keep talking," - the man said menacingly. "Don't think that I won't come for you."

"Look out the window and then get in the line," - I told him before climbing through the hatch. A moment later Pasha slammed it shut.

Only when we stepped outside and saw the sky above us did I start to realize what had just happened. My legs were quaking from stress and shock, and my gut was twisting and churning around, making me feel like I was about to throw up. I had just been threatening five bandits - with a hatchet,

---

[11] Yulia – a female Russian name

no less. Just thinking that some thirty seconds before I was ready to split some heads open - to kill another human being - was making me nauseous. I'd heard before that people can resort to incredible violence when pressured, but until that moment I had no clue how much. Not to mention what they would do to me if they'd gotten their hands on me - no matter how violent and bloodthirsty I'd just been a few moments ago, I knew they could do much worse than that.

But in a few seconds that feeling of dread had passed, washed away by a realization: I was alive! Such a strange, mundane fact to cherish – how often had I been grateful for that fact in the past? Had I ever even been in a situation where me being alive afterward wasn't taken for granted? It was horrible that it was the new norm, but I chose not to think about that. I was too overwhelmed with joy to reflect on that.

And not only was I alive - I had only myself to thank for it. Sure, Pasha was there, too, but it didn't take away from the fact that it was my accomplishment. I could never imagine myself being in such a situation - the old me would recoil in fear or try to talk it out with them. The old me had no claws and could only roll on his back, showing his belly and pitifully wiggling his tail. I had looked death in its ugly, black-toothed jaw and didn't blink. I proved my right to live in the oldest way on Earth - by taking the threat head-on and living on to tell the tale.

Pasha next to me didn't share my enthusiasm - he was still in his dreading phase. The experience had left the man shaken, and whatever had happened back there did not leave him proud or excited to be alive in the same way it affected me. I knew it wasn't my place to question him - back there I was just as scared as he was. But then my newfound vigor and bravery soaked in the rest of the adrenaline still coursing through my body, and I decided to push my luck with him again: "What was that back then? You lost it."

He glared at me with anger, but it wasn't the same look he'd given me during our last confrontation: now, it had a shade of guilt and shame mixed in. I kept staring at him, showing him that it wasn't a rhetorical question and I still expected an answer from him, and the man looked away. "Couldn't keep myself composed when I saw them" - he said, panting. "I don't... I can't tolerate such trash as them."

I didn't say anything, but I could tell that it wasn't all of the truth. His reaction back there had been less of an outrage and more of a panic. What had happened back there had deeper roots, I knew it. A policeman, of all people, was supposed to be used to talking to people like them... Unless his experience in the past had been far too traumatic.

I wanted to say something else, but precisely at that moment the level of adrenaline in my blood went down from red to yellow zone, and my bravado deflated in a moment. *"Who am I to judge him?"* - I thought bitterly. *"I wasn't a hero back then - I was scared witless. It's good that it ended well, but I lost it, too."*

"Listen, I'd appreciate if we kept what had happened there between us," - Pasha told me, still panting. "We'll tell them about the thugs, but not… the rest of it. Alright?"

It almost sounded like he was begging me. And who was I to refuse? No one would benefit from knowing how we'd handled it.

"Sure" - I told him. The man nodded in appreciation.

"Did you know that they live there?" - I asked him.

He threw me a gaze, full of contempt: "Hell no! Had I known that those rats built their nest under this roof I'd have my colleagues smoke them out the very next day. They had never shown themselves before. But then again, you can never tell where they will turn up," - he sighed. "They must've just shown up here a few days ago. Must've been passing through this town on their way from prison. Their ilk does that sometimes - they crash at the houses that their partners outside of prison keep for them, where they can catch their breath before going back to bothering people. I've seen plenty of it back in my days - they harass neighbors and it's very tough to smoke them out of there. Never thought they'd pick the house I lived in for such a place," - he rubbed his temples, showing how much displeasure and headache it was causing him. "If they've had such an arrangement made for them, they must be some big shots - I'm sure they have guns, too."

"Swell" - was all I could answer. Just as we got stuck inside our home and the monsters started roaming the streets, we've gotten such neighbors.

I looked at the forest again. There was no way to tell for sure - the human eye was not so precise. But I could swear that the line of death beyond which all trees were losing their leaves had crept a few inches closer since the last time I'd looked at it.

# CHAPTER 11 – Militia's Finest

We spent around twenty minutes on the roof - instead of going down to the third stairwell, we've decided that it would be better to wait for Maxim there. When he finally showed up, I could tell from the get-go that he wasn't very happy with what he'd found down there, which left me a bit alarmed. What if they'd stumbled across the same people as we did?

"The people don't understand what 'militia' implies," - he complained. "They want us to go outside and raid nearby food stores - they say they're running out of food. How did your trip go?"

"Not too well" - Pasha said before I had any chance to say anything. It seemed that he was back to his confident, arrogant persona. "We've got some bad news for you..."

Pasha told him about whom we'd met there, and I watched as Maxim's face was sinking as he was listening. Pasha, of course, omitted the part where he freaked out and almost lost control, but as per our arrangement, I didn't say anything.

"...They've said that they're going to kill any of us if we show up there again. I know that cowardly scum - they'll do just that, just to prove the point. And when they burn through their food like the parasites they are, they'll go after ours," - Pasha finished.

"We best stay on high alert, then" - Maxim said what all of us were thinking.

"Why, what did I miss?" - Alexei said, approaching us. Just from looking at him, one could think that the man was getting ready for a hunting trip or an expedition into the wilderness, and in fact, that wasn't too far from the truth. We didn't know what he was going to encounter in the sewers, so it was best to prepare for anything - which he did.

He changed his shoes for knee-high rubber boots so that his feet wouldn't get wet, and although he was wearing the same camo jacket, I could see that he wore a thick wool sweater underneath, so that the cold concrete tunnels didn't freeze him to death.

On his back, he had a large backpack, which judging by how it sagged down was full of different things the man deemed necessary for his trip into the unknown. Above his right shoulder stuck out a barrel of a hunting shotgun, and hanging from his hip was a large camping lantern – a bulky thing that must've been uncomfortable to walk around with, but which undoubtedly would provide the man with enough light down below and which wouldn't be affected by the dampness there.

His face adorned a simple breathing mask, like the ones the workers wore when painting indoors, and on his forehead, I saw another, smaller flashlight - no doubt meant to be used if the man needed both of his hands.

One thing was clear: we've got the right man for the job. He was our representative, our brave stalker meant to traverse the unknown and map the route to safety for us.

"Nothing, don't sweat it," - Maxim told him. "You've got other things to be concerned with."

"I'm ready to go" - Alexei informed us as if it wasn't clear from his attire. "Let's go?"

\*\*\*

As he was descending through the manhole, he looked at us one last time. It was clear that even a man of his resolve was hesitating before going down there.

"You better guard this manhole while I'm gone," - he told us, looking each of us in the eye. "I don't want to find it welded when I return. And remember: do not tell anyone yet, alright?"

I looked at Maxim: perhaps I'd see his mask crack under the pressure of the moment? But he remained as stoic as before: "Not a word to anyone. We'll keep a lookout."

"Good, good," - Alexei sighed. "Well, wish me luck."

He crawled down into the sewers and we closed the manhole after him - in case someone came down there we wouldn't want them to pay attention to it.

"You all go," - Pasha told us. "I'll stay here and watch over it."

"Why? There's no need to freeze yourself" - Maxim said, instantly making my suspicions of him spike. Why would he be opposed to the idea of someone staying to guard it? If my suspicions were correct and he was indeed the welder, then wouldn't he want to seal the manhole as well? To cover the only exit left that he'd missed during his midnight rush to seal all the doors?

"That bastard who has sealed us all in here might come here to finish the job," - Pasha grimly said, as if mirroring my thoughts. "I want to make sure that doesn't happen, especially now that we've got such unpleasant guests nearby."

"You really shouldn't," - Maxim wouldn't give up. "No one knows about this manhole yet. It is possible that the welder himself doesn't know about it, either. You shouldn't torment yourself like that."

"I'm staying" - was all that Pasha said. It was clear that the man wouldn't budge.

Seeing that there was no swaying him, Maxim shook his shoulders: "Suit yourself. I'd hate for you to catch a cold right now, is all I'm saying. We need every man now."

With that, he headed for the exit and the rest of us followed him.

I knew that my hunch didn't have any solid proof - it was based on just a single coincidence. After all, Maxim did look like he was genuinely concerned about Pasha's health, and to use that against him felt dirty. Yet at the same time, I knew I had to do something, to somehow look into that possibility while there was still time.

It took me a few moments to come up with a seemingly innocuous question, and much more - to gather the courage to ask it. We were already on the third floor when I finally decided: it's either now or never.

"Say, Maxim, I've never asked you what you do for a job" - I tried to make it sound as casual as possible while the man was pulling his keys out of his pocket.

"I'm a car mechanic. Have I never told you that?" - he wondered.

"I don't think so" - I shook my shoulders, trying to show that I really didn't know. Truth be told, I remembered something like that from our midnight conversations, but I rarely listened to him, and I was sure he had never listened to me, either. Those were just the ranting sessions.

"No, I'm pretty sure I've told you many times about my job while we were talking on the balcony. So… why are you asking?" - Maxim suddenly switched on the offensive, his voice cold and inquisitive.

*"Busted!"* - I thought, but on the outside, I tried to remain calm. I was just internalizing that. There was no way he'd figured out that I suspected him.

"I was just wondering what is your line of work, and maybe if you had any tools to open the door" - I said as nonchalantly as possible, but at the last moment my voice betrayed me and the last few words came out as a squeak.

"If I had those tools I'd have already used them" - Maxim said, looking over his shoulder at me and squinting his eyes. He suddenly turned around to face me and made a step closer to me. I involuntarily took a step back, my right hand carefully reaching behind my back - where my hatchet was.

"Yura… Why do you ask me that now? You don't think I was the one who's welded the doors shut?"

*"Goddamn it"* - I thought. This was bad.

"What made you even think that? There are families here. People I've known my whole life. Do you think I'd really do something like that - put them in jeopardy?" - Maxim kept on questioning me. Seeing no other way out of it, I've decided to come clean with what I've known. Suddenly, when I was pressed against my very own door, I've found some bravery to tell him how it was. To confront him like he was confronting me.

"I found cigarette butts near the welded door" - I confessed to him. "They were pretty recent - I think it was the welder who'd left them. The brand was "Soyuz-Appolo" - and you're the only one I know who smokes those" - I told him, looking for sudden changes in his facial expression. Was he going to admit it when presented with the proof of his involvement? Or was he going to make me shut up - the same way he'd done with that elderly lady on the first floor?

Maxim was in disbelief.

His eyes went wide when he heard what I'd said, and then he let out a long, lasting sigh of frustration, before turning around to go inside his apartment.

"You're losing it, man," - he told me, not looking at me. "Confinement has made you paranoid. Go clear up your head."

With that, he slammed the door behind him. I felt a bit of guilt for blaming it on him like that - the man trusted me, and I humiliated him with such a ridiculous suggestion. It was a good thing I hadn't done that in front of the rest of the militia.

"No" - I suddenly told myself. "This isn't some argument of neighbors. We're all stuck in here because of someone, and no one is above suspicion. If he is not to blame, he should understand where I'm coming from."

With that, I opened my door, intending to have some rest. I've had a crazy day. I felt like I deserved a cup of coffee and a nice book. To hell with Maxim and his militia! My shift was over for the day.

But it was not meant to be. The moment I opened the door, I heard a familiar voice call out my name through static.

"Yura, come in! It's Leonid! Come in, goddamnit!"

\*\*\*

I had already lost hope for the man to contact me, but hope never asks us to come in. It barges into our souls and occupies its familiar spot. Truly, it was the most resilient of all human feelings - a cockroach that you could never get rid of.

It was that blind, chitinous hope that had made me leave the radio on and tuned to the frequency which Leonid had said he would use to contact me.

Not bothering to take off my shoes and dropping dirt from the basement, I rushed toward the guest room, where my only ally on the outside was trying to reach out to me through the radio waves.

"I'm here! I'm here," - I said the second sentence quieter, remembering that Leonid could get into trouble if his superiors found out that he was contacting people outside of the base.

"Yura, is that you?" - the man asked me. He sounded like he was in a hurry. "Sweet Jesus, man, I thought you'd told me that you're stuck inside your homes, where the hell have you been?"

"We've got some business here to deal with. It doesn't matter. Where have you been? I'd been waiting all day yesterday for you to reach out to me," - I asked him.

"Things are going huyovo[12] here, mate. Everything's crazy, I didn't have any time to tell you - listen, it doesn't matter at the moment. I don't have much time. If they catch me contacting you, I'm a dead man for sure."

---
[12] Huyovo – a Russian swear word, means "very bad"

I raised my eyebrows in surprise: it was already clear that our situation had gone from bad to worse, but I didn't expect him to put it like that. Sure, the military likes to keep all of their info under wraps and punished whoever disclosed them, but somehow, I'd gotten the feeling that he wasn't speaking metaphorically.

"I'm listening" - I told him, grabbing a notebook and a pen while trying not to make any noise. It was clear that he wouldn't repeat himself, so I had to get everything down so that I wouldn't forget anything.

"Listen - the military isn't coming for you guys. They have their hands full here with the escapees. They're putting them into camps, I don't know why, and from what I hear they're not treating them well, either."

The military wasn't coming. It wasn't just a guess, a wild theory. There was no more room for speculation. It was one thing to suspect that your partner doesn't love you anymore, to suspect that the pain in your chest is something worse than just the old age creeping closer, and completely different to see the familiar lips spell it out to you, to see the doctor come into the cabinet with your X-Ray in hand and a somber look on his face. It was the sentence.

They weren't coming. Leonid had confirmed it. I knew I ought to write that down, but my pen didn't move. I knew I wouldn't forget something like that, anyway.

"So, we have to get out on our own?" - I asked aloud. I wasn't even asking him - even though he was my ally, I knew it was not up to him to answer such a question. I was just voicing the most terrible conclusion, which was too big, too grand to just sit quietly on my mind.

But he answered anyway.

"No!" - he shouted into a radio. For a few seconds he went silent - no doubt he was trying to figure out if anyone had heard him because the next sentence was spoken in a barely noticeable whisper: "Listen, whatever you do - don't try to approach the military base - or any military outposts, for that matter. We have new orders to shoot down anyone we see. Civilians, familiar faces - it doesn't matter. We're told to fire on sight."

"Why?" - I wondered. That didn't make any sense. Sure, the creatures were dangerous, but what about people? What about refugees? Wasn't the army supposed to protect us? Would they really go so far to keep the information about the incident from leaking?

"I don't know," - he whispered. "They didn't tell us. All they've told us is that everyone who's still inside the town is our enemy now. I've heard over the grapevine that there are more people like you inside the town - they're calling non-stop. Listen, I don't know what to tell you, mate. I'm sorry things ended up like this. All of you there are on your own. I gotta go - don't try to contact me again. I've risked my life already to tell you this. Don't put my life on the line... I'm sorry."

With that, the transmission ended. I had been expecting Leonid's message for days, hoping that he would bring me some good news and let me know that I didn't have to play the police anymore. But instead, he swooped in to bring me nothing but dread, and after that he awkwardly left, apologizing for the mess. I didn't blame him, and I knew that it was better than to be in the dark…

I had to share it with someone. The day had been overwhelming for me. The militia, suspicions rising over whether Maxim had done it or not, the news from Leonid… It was too much to keep bottled up.

I stood up and went outside. I had only one person to share my grievances with, and besides, she'd invited me to come to visit her earlier.

Quickly rising to the fifth floor, I pressed the buzzer near Natasha's door.

"Hey," - she greeted me. "So how did your first day go?"

"May I come in?" - I bluntly asked her instead of answering. I wanted to settle down before I'd start pouring it all out.

"Sure, sure," - she stepped aside to let me come through. "I was just going to go invite you, anyway."

We went to the kitchen where Natasha put the kettle on to make some tea for us, which she filled from the bathtub. I raised my eyebrow and nodded toward the tap, but she shook her head: "I don't use the tap water anymore. I tried to brush my teeth with it this morning but it had such a foul smell… Did you notice it?"

"Yes" - I quickly lied, realizing that when the militia had come for me I was in such a hurry to join them I forgot to brush my teeth.

"I think the water's going bad without the maintenance," - she sighed. "Too bad: I thought it'd be the last thing to go, right after the electricity. A miracle we still have it."

"One old-timer had told me that the water's taste had gone bad because the military had added toxins to it to poison all of us," - I told Natasha with a smile.

"Honestly, at this point, I wouldn't even be surprised if that was the truth," - she sighed. "These past few days have been crazy..." - she said before getting up and starting to prepare some tea for both of us.

Hearing the water slowly boiling made me relax a little bit: after crawling through the building, I could use some tea to relax. And it was reminding me of the time when I could take a hot, bubbly bath: back in the day I used to complain that it was barely long enough to stretch my legs, but now I'd give an arm and a leg for just an hour in it. Too bad that it was filled with drinkable water.

"So how was it?" - she wondered without turning around. I sighed and leaned back. "You're not going to believe this day, girl..."

She was thrilled to find out about the manhole and the "expedition" Alexei was on. Furrowed her eyebrows when I told her that I suspected that Maxim was the welder. Gasped and covered her mouth when she'd heard about the thugs and gave me an approving smile when I told her how I'd handled it. Telling her about those things and reporting our relative progress was not only showing her that we'd got it under control - I was starting to believe it, too.

After that, we switched the topic of the conversation. We started talking about things from our previous life, about celebrity gossip, about our plans and dreams (Natasha had always wanted to purchase the biggest telescope she could afford so that she could take a photo of Saturn in the night sky), about the latest books I'd read… It was surprising how easy it was to talk to her and the many things we had in common - during our previous meetings she was just my neighbor's girlfriend, and I was usually talking to him and not to her.

Throughout the conversation, we hadn't once mentioned or discussed our situation. We were willfully ignoring it, instead preferring to focus on other things - things that were far away from us, both in space and time.

And throughout all of that talk, she didn't mention Nikita once. As strange as it sounds, I was glad - at least she wasn't tormenting herself thinking about his fate. Her own situation was already as bad as it could be.

Keeping up the casual conversation, we didn't even notice how time had flown by and the sun had set beyond the horizon. We were too focused on the conversation, so when I finally glanced at the clock and saw that it was half-past nine, I raised my eyebrows in surprise. Excusing myself, I started preparing to leave.

"Hey," - she told me as I was heading for the door. I could see that she was feeling very awkward. "I know it's really strange, but… Would you mind staying here tonight? I could make a bed for you out of our sofa in the guest room," - she quickly added, realizing how it sounded. "It's just that… I'm not used to living alone, and these past few days it's been really lonely in here. And… it's been really scary," - she added with a bit of shame in her voice.

I considered her offer. Although it was true that she was living just two floors above me, staying together for the night made more sense. We'd go to sleep together, wake up together, cook breakfast together…It would be indeed less lonely that way.

"Sure" - I told her. She was clearly glad to hear it: she smiled and started hurriedly preparing a spot for me as if worried that I might change my mind any minute.

It was strange to stay over at your friend's place when only his girlfriend was home. During any other time, it would make people raise their eyebrows. But we didn't have the luxury to choose our company for the night.

I was worried that I might miss another transmission - but then again, who was going to try and contact me? Besides Leonid, I had no one left on the outside. The rest of the survivors - if there were any - wouldn't try to contact me either. The only transmission I'd heard since the incident that'd started it all was that weird cult speech - and I didn't feel like listening to them again. The air was dead - just like our town.

Getting ready to sleep, I suddenly remembered something: excusing myself for a minute, I jumped outside and rushed downstairs - toward the basement. While I was heading there, I couldn't help but notice that I had a hint of regret that she specified that I'd be sleeping on a separate bed. Swaying those thoughts away, I entered the basement to check whether Alexei had returned.

Pavel was still there, sitting next to the manhole. He must've gone back home to get a blanket - or asked someone to bring it because he was sitting there wrapped in it. When I stepped into the basement, he jumped to his feet, but then relaxed when he saw that it was just me.

"Alexei hasn't come back?" - I asked him.

"Why would I be sitting here if he did?" - he barked at me: the cold was making him even more irritable than usual.

"I don't know, maybe you've decided to guard it so that welder wouldn't show up" - I snapped back at him.

"Makes sense" - Pavel grunted, accepting my point of view. "No, he hasn't come back yet. God knows where he is… Or whether he's even still with us."

His words made me shiver, but I didn't want to give in to the man's fatalism. I wanted to believe that Alexei was alive somewhere out there. Not just because I was concerned for him - though, of course, that was also a part of it. I wanted him to come back because it would mean that there was at least some hope of getting out of there. Even if upon return he'd inform us that there was no way out, at least I'd know that there were still places left in the world beyond our building where we could go. That the world I'd been used to wasn't filled to the brim with mutants or angels of death or whatever those creatures were. The position of a dominant species on the planet, of a rightful owner of the town, was far too comforting for me to surrender.

"He will return, I'm sure of it," - I told Pavel, trying to sound as confident as possible. "I'm sure he's just camping somewhere for the night. If he hasn't come back, it means that he's still exploring the tunnels and they're not all dead ends."

Pavel just grunted: I could see that he was not convinced but didn't want to argue with me. I wasn't in the argumentative mood, either.

"How are you holding up?" - I asked him, trying to change the topic.

"Cold," - he grunted. "Scared. This manhole is giving me the creeps. Since Alexei hasn't shown up I keep thinking: what if there's something underground, too? What if it decides to pay me a visit? I haven't been so tense in years. Even when the bandits ruled the streets and me and my boys were sitting in an ambush. The bandits are still humans, but this..." - he pointed at the manhole with his chin. "This is something else."

"Well, don't shoot Alexei by accident when he does come back" - I grimly joked. Surprisingly, the joke did its job: the man let out a short laugh. His former job had left him with the strangest sense of humor.

"Thanks for coming by," - he told me. "Now go, run back to your place. No use two of us freezing down here."

His joke was demeaning in nature, but I didn't pay any attention to that. Throughout the day, I'd already gotten used to the man's manner of speech and didn't take it personally.

"Don't lag behind" - I told him, making him chuckle once more, and left the basement.

*"Please return"* - I thought to myself as I was rising to the fifth floor. It was hard to remain hopeful in the face of the facts, but I denied the alternative. I didn't want to think that Alexei didn't return because something had gotten a hold of him in the sewers. I wanted to believe that he - and by extension us, the people who'd entrusted him with finding the exit from our hell - had it under control.

"Everything's alright?" - Natasha asked me with concern in her voice. I realized that she must've read from my face that something was wrong,

I didn't want her to get worried about anything. Natasha was slowly recovering from the shock of being stuck inside her apartment and returning to her usual, chipper self. It was pleasing to be in the presence of her - her optimism was helping me recharge, helping me forget about the horror of our situation. So, I wanted to repay her with the same coin.

"Yeah, you know - just the militia thing" - I told her with a smile. The muscles of my face didn't obey me and tried to rebel, wanting to show her the real state of my emotions, but I managed to keep them in check - until she looked away and my smile finally twitched, as if letting me know that it wasn't okay with me lying.

We exchanged some pleasantries before going to sleep and she turned off the light. I closed my eyes and tried to get some sleep. It was proving to be surprisingly difficult: the sofa wasn't very comfortable, and while thinking about that fact, I started day-dreaming about what I was going to do about it. Those were silly, naïve, and even shameful thoughts, thoughts that were unbecoming of a decent man - but while I was alone in the darkness, I allowed them to stay.

I was thinking that, perhaps, I should let Natasha know that the sofa wasn't comfortable and ask her if there was some other way to accommodate me. Perhaps we'd be able to fit onto a single bed without touching each other, or maybe she'd even ask me to hug her for comfort and I would reluctantly agree. Perhaps any moment now, I was going to hear her soft footsteps approaching the guest room, and she'd turn on the lights, before asking me with that sweet, awkward, and somewhat guilty look if I'd agree to sleep with her because she was scared...

My waking dreams were interrupted by a sound coming from above. For a moment I ignored it, being used to my neighbors above shambling their feet while they were going toward the kitchen at a late hour... But then I remembered that Natasha's floor was the last one.

Above us were only the roof and the indifferent skies. Or, at the very least, it used to be that way. Now, there definitely was something else.

My breathing became erratic when I realized that the sound was coming from directly above me. As I was drilling the ceiling with my now wide-open eyes, I wished that I could see through the walls for a moment, to see who was walking on the roof at such a late hour... Before thinking that I could really live without that information.

Had the steps sounded human, I'd think that it was the welder, and then I wouldn't hesitate to run out there with my hatchet ready. A thug doing reconnaissance for his friends would be another strong suspect. But the nature of those sounds made it painfully clear - whatever was walking on the roof in the middle of the night had too many legs to be a human being.

Was it the strange cyclopean creature I'd seen the night before? No, that didn't seem right - if it was anything like I'd imagined it to be it would be bulky and heavy, with the roof trembling under its feet. I doubted it could even climb onto the roof, seeing as it was incredibly heavy. No, it was something else. Something new.

I could hear a soft rustling sound as if something was being dragged across the roof's surface, as well as the pitter-patter of many pointy legs. My imagination painted me an image from my childhood when my grandpa took me out of town to a zoo where, in an aquarium set in the corner of the main building, I saw a centipede drag its body across a blade of grass. The thing was ugly beyond belief - and I was sure that, no matter what the creature above me really looked like, it was not pleasing to the eye, either.

At that moment another thought crept into my mind, just like that cryptic thing's lesser brother: did it know that I was just below it? Perhaps it could hear my breathing, or feel the vibrations of my beating heart travel through its legs.

Carefully turning my head, trying not to make a sound and cringing when the pillow's fabric rustled under me, I looked to the window. The curtains were wide open so that during the day whatever little light that had passed through the clouds could find its way inside the apartment. Could the creature look through it and see me - a clear black silhouette on the white sheets? Would it see me as a meal on the plate?

I could stand up and close the curtains so that it wouldn't see me, but there was no way I'd be able to do it without making a sound - their rustling would no doubt alert even a human, never mind a monster.

"What about Natasha?" - I suddenly thought. "Are her curtains wide open, too? What if it's looking at her at that very moment? What if she looks back at it, too afraid to move even a single muscle?"

I was confident that the thing could scale the walls - there was no other way it'd be able to get up on the roof otherwise - unless, of course, it also had a pair of wings. So, it meant that the creature could easily crawl through the window - I was sure the thin glass wouldn't be an obstacle for it.

"Should I go get Natasha and leave the apartment?" - I considered that option for a second. It was true that we would be safer outside the apartment. But the stairwell had windows, too, and once again, I knew there was no way I'd be able to get Natasha and get out of there without a sound, so the creature could follow us there. Even though it hadn't made its move yet, it had already gotten us cornered.

But I didn't get to act: letting out a familiar sound, the creature scuttled away into the night. It was a good time to stand up and close the curtains - if not to hide myself, then at least to make sure I wouldn't see it. I now understood why kids were closing their eyes while watching scary movies -

they were relying on an ancient coping mechanism. "If I can't see it - it's not real."

Catching any sleep seemed out of the question: I spent the next hour lying awake, listening to the outside. I had a good reason to be concerned, too: as I was laying there, I remembered where I'd heard the sounds before.

It was the very same sound me and Natasha had heard over the radio when we were listening to the man who tried to reach the military base on the day it had all started. The last sound we heard before the transmission cut off and the man was gone.

# CHAPTER 12 – Attack

"Wake up! Yura, wake up!" - Natasha was shaking me, trying to get me to wake up.

"What? What's going on?" - I jumped to my feet, looking around. My gaze was instinctively attracted to the window, where I expected to see a multi-legged shadow. There was nothing there - the only thing out of the norm that I'd noticed was that the window was open, letting the cold air in. Natasha wasn't exactly whispering as she was talking to me, either. Which meant that she wasn't hiding from anything.

"Yura, it's… Oh my god, it's so terrible" - she couldn't put it into words. As I got up from the bed, she called me over to the window. "Take a look for yourself."

She must've seen something outside - something that had put her into such a worried state. I didn't know what it was, but I had a few guesses. Another victim? A trail of blood leading away from one of the windows? Some new, even more terrifying monstrosity which, unlike the rest, didn't hide in the shadows?

I got up from the bed and stood next to her, looking outside. Standing near the open window in nothing but my trunks and t-shirt wasn't exactly comfortable - the air outside was quite chilly. But if I decided to go put some clothes on, I risked missing something happening outside.

At first, I didn't see anything - the yard in front of the building which Natasha's windows overlooked seemed the same as the day before. It wasn't until I noticed something white waving in the wind a few floors below that I started putting together what was going on.

The object that I'd seen was a rope made out of bedsheets. Coming down from the second floor, it was shaking in the wind, coiling like a snake and rising as if it, too, wanted to leave the cursed building along with its creator.

"Someone's gotten out?" - I wondered. Natasha nodded, biting her lip: "An old man. He climbed down and ran toward the stores."

"What?" - I couldn't believe my ears. I knew that Natasha wouldn't lie, and I was confident that she didn't misunderstand the situation, but I was refusing to accept it. "Are you sure? Couldn't he get some food from his neighbors, or endure a bit? It hasn't been that long."

Natasha didn't have time to answer: somewhere in the distance, behind the trees, glass shattered. Judging by the rustling of glass shards that followed, the man had reached his destination and was climbing inside.

There was my answer.

"What an idiot," - I sighed, getting anxious. "He'll get himself killed."

How far did the expedition for the military base had gotten? A kilometer, two? There were a dozen people there, yet not a single one of them came back. What chances did one man have?

I glanced down: little by little, people were peeking out of their windows, curious about the origin of that sound. A few of them tried inquiring what was going on, but the rest of the tenants hushed them: they didn't want to miss a thing. The tense silence settled over our building - not the usual silence of an abandoned town. It now had the context of anticipation, it was pregnant with expectation. Only sometimes I could hear someone whispering to their neighbors, defying the silence to satisfy their curiosity.

The silence was broken by the beast's howling: no doubt, it also heard the ruckus the man had raised. When it went silent, so did the last of the whispers I'd heard: people were now waiting to see what was going to happen. The countdown until the beast's arrival had started. The man had to return before it showed up, or he could forget about going back altogether.

"Come on, come on" - I was whispering, counting every second. He heard the howl, didn't he? Why was he taking so long?

I couldn't accept another death. Not after I'd joined the militia to prevent that from happening. But there was nothing I could do at that moment - not anything reasonable, at least. What could I do? Run downstairs, find a way outside and join him there?

A few minutes later, the man showed himself. I gasped when I realized that I knew him.

It was the same old man who'd come to visit me a few days before, looking for insulin. Back then he had said that his own stock had run dry, and he was unsuccessful in finding someone willing to share. Judging by a small package he was holding close to his chest, he had finally found what he had been looking for - but not within the walls he had been calling his home.

The thing he needed to survive was not provided to him by his neighbors who had been engaging in small talk with him for the past sixty years. I slammed my fist onto the windowsill - if the man had gone outside it meant that he had asked everyone inside the building. How could they allow that to happen? I refused to believe that out of eighty apartments, he was the only one with diabetes.

It seemed that I wasn't the only one who recognized him: everyone else must have recognized him as well because they've started talking about him.

"Hey, it's that man from a few days back!"

"Oh Igor, was it really that bad? You poor soul..."

"Hey, Davidich, didn't you have diabetes, as well? I even pointed him toward your door, said that you'd have some insulin for sure..."

"Hurry up, you fool! Didn't you hear that thing?"

"Don't talk" - I whispered under my breath, my voice almost breaking. Were they really so oblivious to what they'd been doing? "Shut your goddamn mouths. You're going to attract the beast!"

I wanted to shout that for the whole world to hear - but I couldn't. If I did, I'd become part of the problem.

The man didn't even waste time to look around: he just rushed straight toward his improvised rope - the only thing in his tunnel vision he could see. He shoved the package he was carrying under his jacket and started scaling the rope. He was moving at a painfully slow pace - the bedsheets were slipping under his fingers and for every three feet he made it upwards he slid one foot downward.

The entire building was shaken by another roar. The sound brought me back a few days when I'd heard it just on the other side of that metal door. That was the only time when the roar had been louder than now. Since then, it was always in the distance, always far away. We had been conditioned to just accept it as the new background noise, we've developed a habit to ignore it.

And now, that habit was shattered. The loud cry of the animal was just around our building's corner. It was coming from the forest - no, it was already there.

I struck out my neck through the window to take a look at it. It had been evading my eyes since day one, and finally, after days of hiding in the shadows and stalking those who dared leave the walls of our building, it showed itself.

From our previous encounter, I knew only one thing about it - it had one disproportionally large eye. Everything else about it had been an enigma, and after finally laying eyes on it, I was confident: my previous estimate that the creature was not of our world was correct. Even if we gave nature a hundred million years, it wouldn't come up with such an abhorrent design: any animal that would give birth to something even remotely similar to that atrocity would kill it without remorse.

It was large - significantly larger than a bear, despite often being compared to it in the past by the people who had caught a glimpse of it. I could see where the comparison was stemming from - the animal had a large bulking body that could put even an actual bear to shame.

It moved around on all four appendages: while I couldn't catch a glimpse of the shorter hind legs, the longer front legs ended in something that, if not for an odd number of fingers that I struggled to count, would bear an incredible similarity to human hands, even though in the case of the creature both sides of the "hand" were sporting opposable thumbs. Sometimes it walked propping itself onto its knuckles, but when it put its palm down onto the ground, stretching its fingers, I could see just how big it was – its hands' imprints were as large as a dish tray, if not bigger.

Had it formed a fist and struck a grown man's chest it would undoubtedly crush all of his ribs at once. I shivered when I remembered the screams of the postman: back then, I couldn't even imagine what he'd been going through. Now I had a vague idea.

The body was entirely hairless, its thick grey hide exposed to the elements, with the only exception being a patch on the creature's back, right behind where its scapula would be if it shared such anatomic features with a human. There, the black fur was thick and long - so long, in fact, that its dirty bangs - each as thick as a rope - were hanging all the way down to the ground, lightly waving left and right as the creature moved forward. Had my eyesight been any worse I'd decide that it was no fur at all, but the tentacles the creature used to grasp its prey.

The head seemed comically small compared to the rest of the body, despite being connected to the rest of the body by a neck so burly and muscular I could see the muscle fibers peeking through the skin…and, once again, it looked remarkably human. Sure, it sported massive thick fangs, the shape of which was nothing like what you'd find in the Earth's animal kingdom, and the nose was just a cavity above it, but the general shape seemed the same.

But of course, the biggest difference was the eye. Massive and bulging, with a transparent eyelid slowly blinking only once every ten seconds, it was so big in relation to the rest of the creature's head I was finding it hard to believe that its skull could fit anything else inside. If the creature even had a brain it must've been the size of a pea…or it was located in some other part of the body altogether.

The iris was bright yellow - the color of a new warning sign. The color was so bright that even when the creature slowly blinked, its transparent eyelid barely concealed it. The pupil, slightly twitching as if to the beat to the creature's heart, was constantly changing shape, one second stretching into a thin vertical line and the next spreading into a formless black spot - either to hypnotize its prey or to look in all directions at once.

"It's no bear, after all" - Natasha whispered. Her eyes were wide open as if hoping to cast a net wide enough to catch every detail, every aspect of the creature's appearance. "It's more like an ape."

It set it's gaze on the man on the rope, who at that moment had only managed to cover half the distance toward his window. Then, turning its head in unnatural movements as if controlled by a puppeteer, it scanned the windows, its gaze shifting from one tenant to the next. Despite having crushed a group of ten people just a few days before it was now cautious: no doubt, the number of people and all the noise they were producing made it wary.

It turned its head toward the nearest window. I didn't envy the people who lived there: even with the steel bars between them, one couldn't feel calm when such a mighty killing machine was peeking at them from the outside.

Then, slowly and carefully, minding every step, the mountain of muscles slowly shifted in the direction of the man who was still struggling for his life. It held its head low, and although its every move was aimed at bringing it closer to the man the yellow eye was wildly darting around, trying to figure out if the people who were out of its reach could harm it in any way. The pupil was changing its form with every face it looked into, almost as if assigning a particular shape to every person so that it would be easier to remember them later.

Upon seeing the creature approaching, the man started squirming, trying to get inside his apartment as fast as possible. But it seemed that his additional efforts were, in fact, detrimental: either he'd exhausted himself or the anxiety was causing him to make the wrong moves, but he actually slowed down.

"Come on, Igor, just a little bit!" - his neighbor shouted at him. "Can't you see that thing there? Come on!"

"Hey! Over here, you beast!" - someone else called the creature over, trying to distract it. The eye reacted and glanced at the man, as if the animal understood who he was referring to, but then kept on spinning wildly, disregarding him as unnecessary.

Someone else tried calling it, but it was now ignoring people, focusing solely on the man in front of it instead. Even though it was clear that it had chosen him as its primary target, it was not lunging toward him, not trying to get to him before he got away, taking its time instead.

Almost as if it was waiting for something.

The man had stopped moving altogether: he was too tired to continue. Old age was not merciful to him, quickly draining him of all the strength, and now all of his efforts were aimed toward just not falling down.

"Come on, Igor! Don't you want to live?" - his neighbor urged him. "Use your legs, for Christ's sake!"

"I'm trying" - the man mewled, pushing against the wall with his legs. The bedsheets the rope had been made of creaked in protest, but still held on.

"There you go, like that! Just a little bit!" - the neighbor was pressing him. "If that thing yanks the rope you're done for! Come on!"

"Come on, Igor! You can do it!" - people were cheering for him. The oldest scene in human history: a man trying to get up towards safety, where the rest of his kin were, while a predator stalked closer with each second.

The rope was creaking so loud I could hear it on the fifth floor. The fabric was tearing thread by thread, and at any moment it could cause a chain reaction, with the remaining threads not being strong enough to support the man's weight.

"Come on, Igor! You're almost there!" - people screamed. "Come on!" - Natasha joined them.

He was right next to his window. All he had to do was reach out, grab the windowsill, and pull himself inside. The tension was so unbearable I involuntarily locked my fingers in a sign of prayer.

"What did he even tie that rope to? How long will it hold?" - was all I could think at that moment.

The old man reached out toward his window. His foot slipped on the wet from the rain wall. He tried grabbing onto the ledge, but his fingers missed it by a few centimeters. He fell down to the ground, landing on his right leg sideways.

The creature's eye followed him all the way down. When he hit the ground, it let out a purring, guttural sound.

Even from the fifth floor, I heard a loud crack - the brittle bones of his hip snapped like a dried-up breadstick. The man moaned in pain and rolled around on the ground, before trying to get up to his feet. A small white package that had fallen out of his jacket was lying on the ground below him, marking the spot where the man hit the ground. He didn't bother to try and pick it up.

Grabbing the rope, the man tried to scale it again, but this time he couldn't make it even one foot upwards. On top of already being exhausted, he couldn't grab it with his legs - his now dysfunctional hip was preventing him from doing so. The best he could do was wiggle left and right, with his feet dangling just a few inches above the ground.

The beast resumed its march toward him.

Someone threw a book at it, and it swooped down on the animal, rustling its pages menacingly, before harmlessly falling onto its back and sliding down its side. The creature paid it no more attention than it would pay a falling leaf.

"Somebody help him, don't just stand there!" - some woman screamed.

"What do you suggest we do?" - someone replied with annoyance as if we were talking about some minor issue rather than the man's life.

"Do something! Go to his apartment!" - the voice from below demanded.

A man's head stuck out of the window to the left of the one the old man had left through; his face was red and his breathing was heavy. No doubt he'd just completed a short but very intense run.

"His apartment's door is closed! I can't get inside!" - he reported to the rest of the onlookers.

The beast was getting closer: only another ten meters or so separated it from its prey.

It was startled when a heavy cooking pot - a massive thing made of cast iron, able to fit around twenty liters and crafted in previous age to provide food for a family of seven - landed near it. Had it found its target, even that other-worldly monstrosity would feel it. Since it didn't, the only thing it had managed to achieve was to startle the animal for a moment.

"Doesn't anyone have a gun?" - the pot's owner cried out in exasperation, seeing that his effort was in vain.

Pavel had a gun, I realized. The clarity of that fact almost made me shiver from the relief of knowing what to do. He could stop the creature, scare it away. He was the only one I knew who could actually save the man!

I jerked to move to the door... and the next moment I froze. I didn't know which apartment he lived in - or whether he even lived in the same part of the building as me. Looking for him was a waste of time - there was no way I'd make it in time. There was only one thing I could do.

"Pavel!!" - I screamed at the top of my lungs, startling Natasha. "Pavel! Wake up, goddamnit!"

The man must've been sleeping - he did say that he was going to pull an all-nighter on his shift. How sound was his sleep? What were the chances that he'd hear me while sleeping after being awake for almost twenty-four hours?

"Pavel!" - Natasha helped me, shouting as loud as she could. She had no clue who Pavel was - she never had the chance to meet him. "Pavel, wake up!"

"Pavel!" - I shouted again. "Does anyone here know Pavel? A former policeman, from the militia! He has a gun on him!"

There was no answer. Someone else in the distance cried his name out, too.

"Does anyone know him, goddamnit?!" - I screamed into the wind, demanded to know. "He's with the militia! He was walking around just yesterday, letting everyone know about us! Pavel, the former policeman!" - I screamed, glancing down at the beast. It was some five meters away from the old man, who froze and clung to the wall, too afraid to even move. Perhaps he was hoping that the beast would leave him alone if he played dead?

"You should know that yourself!" - someone asked in return.

"I've seen him!" - someone shouted. I turned my head: where did that voice come from? Where was that person who could point us toward the old man's only savior?

"Lyuda! Go call Pavel! He's your neighbor, isn't he?" - the same voice screamed. Where was it?! I was ready to go there myself, even if it was a different stairwell, the creature on the roof be damned! I just needed to know where he was!

"I'm going, going!" - a female voice replied. Why hadn't she gone for him when I was describing him!? Surely, she should have recognized who I was talking about!

The beast was two meters away from the man. Someone dropped a frying pan onto it and it landed straight onto its head. The beast wailed - not from pain, but from annoyance. Its eye roamed around, trying to find where the strike came from, but then it turned its gaze back toward the man in front of it.

He finally let go of the rope and collapsed to the ground. Using the wall as a support, he hopped along it, away from the beast. The man was trying to say something, but at that point, his speech was already unintelligible.

"Go to the other side of the building!" - I shouted at him. "There are small windows that lead to the basement!"

The basement, the basement, of course! Why didn't I think of it while I was calling out Pavel's name? He most likely spent the entire night there! If there was a place where I could find him, it would be there!

The beast didn't pursue him, instead just gazed at the man. For a moment I thought that, perhaps, it wasn't hungry. Maybe it only attacked when provoked?

With a mighty leap forward, the creature put an end to that line of thought. Natasha gasped and covered her eyes like a kid.

It smashed the man against the wall with a fist producing enough force to make him cough out blood. People screamed. Not giving the man a chance to recover, it grabbed him by the leg and sped off into the town, pulling him with such ease one could think it was a paper doll in the beast's hands.

Throughout all of his way there, the man screamed. Anyone would if they were in his shoes, but the worst thing was, those weren't the screams of terror. The man was hollering at the top of his lungs because of the unbearable pain – as he was being pulled away the broken femur was thrashed across the ground, sending waves of pain throughout his whole body.

Even after they vanished from sight we could still hear his cries in the distance. For a full minute, his cries echoed across town, until they were suddenly cut off mid-exhale.

Natasha winced, hang her head, and walked away. Some people were crying, others were discussing what had just happened in hushed voices.

We could've saved him, I thought. We could've saved him had we been dedicated to our goal - the goal we had chosen for ourselves. Had Pavel heard our cries for help?

I grit my teeth and tried to calm down. It had the same effect as trying to protect yourself from a bomb by covering yourself with a blanket - a second later I slammed my fists onto the counter, quickly put on my clothes, and headed for the exit. It didn't matter to me whether the man was to blame or not - Pavel was going to get a piece of my mind.

# CHAPTER 13 – Despair

The woman who claimed that she'd known him lived in an apartment on the third stairwell. I knew that the roofs were the dangerous territory now, but I didn't care. I was going to step outside for less than thirty seconds - if the unknown creature was waiting for me there, then it meant that it was simply not my day.

A step outside, a quick rush toward the door in the distance - and I was back to safety. It almost felt like going from one section of a sunken submarine to the other through the ocean. I involuntarily held my breath as I ran.

Once inside, I rushed to the fourth floor - where the woman had lived. The people were already outside of their apartments, discussing the earlier events. I only caught a bit of their conversation.

"What a crazed old man. Why did he even venture outside? He should've waited for the army to come to rescue us," - a man argued, clicking his tongue and crossing his hands.

"Don't be like that. He wouldn't do that if he weren't desperate. Oh, dear, what a horrible way to go..." - another man argued, shaking his head.

"Everything is according to God's will - so it is said" - a woman proclaimed with a benign and wise look on her face.

"Where does Pavel live?" - I interrupted them.

"What Pavel? Who the hell are you?" - she countered with a question of her own, suddenly losing her temper. "What apartment are you from?"

"Pavel! The policeman!" - I screamed at her. The shock of the man's death and the frustration of Pavel's inaction were still fresh in my mind, making me act out. "I was calling for him through the window!"

"Oh, so that was you, making all that ruckus," - she noted with some cold indifference. "Way to make a scene."

"A scene? Pavel had a gun! He could've warded off that creature!" - while I was fuming I was taken aback by her calmness. How could she be so indifferent to that man's fate?

"Are you from the militia?" - she inquired.

"Yes, I am" - I told her, puffing my chest out. She ought to know that I wasn't just a pedestrian, making a scene – I was one of the few people who put everyone's well-being above my own. Not that I needed an ego boost, but perhaps it would make her shut up. "What about it?"

"Hmph! Figured as much. Should've done your job better" – she said bluntly. I started seeing red.

"Pavel lives here" - I heard a female voice to the left of me. Looking there, I expected to see another indifferent face… But all I saw was a concern.

A woman stood at the door of her apartment, giving me a careful look. "You said you were from the militia, right?" - she asked me.

"Yes, I am," - I tried to calm down. "You must be his wife?"

She nodded her head, then bit her lip. As much as I wanted to blow up at him, to make her go wake him up or to enter his apartment and pull him out of his bed, I didn't do any of that. I did not like the look on her face, and her next question confirmed my suspicion that something was wrong, making me shake.

"Do you know where he is?"

"You mean he still hasn't come back from the basement?" - I asked her in disbelief. The woman behind me let out a satisfied grunt, but I ignored it.

"He must've fallen asleep there," - she whispered. Her eyes were open wide, but she wasn't looking at me anymore - she was staring at some point far beyond the walls. "He didn't get much sleep during the day. He's been falling asleep in his office many times back in the day. The night shifts… he never handled them well. Can you go… wake him up?"

"…Sure," - I told her. "I'll go get him." For some reason, I smiled at her - I must've been trying to show her that everything was alright. She returned the gesture, but I could see that she did so on autopilot – her mind was elsewhere.

Awkwardly nodding to her, I went toward the roof: there was a door leading to the basement in every stairwell, but it was locked and I had no tools to pry it open.

Not to mention that it was possibly dangerous to leave it open now.

"He has to be just asleep," - I kept telling myself as I traversed the roof. "His wife said that it's not the first time he falls asleep during the night shift. Once I see him I'm going to give him such a whooping, he won't sleep for days."

He must've been a very sound sleeper if he'd missed everything that had been going on outside. Of course, the windows of the basement were facing the forest, so I could give him leeway. Maybe when I'd find him there, I'd go easy on him, after all...

The forest was getting darker: the dark wet bark of its trees, the skin of the forest was slowly being exposed. Some unseen shears were cutting down the leaves from the trees, cutting deeper and closer to us with each passing day. The yellow leaves were no more than a line, a thin border no more than fifty meters long.

Once back inside our stairwell, I saw Maxim: the man was busy arguing with some of the elderly, assuring them that we were safe. When he saw me, he furrowed his eyebrows: our last conversation still tainted his memory of me. But he must've seen something on my face, so in a second he mellowed out and gave me a concerned, inquisitive look.

I simply nodded for him to follow me and proceeded downward, hearing his footsteps behind me.

"Pavel" - I called out into the basement when we entered it. "Where are you?"

I wanted him to answer, to voice his usual dissatisfaction with me. To come to meet us halfway and ask us what the ruckus had been all about. When my echo was the only answer I'd gotten, I admitted it. I already knew that he wasn't in the basement anymore. The reason I was calling for him was to see if there was anything else besides him down there. Something that hadn't been there before.

We proceeded carefully. Maxim wasn't asking any questions: he must've figured out what had happened.

I was counting seconds until the moment we'd turn around the corner and see if Pavel was actually there. Hope, as usual, clung to me with its insectoid legs, trying to burrow in deeper.

Three...

Two...

One...

Zero.

There was no one. Not even a body, either dead or alive. Just the proof that Pavel wasn't among the living anymore - a large stain of blood, and the drag marks leading toward the window. A thick, straight red line, going across the floor and then up the wall. I never thought that Pavel, with his large complexity, would fit through it. Apparently, with enough effort, you could even pull a hundred-kilo man through a hole half his waistline.

No signs of a fight, no splatters, bloody fingerprints. Just a red line pointing in the direction he had been taken - a red carpet rolled out after him, in spite of the tradition. That, and his gun. The only thing left of a retired policeman.

Maxim brushed his hair with his hand, grabbing it so hard at the end of the gesture it seemed like he was trying to tear his scalp off.

Why didn't we hear anything? The man had a gun on him. Surely, he wouldn't hesitate to use it to defend himself. Even if the creature had appeared completely impervious to damage to him, he still wouldn't go down without a fight.

"He's been falling asleep in his office many times back in the day. The night shifts… he never handled them well," - I remembered the words of his wife.

I had just seen the ape-ish monstrosity that had been terrorizing us with its howls. There was no way it could enter or leave through that window. There was only one possible suspect - the same thing I'd heard the night before, scuttling across the roof just above my bed.

Why didn't I put two and two together? Why didn't I think that it could crawl inside the basement? Even if it wasn't the case, why not warn the only man who was spending the night outside of his apartment, trying to protect the only way out of our building? If the creature could scale the wall, then surely it was nimble enough to fit through the window?

If I hadn't been such a coward, such an egoist, I could've saved him.

"Goddamn," - Maxim took a careful step closer to the puddle of blood, picked up the gun from it, doing his best not to get any blood on his clothes. When he inevitably stained his sleeve, he started rubbing it, trying to get the blood off.

"I better go tell his wife. Someone has to," - he told me, heading for the door.

The roof. Maxim would have to go there through the roof. He could fall prey to that creature, too, if he weren't careful.

"Wait!" - I called him over. Maxim stopped and gave me an inquisitive look.

I didn't know if I was doing the right thing. He still hasn't done anything to prove that he wasn't a welder. But seeing how shaken he was to see traces of Pavel's demise, seeing as he was concerned about the man's wife, seeing how he genuinely tried to do his best to keep it civil within the walls, I decided that he at least deserved a chance to be trusted.

I told him everything I knew: I told him about my radio, about the encrypted transmission and the "Swan Lake." I told him about the conversation with Leonid and that the military wasn't our ally anymore. I told him about the last minutes of the expedition beyond our building's walls and the creature I'd heard on the roof the last night.

When I was finished, I dreaded the moment when he'd ask me one particular question, and then the moment finally came.

"Why didn't you tell me any of this sooner?" - he asked me. I shifted around uneasily but then regained my composure. It was no place for shyness. Whatever happens, happens.

"You know why," - I told him, looking him in the eye. Was he going to get angry at me again for suspecting him?

"This again," - despite the grim setting, Maxim let out a tired smile. "So, you think that I'm the welder just because I smoke the same brand of cigarettes as him? Yura, that's a stretch - I'm not the only one who smokes them."

"Yes, but I couldn't ignore that fact," - I pointed out to him. "Tell me - wouldn't you do the same in my place? Wouldn't it be wise to suspect me if the roles were reversed?"

"I wouldn't keep it a secret - I would approach you immediately," - Maxim argued. That made sense: he was a straight-forward man, not used to beating around the bush. He was the man of action. I wasn't, no matter what I kept telling myself. I felt shamed by his answer: he just wanted me to talk it out with him. In his eyes, I was probably a twenty-year-old kid, playing an investigator. It hurt deeply: the part of my soul that got struck by his words already had a lot of scar tissue there.

Being shamed by an adult was nothing new to me.

"That makes sense, but I... I didn't know if I could trust you," - I told him. Being honest was the only way I could repay it to him. "And if we're being honest, I still don't know if I can trust you - or anyone, for that matter."

"Look, I appreciate that you opened up to me. It's very stupid of you to think it was me - but I appreciate it nonetheless. At least you confronted me about it in the end. If you want to know, if you think it's even relevant, what kind of cigarette butts you've found there and it's your only clue, I'm not the only one who smokes those in this building. Just the night before it happened a young man asked me for a cigarette so I gave him the rest of the pack I had on me - they're dirt cheap," - he told me.

"What young man?" - I immediately asked. Whether the man agreed with my theory or not didn't matter. I needed more information.

"I don't know. He had a scarf on his face. It doesn't matter! The point is, if you think that something so minuscule is a smoking gun, you are mistaken. Coincidences happen. Now forget about it, we have a lot of work to do," - with that, he turned on his heels and headed for the stairwell.

I wanted to agree with him. To let it go, to concern myself only with the pressing issues at the hand. But I knew it was unwise to ignore the identity and motifs of a person who not only sealed us in during such a critical hour but was willing to kill other people to keep his identity a secret.

There was something bigger at play. I had already stopped believing in coincidences, and I didn't think that his appearance was one, either. The welder, the sirens, the monsters, "the Cricket", the military locking down the town and shooting all the survivors… There was more to it, I was sure of it.

So, when Maxim told me that he had shared a pack of cigarettes with some young man whose face was concealed I knew immediately: back then, he had come face to face with the one who had denied us our freedom.

\*\*\*

I told Maxim to go alone: I couldn't face the woman after my inaction had indirectly led to her husband's death. Even if she didn't know that, I would.

Instead, I went back to my apartment. The people all around me were worked up. They needed guidance; they needed to be told that everything was under our control and we could protect them… But I wouldn't be able to muster such a lie. I needed to recharge.

Once back in my apartment, I just sat in my chair and stared into the ceiling. I wanted to take a break from that hell, to pretend that I had been evacuated along with the rest of the town.

All was lost. We've had it under control for no more than a day, and even that was arguable. In just one day, our militia had been cut down to half its strength. Alexei was undoubtedly gone at that point, and although we hadn't found the body, Pavel's fate was also not a mystery. We had failed. I had failed.

Who was I kidding? I was not fit for such things. My mother had been right all along: I wasn't needed because I wasn't anything special. And now even my own town where I was supposed to spend the rest of my life had been rejecting me, summoning the crowds of monsters to either drive me out of there or bury me under the rubble of my own house.

It was best to leave it to grown-ups.

I looked at the radio: just a few days before, it was my tool to uncovering the secrets of our town. Well, not uncovering, per se: I'd had around as much success with that as with trying to find out the welder's identity. But it had been fun to pretend that I could peer behind the veil. It had been my old friend that had always been there for me after another dull day of work. Nowadays, it was nothing but the bringer of bad news. Even that sacred piece of my own tiny world I'd built for myself to take cover in from the world outside had been corrupted.

I looked at the clock: the position of arrows was reminding me about something. I'd long since lost the track of time and wasn't even sure what day it was anymore - the date had no more significance to me than it would to a caveman, yet somehow, I knew that something was supposed to happen at that moment. My internal alarm was ringing, the springs of my internal clock winding it into motion, but the notification on my mind's screen was blank.

"That's right," - I remembered. "Those religious nut jobs said they'd be broadcasting about now."

I thought about it, and then sat in front of the radio, turning it on and tuning to the right frequency. I could use some God in my life.

As I'd expected, I'd missed the beginning of the transmission: another kick to my self-esteem. I couldn't do even that right. Taking a deep breath to calm myself down, I honed in on the frequency and started to listen.

I expected the voice of the unseen narrator to soothe my nerves, tell me that at least my end days were going to be calm, but he sounded surprisingly agitated. Even he refused to grant me any peace of mind.

"...for your hard work.

The aggressors, the traitors of our plan that had spread across the entirety of our country are trying to oppose us, but rest assured - it will be all for naught. Forty years! Forty years we've spent on this plan, waiting for his arrival. It is through the brave sacrifice and willingness to keep his secrets that the first explorers of the outside had shown that we've managed to keep this event concealed.

We've been denied our chance to keep talking to him when our old god - the mighty red titan of fifteen bodies - had collapsed thirty years ago. The traitors of his faith had reverted to our old ways of the cross - the ones that we'd rooted out a century ago. They live in palaces while the common people keep on struggling. They've forgotten their oaths they've been giving to keep all the workers fed and housed. They've left abandoned our hometown and left it to rot after everything we'd done for them. Well, no more! The King in Rags is here. He is among us. His blood may not be red like that of a worker, but it now runs in our veins all the same. He is one of us now."

He didn't sound calm at all, I'd noted. Hell, he didn't sound very religious, either. From what I could piece together, he was talking about the Soviet Union - what else could be that "fallen red titan of fifteen bodies"? I had never heard anyone refer to it as an "Old God", though it was an incredibly apt description. I could see how some people, who had denied faith in their laborious fervor, could replace it with loyalty to the Party instead.

However, what was the plan that he'd been talking about? What kind of plan could they be nestling for forty years? Who even were these people? From the context, it seemed that they were native to my town – most likely some of the old-timers, who had lived there since the town's foundation and that had been privy to the secret of its foundation. Those folk could always be counted on to tell how glorious the times of the old had been, when the USSR was still a thing.

As for what their plan was, I had no idea. I could only keep listening. For once in my life the radio was broadcasting not some encrypted messages but actual words – I just had to use my wits to piece their ramblings together.

"My comrades, I've been receiving your reports about the good job you've done. By now, you should've acclimated to the changes. You've accepted him as your kin. You've been getting ready for this moment for many years - some of you since your birth. The time has finally come. Seize your people. Show them the truth. Convert the rest, convert them back to the one true faith. And once you're all ready - lead them outside. Unseal the doors. The time is nigh for our faith to spread. Do not fear the beasts - we will distract them."

His words made me choke on air, my throat tensing from the shock. Seize your people? Unseal the gates?! After listening to him for a bit, I'd gotten acclimated to his manner of speech, full of analogies and metaphors, so I was confident: the man was talking about the welded doors.

Leonid had said that there had been more people like us in the town. Back then I'd thought that he meant just the people who couldn't evacuate in time - the sick and elderly, who couldn't get out of their houses on time. Could it be that some of them had had their doors welded shut, as well?

Had all of us been the victims of some enigmatic cult, working from the shadows? The cult that somehow knew what was coming and prepared accordingly?

I didn't know what their plans for us were, but I could think of only one thing: we were left behind to be a sacrifice. An offering to their King in Rags, whatever that was. I wouldn't even be surprised to find out that it wasn't some abstract entity, but an actual creature of flesh and blood.

But what did they mean by "lead them outside"? And how was he going to distract the beasts that roamed the streets?

The answer to that question came immediately: although their sleep was not too long, they had been awakening just as slow as the first time a few days before – and just as loud. The sound which I had hoped to never hear again in my life was slowly gaining volume, breaking through the silence.

The sirens. Following the command of their new masters who had somehow pried the control over them from the military, they were coming back to life again - although this time, they were distant, as if they were crying for another town, and serving a different purpose. Where before they were the means to alert the populace, now they were a distraction. A loud noise meant to attract the beasts and draw them away from certain parts of town - the parts where no living soul set foot for the past few days.

At that moment, I was one of the two people who knew what was going on - and even armed with that knowledge, I still couldn't help but panic. The dread spread through my veins like oil, clogging the heart, and making it work harder. My breathing had sped up as well. I was hearing the sound which every person had been conditioned to associate with one thought: "run."

Yet I couldn't. I could only sit and desperately try to calm down, waiting for what was coming next. And I could only imagine what the rest of the people in the building had been going through.

The last time the sirens had been sounded, the town turned into the hellhole. What was going to happen now?

# CHAPTER 14 – Believers

The sirens were wailing in the distance, announcing the beginning of something. The people in our building answered with the same call: some were crying in fear and distress, others - panicking.

The radio followed. Disturbed by the sirens, it started screaming as well. Screaming in a way I'd never heard a radio do. The very white static, the oldest noise in the universe which only those with mechanical ears could hear, was twisting and whining, becoming high-pitched and fast; the next second - low and slow. It seemed as for the first time since the big bang something disturbed it, uprooted it from its primeval roots. Some unknown, unearthly energies were traveling through it, making it squeal under their heels.

A blinding headache split my head – only for a moment, subsiding so fast I barely recognized its presence. One moment I felt like tearing my hair out and the next one it was already just a memory. I felt something swell within me as well. For a moment, so short I barely registered it, the meaning of those strange sounds became clear to me, before that knowledge retreated into my subconscious. It felt like something reached out to me, but I wasn't ready to accept it yet.

I knew for sure that the sirens had nothing to do with it. No, it was… something else. Something that my radio could detect, but not explain. It just screamed that gibberish at me, without translating, without explaining anything. Just bringing my attention to it.

Something else was going on at that very moment. Something for which the strange radio cult had created a distraction.

Outside my apartment, people kept on wailing and shouting, completely oblivious to what was transpiring yet feeling with their guts that it was nothing good. I didn't see the point of interfering: I doubted they would listen to what I have to say, and I didn't have much to say on top of that.

Then their screams changed: someone cried out aggressively, provocatively. A female voice, muffled by walls, wordlessly cried out in shock, in fear. Another voice grunted as if resisting something - or someone. "Stop!" - I heard a man shout with a sudden clarity: the walls failed to contain his call.

*"The bandits?"* - I thought, feeling my knees shake. Were they agitated by the sirens and decided they had nothing to lose? Were they waiting for it to happen? Were they in cahoots with those who sealed us in? Were they doing their bidding?

I remembered the words of that man, back there when I was threatening to carve their heads open. Would he remember my face? Would he remember his grudge?

The hatchet was still behind my belt, its short handle rubbing against my leg. "I'm here", it was telling me. "I'm with you."

Pulling it out, I headed outside.

On the stairwell, things had gotten clearer: someone was fighting a floor above. I didn't hear the swearing of the bandits, didn't hear any heavy blows landing on someone's head. Just struggling.

"What the hell's wrong with you? Snap out of it!" - some man grunted. It was tough for him to speak. The breath was raspy, uneven. No doubt he was wrestling with someone who those words were aimed at.

Someone must've lost their mind from the sirens. That, or dementia. Perhaps the second round of sirens had awakened the deep trauma - the memories of an airstrike from some war of the last century?

Or maybe the transmission I had eavesdropped on had such an effect on them? Maybe they were one of the intended listeners and were doing whatever it was prescribed for them to do?

Either way, it was worth investigating. I headed upstairs.

My prediction turned out to be true: two old men were wrestling with each other. Neither of them knew how to fight, and they were engaged in that weird bar dance the drunkards sometimes partake in when they want things settled. Arms on the opponent's shoulders, trying to both push them away and wrestle them to the ground. Legs wide. It looked more like two bulls crossed their horns, trying to find out who among them was the strongest.

Two people - an old man and a woman - were trying to pull them apart. The rest of the people just silently stood around them, observing them. Their dance had no more open spots. Even if they tried to help, they wouldn't be able to get close enough - all the space around the fighters was already occupied.

I tried to chime in anyway.

"What's going on here?" - I demanded to know, trying to sound confident and louder than the noise. The noise of fighting, the noise of sirens.

"Get him off me!" - one of the fighters grunted. His opponent's fingers were getting dangerously close to his neck.

"What are you standing there for? Pry them apart! We have bigger things to worry about!" - one of the women who were observing the fight scolded me, pointing at the window where the sirens were still screaming.

"Right..." - I went behind the other fighter, tried to pull him. His skin felt hot to the touch: the man seemed to have a fever. No dice: the man wouldn't budge, despite being a whole head shorter than me. His old muscles and ligaments, which I had expected to be weak, were surprisingly tense and strong, like a bark of an old tree.

"Hurry! What's taking you so long? He'll strangle me, I tell you!" - the other man wheezed. I took a glimpse at him: the man I was wrestling with indeed already had his fingers on the old man's neck. Squeezing it so hard they were almost drowning in the wrinkly skin.

"One sec! Let me… What the hell are you standing around for?" - I shouted at the rest of the observers.

"I'm not coming closer to him - he might have rabies" - someone commented. Still, I felt another set of hands join our struggle and nodded in appreciation.

The man still wouldn't budge. Where was he getting all of that strength?

I heard the answer a second later: one of his bones cracked under our combined assault. The man paid it no more attention than he was paying to us. He was going all out, disregarding the injuries.

"Help…" - the man wheezed weakly. He was starting to sink to the floor, his grip on the assaulter's hands getting weaker by each second.

"Pry him off, come on! You're killing him, old man! What are you doing?" - one of my helpers addressed the assaulter, but he remained mute.

It was time for drastic measures. If he was ready to strangle that old man, then I had to be ready to do the same to him if I wanted to stop him. Letting him kill him would feel like being an accomplice, yet I couldn't imagine actually hitting him. Taking my hatchet, I put it across his throat and started pulling it. I was careful not to crush his windpipe, but as even those measures proved to be ineffective I was drawing more and more of my power with each second.

"Yes! Like that! Pull him!" - someone shouted. I doubled my efforts, feeling the warmth of their approval spread through me. I was helping them. I was valuable.

Just a little bit more...

The old man suddenly let go of the man and turned his face to me. Before that, I didn't get a good look at it. Now, I recognized him.

It was the same old man who, just a day before, was telling me that the water was fine. That you could drink it without any problems.

The man didn't look healthy. His skin was sickly pale, and on top of that it had a strange texture to it. Like paper that got wet and crumbly and then dried up. But only when he looked me straight in the eye, only when his face was right next to mine, did I see what was really wrong with him.

His skin was covered in strange dark spots – or rather, there was something underneath his skin, some strange growths that were giving it dark pigmentation. Those weren't bruises for sure – I could see the skin slightly bulging as if something was pushing against from beneath. Something strange, alien had settled there – and it was now pulling the old man's strings.

He opened his mouth and let out a guttural sound. The growth on his left cheek twitched in response and moved upward, toward his eye, moving the skin with it – it looked as if the man had a tic. It stretched his lower eyelid to its limit before finally poking from underneath it, rubbing against his eye – a bizarre lump of flesh, almost completely black and clearly with a will of its own.

It stretched toward me as if it wanted to reach out to me. As it moved, the old man let out another moan, obeying its new master's will.

I leaped back in disgust. The other tenants followed. The man whose neck the afflicted old man had been squeezing managed to break free from his grasp, coughing and wheezing, but the old man didn't pay him any attention. He had a new target.

He - It - opened its mouth. Said something to me soundlessly, like a fish in a tank. Twitched, as if realizing its mistake, and tried again.

"Yyuuuuuuuuuuuuuuuuuuu..." - it groaned. Its voice was normal - just a little bit coarse. In a moment, the meaning of that sound became clear, making my skin crawl.

It was trying to say my name. How?! How did it know me?

"Yuuuuuriiiiiii" - it repeated itself, a bit faster this time. pulling every syllable. It wasn't the old man speaking - something else had possessed him. Something was within him, running with his blood, sharing his flesh. Observing me. Gauging how much of a threat I was.

"He is among us. His blood may not be red like that of a worker, but it now runs in our veins all the same. He is one of us now."

The answer came to me on its own. It was Him. I was among those who had come face to face with that cult's messiah. The King in Rags. The one whose blood was running among their own. He had come to fulfill his promise.

"Jesus Christ" - one of the men whimpered and disappeared within his apartment. The others, seeing that it was focused solely on me, followed his example. Not a single person stayed around to help.

"Stand back!" - I screeched, realizing that I was left all alone. I raised my hatchet over my head to try and look more intimidating. "I'll do it, I swear!" - I promised the old man while doubting if I really had it in me.

Was the old man nothing more than his puppet? Was he like a zombie from those movies Nikita and I liked to watch and laugh at? He wasn't dead - that was for sure. The dead lack the warmth in their touch. The old man, with his fever, had plenty of that.

Did it mean that he could still be in there? That he was just under some sort of mind-control? They had always made it look easy in the movies. "The man you've once known is gone." How could I restrain him without hurting him? Was there even a way to deal with it in a humane way when all I had was a hatchet for meat?

In the distance, I heard the sounds of struggle and fight. Judging by the sound, the fight was in the next stairwell. Were people there facing the same threat as I was?

And then - a gunshot. Clear as a day. Then another one, and another one. Was it Maxim?

He had just taken the gun from Pavel. Did he know how soon he'd have to use it?

Did he really have no other options than to use it against the people he called neighbors just a few days prior? Did it mean that I also had no choice?

Was I going to die, if I hesitated to act?

The oxygen and horse-load of adrenaline that had been pumped to my brain with another heartbeat, combined into an igniting concoction that exploded in my brain and lit a blue fire deep inside. "It's him or me!" - I decided with sudden ferocity. Fear of the man in front of me, of what I had to do became so enormous, stretched so far inside my mind I couldn't even feel it. It was just a background at that point. The front row, the driver's seat of my head was occupied by things like fury, bloodlust.

"If I have to cut off a few of his limbs to subdue him alive - so be it. He won't mind, will he? He'll live," - I decided the man's future for him.

My hand squeezed the hatchet so hard I couldn't tell where its metal ended and my bone began. It was as if I was born that way. Born to kill.

The man's eyes remained blank: his passenger had made a decision for him. Letting out a terrifying, blood-curdling groan, the man rushed at me.

There wasn't too much space to avoid his charge: two steps back and I would fall down the flight. Perhaps that was what the man had aimed for when he grabbed me with two hands and started pushing me there.

I was keeping him at a distance with my free hand. Without even realizing what was I doing, I raised the hatchet above my head and, before he pushed me off the stairs, brought it down on his shoulder.

For a split second, for a moment shorter than a heartbeat of the man's racing heart, I saw the pure, pink color of his flesh as it was separated by grey steel. Saw the white of his bones, felt their rigidness put my motion to a halt.

Then his heart pumped blood again and turned his flesh red. Pulled a crimson veil over his wound.

He screamed in pain, hissed like some nocturnal creature, wiggled his whole body to get out of my grasp, moving with surprising speed for his age and agility. His animalistic cries made me snap out of my rage for a second - I had never laid a hand on another human being before. To see one bleed from such a gruesome wound, to know that I was the one who put them through such pain, was quite a shocking experience. I felt like a criminal, an enemy to humankind.

But a few seconds later the red thick fluid - the same as the one that was running through my veins - suddenly changed to a black gelatinous ooze that was coming out in clumps. The substance started to bubble, to rise up and down in an effort to cover his wound. It was behaving as if it had a will of its own, separate from its carrier, and was haphazardly trying to heal the damage to its vessel. The man scooped up a handful and hungrily licked it, the strange ritual seemingly making his pain subside, before hissing at me with his now black mouth and retreating back to his apartment, dripping red and black.

The door closed after him, and I heard the lock click - he locked himself to either heal his wounds or die in peace. A few moments later the door to the right of me opened: a scared tenant peeked outside.

"We need to barricade his door!" - I commanded him. The man was too scared to object: he just nodded in agreement.

"Do you have a hammer and nails? Some planks?" - I inquired. He shook his head: "No. But Mihalich does. He's a carpenter."

"Go fetch him and get to work" - I told him before running upstairs.

"Wait, aren't you going to help us?" - I heard his confused, scared voice. "What if he comes out again?"

"You better finish before he does, then" - I answered, not even slowing down. I had heard the gunshots coming from the next flight of stairs, where Maxim was. If the same thing was happening there, too, then we needed to unite to fight them back together.

On the fifth floor, a group of tenants grouped up around a sobbing woman, trying to console her. Her shoulders were shaking, and in the moments when she took her hands away from her face she revealed not only tears but a stream of blood coming from her split eyebrow. The door next to them was shaking every few seconds under blows of someone who remained locked within the apartment - I could see the key still sticking out of the keyhole.

"He never raised a hand on me, and now… It's like he wasn't himself! Like he was sick or possessed," - she was telling everyone willing to listen.

"Must've been drinking behind your back, then" - one of the women deduced with confidence. "I'll let him have the piece of my mind when he snaps out of it" - she told her, before noticing me approaching. Her confidence disappeared in a second, giving way to terror, and it took me a moment to realize why: I was holding a bloodied hatchet, and my clothes were covered in blood, too. In the heat of the battle, I hadn't noticed it, but now, as I was standing in front of the people, I was quickly becoming self-conscious about how I looked.

Someone screamed, but I quickly raised my hands to show that I wasn't a threat to calm them down: "I'm okay! I'm not one of them. I'm from the militia."

"Don't walk around looking like that - you'll scare people!" - she barked at me, but I didn't have time to argue with her.

"No matter what you do, do not open that door" - I warned them before starting to climb up the ladder to the roof. I didn't know what strange affliction had stricken down the people, but I had seen firsthand how they behaved. If they opened the door, they would release the man inside. And I didn't want to fight another one of my former neighbors if I didn't have to.

"But… How will I get back home?" - the wounded woman asked me. Somehow, she was looking up to me as if I was some sort of authority - I was sure the bloodied clothes and hatchet made it hard to argue with me.

"You don't," - I said, climbing all the way up, before giving them one final look. "Your husband is a goner. Barricade the door - the men from the floor below you can help you with that."

I didn't stick around to see if they followed my instructions - I was needed elsewhere. Climbing to the roof, I quickly covered the distance toward the entrance to the third flight, only stopping at the door. Something had attracted my attention.

The sirens were still blaring somewhere in the distance, intending to draw in the monsters out of the town like the Pied Piper led the rats out of the village. I didn't see any of them, but…

From where I stood I could see a street stretching into the distance. Was I making it up or did I really see a procession of people going around the corner?

There was no mistake about it - a few dozen of them were following a hooded figure. Even from such a distance, I noticed that something seemed off about it - aside from the fact that it was outside at such a time. It was a full head taller than even the tallest of its followers, and very bulky on top of it, too. As for its movements... I wouldn't call them inhuman, but there was some strange mixture of both awkwardness and strength to them - something I couldn't quite pin down but stood out nonetheless.

The people following the figure didn't seem alarmed or scared. I would've expected them to constantly look around, searching for beasts to leap at them around every corner, but all of them seemed to be entirely focused on the stranger that was leading them. It was as if his confidence was giving them faith to carry on without fear… Or as if they were being led by him. Like the entranced kids led by the disgruntled artist from the infamous fairy tale, they followed the figure's every step to the sound of the sirens.

A strange procession, almost religious by how it looked, with the sirens being their only hymn.

Bizarre and curious as it was, I had no time to think about it. I had made a parallel to the last transmission I had received, but it was not the time to analyze it further. The procession was far away anyway. Staring at it would not give me any deeper insight into what it was.

Opening the door, I rushed down the creaky ladder; the sirens getting duller as the walls got in the way of the sound spreading but not disappearing. New sounds from below joined them: the sounds of struggle and fight, and just as I put my foot down on the floor another shot echoed through the corridors.

I looked over the railings to assess the situation: if there was a fight still going on, then it meant that someone was still fighting back.

Just as I looked, someone ran from one apartment to the next. I didn't get a good look at them, but what I saw sent chills down my spine: the person moved with a strange ferocity in their moves as if driven by animalistic instinct alone.

They were everywhere. The people who had been brainwashed into becoming ferocious killers. I didn't know if they could be brought back from beyond that threshold, but it didn't matter at that moment. What mattered was we had to stop them - then, once they were subdued, we could think about what to do with them.

I had to be careful: it was hard to pinpoint where exactly anyone was - or who anyone was, for that matter. The paradigm has shifted: now the threat wasn't just outside. Any person, no matter who they had been just an hour ago, could now be a threat. Anyone could now be something else other than human.

A shot echoed through the stairwell and someone cussed and cried out in pain. I froze in my tracks: did that mean that the other side had guns, too? Or did the pain make them remember how to swear?

"Stop cowering there, you son of a bitch! Come here, I've got something for you!" - I heard a familiar voice. Maxim! He was down there, and it seemed like he hadn't given up yet. He must've been down there, at the third stairwell, when the sirens signaled the beginning of the assault. I felt relieved: so not only people were fighting back, but I also knew those people! Which meant that they wouldn't shoot me on sight, thinking that I was one of the possessed.

I was afraid to descend. I was still shaken up by my earlier confrontation. But I knew that just standing around wouldn't do me any good - I had to either leave or come down and join the fight. My fury was running on fumes, and yet there was enough for me to make the decision: I quickly ran down the stairs, trying to make as little sound as possible, and looked around.

Some of the doors to the apartments were wide open and judging by the chaos inside and occasional blood splatters on the walls, I could tell that the fight broke out there very recently. It made sense how the assailants made it inside the apartments - over the last few days, people started leaving their doors open so that their neighbors could come in at any time to have a talk or share the news. It was heartbreaking to see how horribly their trust backfired on them, but it wasn't the main thing that concerned me.

Back at our flight, from what I'd seen, only two people had become possessed, but just two people couldn't cause so much chaos in such a short amount of time. Had the third flight had more cases? Had there been a horde of mindless zombies just a few floors below me, rummaging through the apartments on their way down and tearing everyone limb from limb?

How soon would they reach the first floor and turn back?

I could definitely hear the sounds of struggle down below, but the wailing of the sirens was making it hard to focus.

"Are you holding him? Are you holding him good? Stay here, I'll go check out the others!" - I heard a familiar voice coming from one of the apartments before a man holding a gun stepped outside. He raised the weapon to shoot me down, but a moment later he recognized me and lowered the weapon.

"Yura! Don't stand there, hide! They have the guns!" - Maxim shouted at me.

"Guns? Where did the possessed get the guns?" - was all I could think before one of them appeared around the corner of the stairwell.

I recognized him by purple inky spots under his skin, by the neurotic, twitchy movements of his arms… But I also recognized the bald head, the tracksuit, the pale skin which hadn't seen the sun in decades… A bandit. One of those who had threatened to kill me if he'd ever see me again just the day before.

In his hands, he was holding a pistol - similar to the one Pavel had had, and in his other hand, he had an awkwardly big checkered plastic bag - like the ones old people use when going to the market for food, and from a short glance I could tell that it was filled to the brim with food of all kinds. If not for the gun, on any other day he would seem like a man coming back home from grocery shopping, but I knew that it wasn't just a purchase - it was a trophy.

What Pavel had been so afraid of came true, and on the very next day at that. Running out of food to eat, they turned to the rest of the flights, and we were powerless to stop them. I wasn't sure if they were acting on their own accord or their strange ailment was making them act up, but that didn't matter at the moment. What mattered that they were in there with us. A tumor spreading through our building and consuming everything it could reach.

He - it - glanced at me, and for a moment, it seemed like it recognized me. For a moment the primal darkness in its eyes lit up with a spark of realization that he knew who I was, before reverting to his violent side and aiming a gun at me. The shot knocked a piece of plaster out of the wall behind me - just a bit to the left of my head.

"Take cover!" - Maxim shouted at me, hiding inside the apartment. He raised Pavel's pistol and took a few shots at the bandit, but none of them had found their targets.

"Blyat[13]!" - I screamed, hiding inside another apartment. In an attempt to get out of the line of fire, I dramatically leaped inside one of the open apartments and crawled away from the door. My heart was racing and my thoughts were a mess. What the hell was going on? First the creatures were outside, and now the bandits were looting us during what seemed like a zombie outbreak? It was bad enough to get eaten by the creatures outside, but now I had to be afraid of getting shot, too?

Maxim was heavily involved in the shootout, trying to hold them back. He had a better cover than the other man: while he was peeking around the corner to take a shot, the bandit was out in the open, with nowhere to hide on the landing between the floors. It almost seemed like Maxim could win this, but then a third gun joined their firefight, and the number of new holes on the walls near Maxim started increasing at double the rate. The thug had an ally coming to help him, and it was only a matter of time before Maxim would run out of ammo.

"Blyat!" - Maxim screamed as the bullet grazed his forearm. "I can't hold them back, Yura! Close the door!" - with that, he slammed his door shut. I heard the lock click as he locked himself up, and not a second later I heard two sets of footsteps. The bandits were coming up. How much time did I have before they'd see me? A second? Two seconds?

---

[13] Blyat — a Russian swear word, bread and butter of Russian swearing. In this context it means the same as the F-word, and is meant to imply the immense frustration of the speaker.

I jumped from my feet to close the door, but just as I stood up, the possessed thing entered the stairway - just in time to see me stand up. Had I remained on the floor he wouldn't have noticed me, but it seemed that my luck was finally running out. He sent a careless shot in my direction, meant to scare me away from the door, and I had to quickly scuttle away, into the depths of the apartment. Into a dead-end.

The room I ended up in was a kitchen. It seemed my earlier estimate was the correct one: they had come there to take away the tenant's food, and they had been going from one apartment to the next. The cupboards were wide open, with some missing the doors where the burglars tore them out in a rush to get as much food as possible. The fridge was wide open, too, demonstrating its empty, pristine white insides.

They had already been there. They knew the layout of the apartment. And nothing was stopping them from coming inside.

I could hear them right outside the apartment. At least two of them. They quietly made their way into the hallway, the careless shuffling of their feet heard even through the distant sirens.

It was so strange and bizarre: the sirens were warning me of danger far away, while the actual threat was just a few meters away from me. I was involved in a very small, almost domestic act of violence. The intruders were at my doorstep, and I had to do my best to defend myself. No police were going to help me. The neighbors wouldn't call them. There was no one to call.

I was on my own.

What was the plan? Suppose I'd be able to ambush the first one. Since I was hiding behind the corner, he wouldn't be able to shoot me before entering the room, and I wouldn't be able to hit him with my hatchet before that. The moment he'd step beyond the kitchen threshold, we'd be locked in a bizarre version of a Mexican stand-off. The difference was, of course, that I wasn't packing a firearm… and that there were at least two of them.

Suppose I'd be able to land my strike on the first one before he'd have a chance to shoot me. What was I going to do about the second one? Was I going to use the body of the one I'd killed as a meat shield? I strongly suspected that it only worked in the movies. Once I'd deal with the first one, the second one would finish me off. He would know where I was hiding and there wasn't too much room in the kitchen to hide or jump out of his line of fire. I was a sitting duck, waiting for them to strike.

I heard one of them slowly head my way. Our confrontation was maybe seconds away. He came closer to the door. It shook gently when his hand touched the doorknob. I raised my hatchet above my head, afraid to even blink.

At that moment, the howling of the sirens suddenly stopped. In the abrupt silence, every sound suddenly became crystal clear. I stopped breathing mid-breath so as not to alert the intruder outside the kitchen door.

He stopped, too. Made another step. And another one. I was scared that he was going to hear my heartbeat.

The steps were subsiding, I suddenly realized. The man was walking away as if the sirens going quiet were some sort of signal for him.

He let out a groaning sound, his companion answered with the same one.

"Let's go," - one of them suddenly said. "The boss says we're done here."

Slowly, they walked out of the apartment where they, judging by the sounds, seemingly joined the rest. I heard the echo of their steps as they were going upstairs, heard the ladder quake and rattle under their feet as they were ascending to the rooftop, heard the hatch close after the last of them. They were gone. As mysteriously as they had arrived.

Their sudden regaining of humanity alarmed me - so they could revert back! That meant that the man I attacked was not like that permanently. I had almost killed the man who was going through some sort of episode.

But then again, they were talking about their "boss" in the present tense. I didn't hear the whizzing of radios - so how could they know? Did they have an agreement of sorts, to leave once the sirens would go silent? Or was there something else going on?

Or maybe, their boss was always with them? Hiding right under their skin and commanding them all at once?

"Everyone alive?" - I heard Maxim call out.

"Yeah, I'm fine" – I shouted, trying to keep my voice even. I didn't want to show anyone that I was scared, even if it would be nothing unusual in such a situation. Somewhere on the floors below, someone cried out in pain – not everyone had come out of the confrontation unscathed.

Maxim was already on the staircase when I walked out of the apartment. The man seemed shaken.

"They've taken the food," - Maxim said, gritting his teeth. "And drained the water from the bathtubs where they've had the chance. Bastards want us to starve here."

They've drained the water… Once again, it seemed like there was some connection between the water and the strange epidemic of madness that's gotten to them. The people had been complaining about tap water's taste, the old man who I had been fighting was saying that the tap water was fine to drink, and now the thugs, stricken by the same strange disease, were wasting their time trying to leave people without the water they had stocked up on. What was going on?

"I think there's something in the tap water," - I've voiced my concern to Maxim. "Something that makes people go crazy.

Only those who were drinking it were affected by it, and those guys had the same signs of infection as the other infected."

Maxim stood there for a few moments, pursing his lips, before saying with a sigh: "just a coincidence."

\*\*\*

For the remainder of the evening, we spent our efforts trying to barricade the doors to the roof. From that moment on, we were facing off against the beasts for which the locked door was not an impossible obstacle, so we had to make sure to guard against them. It would make communication between flights even more difficult, and we were all on our own, splitting into three segments, but it was the only choice we had. We couldn't ignore such a blatant hole in our defense. Our only choice at that point was to split our forces and hunker down.

Our situation seemed to be getting worse with each day. Not only were we besieged by the monsters from the outside, but now the other-worldly threat had found its way inside the building as well. Before that, we were toying with the idea that we could keep the bandits at bay. But now, as some new life was circling through their flesh, it seemed that they had abandoned their fear of death.

It was as if the very building we were residing in had gotten infected. A quarter of it had become a tumor, draining the rest of its resources and doing its best to speed up the whole organism's demise. The world, which in the last few days had shrunk to the size of one Khruschyovka, shrunk once more. Now, the fourth flight was a white spot on its map. "Here there be monsters."

The people who had been robbed of food had been complaining to everyone with ears about their situation. Some of them were doing that just for the sake of it, while others, keener ones, were trying to get their luckier neighbors to share some food with them. It wasn't rare to hear people argue over a loaf of bread. Eventually, I caved in to their pleas and gave an old man half a kilo of buckwheat. I quickly regretted that decision: for the next hour, the door of my apartment was besieged by people who had heard that I was sharing food. They didn't care that I already had less than those who hadn't shared – all they cared about was that I was seemingly willing to part with it, too. In their eyes, I was someone who was putting their well-being above my own, and thus could be exploited. Perhaps they were right. Their shouts and demands echoed through the stairwell outside for an hour until Maxim came and told everyone that the barricade was almost ready and if they wanted to sleep in their beds instead of cold hard stairs they had to leave. Only then did they leave me alone.

We also had to take care of the dead: as their numbers were growing we had to come up with a way to store their bodies more efficiently. We couldn't just throw them over the edge of the roof - it would only serve to attract more monsters to us. Laying them in the basement wouldn't work for the same reason, either - we had already seen that the basement wasn't safe.

In the end, we had to pile them up in the apartments of one of the deceased tenants. The old man probably hadn't had so many guests in many years, so he would at least have some company in the afterlife. He probably wouldn't appreciate that he and his guests were stacked like logs, but you know what they say: "the more the merrier."

As we were leaving that apartment, I made sure to check if all the windows were closed. The last thing I needed was one of those wall-crawling creatures to find its way inside to feast on them.

We also had to take care of the people who had been locked in their apartments by their neighbors, but it seemed that they had taken care of that for us. Once they had realized that they couldn't escape and that their doors were locked from the outside, they simply jumped out the windows. The witnesses said that they all had done it simultaneously, at the same time - as if the same fatalistic idea had struck them all at once.

I wasn't very surprised by such a revelation. After all, their symptoms had also appeared at the same time. Those people had some sort of uniformity to them. Perhaps the cultists who had summoned the sirens that heralded the madness of the afflicted used the radio to spread their word, but the possessed men and women seemingly used something else entirely.

Despite Maxim's protests, who believed that my paranoia was acting up again, I decided to look into my theory that something in the tap water was causing it and ask around. It was easy to find those whose families had been affected by the event: they were the ones who grieved. What was hard was to approach them and ask about this matter.

People were unwilling to open up and talk about it, their grief making them unresponsive. In some cases, they'd snap at me for asking seemingly absurd questions at such a critical hour, and each time that happened I wanted to give up my quest and leave them alone, and only my desire to get to the truth was pushing me forward.

But an hour later I'd finally managed to confirm my hunch: the people who had been affected by the sudden onset of madness had been drinking tap water despite the protests of their cohabitants. I made an announcement and made sure that the information reached everyone. Some people were doubtful, but I could see in their eyes that the events of the day had scared them enough to follow my advice – just in case.

It felt like a hollow victory – that revelation had come at a great cost, and it seemed insignificant when compared to everything we'd gone through. Besides, even though it answered some questions, it also brought up new ones: how did that thing get into the water? Was the cult behind it or were they just going along with what was happening?

The only good thing to come out of that day was the new recruits, as Maxim liked to call them. A few disillusioned men, whose feeling of having control over their lives had dwindled during the events of the past day, and who decided to do everything in their power to take it back.

I left it to Maxim to show them the ropes and share with them what we'd found out. I could tell that they didn't see me as a figure of authority anyway, so leaving it to him I went to Natasha's apartment. Despite living alone for many months, I couldn't endure another night in solitude. I needed some company. I wanted to pretend like everything was how it used to be in the old days.

\*\*\*

"You know, I can't believe that this is happening to us" – Natasha complained to me over a cup of tea. By the time that topic had come up, we'd spent a good few hours talking about everything else, playing out our old conversations about politics and news. As if the world we had lived in had still existed. So finally, when there was nothing else to talk about, Natasha decided to raise this question.

"I hear ya" – I told her. "Between the monsters, the weird transmissions on the radio, and the possessed people I don't even know what to think anymore."

"I've never thought that living here would come to bite me so hard" – she kept on talking as if she didn't even hear what I've said. "I've always thought that I'm missing out on life in a big city, that I could find a better job out there, that I'd be able to go on vacation more often if I didn't live in the middle of nowhere where decent pay is unheard of… But I never imagined that something like this could happen. I mean, they wouldn't lock down some big city, right? Would anything like this even happen in a big city?" – she asked me.

"No, I guess not" – I answered, taking a sip of tea. "It's one of the perks of living in the middle of nowhere."

"It's not just that, I think… I think this whole phenomenon has happened here because it was bound to happen here, of all places. You know what I mean? If you live in a moldy house, you're bound to get sick more often. And if you live in a town that used to be missing from the maps a few decades ago… You end up in our situation. As unreal as our situation is, it is real, it just had to happen somewhere, sometime. And this is the place. This is the place where the world ends – and no one outside even notices it. Am I making sense?" – she asked me.

"I struggle to follow you" – I honestly admitted, though there was some truth to her words. The roots of the catastrophe we'd found ourselves involved in definitely stretched into our town's dark and mysterious past – of that I was sure.

"And to think that I could be far away from here right this moment" - Natasha let out a bitter, hollow laugh. "Nikita was offering for me to go somewhere for a vacation. He said he'd join me in a few days, after he'd get everything settled with his boss. But I didn't want to leave him alone here, so I decided to stay. I've always been here for him," - she whispered.

"You're a good girlfriend" - I awkwardly pointed out. Somehow, I felt like she needed to hear that at that moment.

"Oh, am I?" - she smiled at me, but the smile was crooked as if she'd forgotten how to do it. "I've wanted to leave this town for so long… I've been telling him that for years. But I've decided to stay here. And not because I love him, but because... Because he needed me. I could feel that he was yearning for attention, like a child, even if he never voiced it or showed it in any way."

I could relate to what she was saying. I knew the feeling of being anchored down by your relationship with other people. To feel like you can't leave because they needed you where you were. I wanted to tell her that it wasn't her fault, or that she was doing him a favor and that she was a good person for doing that for him… But the words were not forthcoming.

Suddenly, those words just didn't feel right to me anymore. I could lie to myself, but I couldn't bring myself to lie to her as well.

A few minutes later, I went back to my apartment – alone. When Natasha asked me if I wanted to stay, I just came up with some lazy excuse that I wanted to clean up at home. I could tell that she saw right through it, but I simply couldn't stay there with her. I needed some alone time.

# CHAPTER 15 – A Breach

When the morning came, Maxim had invited me to join them in strengthening the perimeter, but I declined his offer, telling him that I had something else going on. He gave me a disappointed look but then just silently turned around and left. His sigh stabbed me like a dagger between the ribs but I knew that I had important things to do. I had to keep the big picture in mind – I had to find out something about our situation.

I spent the entire morning listening to the broadcasts, trying to eavesdrop on another transmission, but it seemed that my luck had run out. The strange cult which seemed to have an insight into what was going on had seemingly disappeared. It made sense, too: the transmission I had received the day before seemed to carry great importance, and unlike the first time, they didn't leave a time and date of when they would be broadcasting again. It seemed that their job there was done.

Leonid wasn't heard from, either. I didn't know what that meant: perhaps he wasn't ready to risk sticking out his neck for me anymore. Perhaps their base had already fallen to the onslaught of those creatures or they had gotten possessed, too. Perhaps his higher-ups found out about our exchange and sentenced him to a tribunal, which, considering that we were in a de facto war, meant a death sentence.

Nevertheless, I spent one hour after the other listening to the radio waves, trying to pick up something. Trying to guess the frequency, trying to hear the words where there were none. In the past, the radio had served me well to warn me about the upcoming threat, and so I felt like I needed to stay vigilant for more clues. That it was my responsibility as a sole man with a radio. I felt like our building was a submarine, submerged in the ocean of madness that swirled and whispered to me just outside our walls, and I was the listener, trying to hear the soft purring of the enemy's engines. Trying to guess their maneuvers and warn the rest of the crew ahead of time.

Little did I know that our submarine would soon take another blow to its hull, and no amount of me listening to radio waves would warn me about that.

After countless hours I was already dozing off. My mind was starting to play tricks on me and I was having a hard time discerning my dreams from reality. So, when I heard the distant screams of terror and panic, at first I thought that I must've finally picked up hell's radio frequency and could hear the voices of those who weren't lucky enough to escape in time or find a safe space like us.

Only after a few seconds, I realized that the screams weren't coming from the radio. They were coming from outside of my apartment. From the stairwell.

"The bandits?" - I jumped to my feet and grabbed my hatchet from the table near me: since the last few days, the thing wasn't leaving my side. Even when I was sleeping I was putting it somewhere within my reach, and if it wasn't so hard and sharp I'd be hiding it under my pillow.

I had spent a good amount of time the day before washing off the blood and that black ooze from it, and as it was running down the drain I couldn't stop thinking that I had used it to harm another human being. But the moment I felt its weight in my hand all the doubts and guilt disappeared as if they too were washed away. I knew that it was my time to act.

Rushing to the door, I stepped outside, holding the weapon ready - just in time to see an old woman running up the stairs. For a moment, I prepared to tackle her, to bring down the blade on her head, but then I noticed that she wasn't like the man I had faced off the day before. Her skin didn't have the same dark purple patches on them, and her facial expression was not of anger or disdain - only pure horror. For a moment, she froze in her tracks, noticing the hostile look in my eyes, but then she kept on running upstairs - away from something that terrified her far more than someone like me ever could.

I recognized her. She was the same woman I had been talking to a few days ago. The one who asked Pavel's help to move her strangled neighbor to the bathroom. The one who had said that she intended to stay with her and pray for her soul. It seemed that the time for prayer was over.

For a moment, I wondered what could it be that scared her so much. A moment later, I didn't have to guess anymore.

I heard it.

Down below, on the first floor. They say that humans react to sounds faster than they do to the things they see, and now I understood why. It was the primary tool of notification for our ancestors, who had dwelled in the jungle, that something was approaching them. It was the main tool to let them know: there is something near that you don't yet see. The hearing was the eyesight which could penetrate through thick leaves and look around the corner.

And it was very well refined.

All the way from where I was standing, I could tell what was going on. The way sounds reflected from surfaces, the way sound waves curved around the stairwell on their way up - I could picture things I hadn't yet laid eyes on just from those minute details.

The bestial ape that had claimed a life a day before was back - and judging by the sounds it was making, it was already inside the building.

Its grunts and hissing were loud and audible, but they lacked a certain ring to them - the ringing that a clear echo would give them. The beast was not on the stairwell - not yet. But its sounds weren't muffled either, which meant that nothing stood in its way.

Did it somehow break the door? No, the sound of its grunts was somehow soft, uncertain around the edges. As if it bounced from the soft surfaces on its way to me and lost some of its crispness. Soft surfaces like the foam that covered all of the doors from within, or the wallpapers and cushions on a sofa. The beast was in one of the apartments. An apartment that remained open when the woman escaped it, running for her life.

How? I didn't know for sure, but I didn't have to ask, either. There was only one certain way it could have entered the apartment - by tearing the grates off the windows. With how much strength its body carried, I was surprised it hadn't done that already. Barring any miracles or hidden abilities the creature possessed, it was the only way it could've found its way inside.

How many steps I'd have to take down those stairs to stand in front of the door to the apartment where the beast was? Forty, fifty? How many more steps I'd have to take to stand before it - another ten?

Sixty steps. At that moment, that was the maximum distance between us. A completely unobstructed path that both of us could walk.

Sixty steps to death. Sixty human steps - the beast would no doubt need even less.

My first instinct was to hide inside my apartment. If it hadn't been able to break through the main doors, it wouldn't be able to break the doors to my home, either. The grates on the windows were different - it just needed to figure out to pull on them instead of pushing.

But what would I do then? What would we all do if it started roaming the stairwell? Hope that it would eventually leave? What if it wouldn't be able to find the exit?

Letting things run their course meant an eventual hungry death. The only way to prevent that was to keep the beast out of the stairwell. To lock it in the apartment it was in. Deny it any more ground. I looked around to see if anyone was willing to help me, but I was all alone. The rest of the tenants had already done the obvious thing and hid in their houses.

It was all up to me. I had to go down there and close the apartment's door.

I wanted to bargain with fate, to offer it someone else in my place - but I was out of bargaining chips other than my life. And every second I spent thinking about it was drawing closer to the moment when the beast would inevitably start roaming between the floors.

Cursing myself, I slowly made my way downwards - toward the source of those horrible, alien noises.

It wasn't bravery that pushed me to such a reckless action - it was desperation. I was facing a paradox - stay safe and die or risk your life and live - and my body was telling me that it wanted to live some more.

With each step, it was getting louder. What was it so busy with down there? What were those sounds?

I made it to the second floor without making a sound. Shambled my feet by accident while descending to the first and resisted the urge of running away. Did it hear me? Didn't seem like it - the sounds it was making didn't stop or get closer.

I was just one flight of stairs away from the apartment. The door was wide open, exposing what was inside: the yellowing wallpaper, the old rotary phone on a decorated shelf. Something I had seen before.

Just like I had thought, it was the apartment where the welder had killed the woman. Where Pavel had been helping to move the deceased woman's body.

The sound coming from the apartment was now clear: it was munching. It seemed that the beast had developed a taste for human flesh. How long had it been since that woman had died? Three days? Was that enough for it to start to decompose? Could it be that her neighbor, who had been willing to stay with her and pray for her soul, decided to open the window and let some fresh air inside because the smell was already unbearable? It would explain how the beast sensed it and decided to pay it a visit for a quick bite. It was that smell that guided it, revealed to it that the strange concrete monolith it had been circling around was, in fact, hollow and had sustenance inside of it. The bodies of the dead and, if I didn't act fast, the living.

The door was right in front of me. Just nine more steps toward it. The key to the apartment was still in the keyhole - when the woman had been fleeing she didn't bother to pull it out. A plan hatched in my mind. Get to the door. Pull the key out. Close the door. Lock it with the key. All without making a sound. A crazy, tense plan - but the only one that could work.

Carefully, trying my best not to make a noise, I inched towards the door. I wanted to scream in terror from the fact that my steps weren't completely soundless, but I guess the creature didn't hear it over the sound of the bones breaking under its bite.

I was now right next to the door. One more step and I'd be inside the apartment. The beast was now mere meters away from me, in the guest room somewhere around the corner. If I messed up, I'd have a second, maybe two, to say my prayers.

There was no going back now. Carefully, I slid the key out of its keyhole. On its way out, it clanked. The munching stopped.

It growled and took a step.

I slammed the door shut and started shoving the key into the keyhole, but my trembling hands couldn't pull that off. A muffled roar came from within the apartment and I felt a massive body slam into the door from the other side. Luckily, the door seemed to be reinforced: the ex-tenants had made sure to protect themselves from burglars as with them living on the first floor they were the prime targets.

My legs were twitching from all the adrenaline in them, begging me to run away. I knew that if the creature somehow turned the door's handle - even by accident - it would break out that instant, leaving me no chances to survive.

I took a pause, took a deep breath, and then slid the key in. A moment later, I turned it, locking the door. The beast was now subdued.

I immediately leaped back from the door as if it was blazing hot. Seeing its metal frame shake with each of the beast's strikes was making me tremble along with it. The durable sheet of metal, meant to protect the people inside from the invaders, now contained the threat within instead. I doubted that the door's manufacturers considered that it would one day have to endure the onslaught of an other-worldly beast, and thus I wasn't sure how much longer it would be able to hold.

The door bulged, the plaster was falling from the ceiling after each bang, the very door frame seemed like it would finally separate from the wall and unleash the evil within onto me… but the door withstood its assault. Whoever had sold that door to the apartment's owners had done so with a clear conscience.

I let myself relax only for a moment. After that, I started waiting.

The beast threw itself at the door, again and again, hoping to break through to the other side. One strike after the next. I wanted to run away. My skin was crawling from the realization that death was separated from me by a thin sheet of metal - but at the same time, I needed to see with my own eyes that I had succeeded in stopping it.

If it broke out, what was I going to do? Stop it with my hatchet? I had already received my fair share of combat that day, but even so, I doubted I'd be able to fight it back.

Even so, I stayed. I felt like I had to stand my ground. To face that abnormality that was at my home's threshold. Not because I valued it - but because it was *my* home. I wanted to push back at the world.

After a minute or so, the beast gave up. I heard it move deeper into the apartment. Carefully getting up from the steps I was sitting on, I sneaked closer to the door and pressed my ear against it.

I could hear it within. Just there. On any other day, I would look strange, as if I was eavesdropping on my neighbors. But now that apartment wasn't a place where humans lived. There was no privacy to violate. It became a beast's cave, and I was listening to the unknown within to determine whether the animal within was of any threat to me and my tribe.

Above me, people were carefully coming out of the apartments. No one dared to come down to the first floor. I only heard someone make it to the last flight of stairs and then hurriedly shuffle away when they saw me and realized what exactly I was doing. No one else dared to come down there while the beast was still there - and not later, either.

After half an hour, I heard the beast leave through the window - the apartment had exhausted its curiosity and it moved on in search of its next prey. Luckily, it decided against prying off grates on other windows. I suspected that it was due to the fact that the tenants had already left the apartments there and there was nothing that could attract its attention.

Only then did I relax and sit down on the steps. The concrete was cold and hard, but I was too drained to find the strength to move up to my apartment. I was just sitting there, thinking about everything I'd gone through.

Our submarine had another breach and sunk even deeper – by exactly one floor. The entire first floor was now unsafe, too – as it turned out, the grates on the windows were just an illusion of safety. It felt like with each day, the hostile environment was seeping in more and more, and the best we could do was patch the hull up and hope that it was the last such case. We were slowly being cornered in our own apartments.

It was while I was sitting there when I heard another noise: someone was approaching the door to the basement from the other side.

I jumped to my feet: was it one of the beasts? No, it didn't sound like it. The steps sounded human. One of the possessed, then? The thugs coming back for a rematch through the basement?

The exhaustion suddenly vanished, my body revitalized, tapping into some hidden resources. Just a few moments before I had felt like I couldn't even get up to my feet, and now I was feeling like I could fight for days. I clutched my hatchet and prepared for a fight.

The steps neared. The door opened.

The first thing I noticed was the stench. I had never met a human who smelled so horribly.

It filled me with the dread of anticipation. I expected another monstrosity or a mutant, or who knows what else - but then I realized that the stench was actually quite familiar. Not the unknown smell of other-worldly miasma I had thought it to be, but the easily recognizable smell of human waste.

The human that came out of the basement was dirty from head to heels, so it was hard to recognize the camouflage pattern of his clothes. When the person saw me, he tensed up for a moment, seemingly alarmed by how I looked, before easing up and waving at me.

"I see you had a tough day, too" – the man noted, no doubt noticing my worn-out look.

"Alexei?" - I finally recognized the stranger, putting my hatchet down. My tension changed for euphoria - every fiber of my body was rejoicing that I wouldn't have to fight anyone, after all. I felt so relieved that I wanted to hug him, and only the putrid smell of the sewers coming from him was stopping me.

"You're alive!"

He has returned from his expedition beyond our building. An expedition that lasted for more than a day. There could be many ways to interpret it, but to me, it meant one thing: it was possible to survive beyond the walls we were confined in. There were places to go to. Otherwise, where had he been all that time?

It was a silver lining I was clinging to, a tiny flame of hope that was struggling against the winds of reality. I wanted him to tell me the good news. I needed it.

"Barely," - he grunted. "The sewers are crawling with some things. I haven't seen those before. One almost got me once, but I was lucky to shoot it down before it gained on me."

"Where have you been all this time? We thought you were dead!" - I told him.

"I couldn't get through to here," - he explained. "There are many things, even in the sewers, and I waited for them to leave. Luckily, I had found the manhole which led to a Khrushyovka's basement - just like that one," - he nodded toward the door leading to the basement behind him. "So, I spent two nights there - many people left their houses unlocked when they evacuated, so I bunked in one of the abandoned apartments. I got stuck there when one of the creatures found its way in."

"Horrible" – was all I could say. What he'd gone through must've been terrible, but I couldn't be bothered about that. I wanted him to get to the good news. I wanted to hear him get to the part where he'd found the exit, but I also was afraid to rush him, as if that would somehow scare the good fortune away.

"When you hear something outside of the apartment and you go to take a look through the peephole, and you don't see anything, and then you realize that you don't see anything because one of those things is crawling across the door at that very moment… It's a horrifying feeling, Yura" – Alexei continued droning on. "And when you look out the window… They are everywhere, Yura" - he told me, staring right through me. His gaze became hazy. At that very moment, he was recalling the things he wouldn't be able to even describe. "We've got it easy here."

I didn't say a word. I didn't want that conversation to continue. I already had a clear idea of how bad things were. I didn't need a first-hand account of that.

I wanted him to tell me just one thing. But he was taking his time to get to the point. Why? Did he really need me to feel pity for what he'd gone through? Everyone had had it rough these past couple of days. He wasn't special in that regard. So why?

He didn't answer my silent question. He just tried to squeeze past me to go upstairs.

"Excuse me, Yura, I want to go take a shower."

A few days ago, I wouldn't object. I would just put his interests before mine and patiently waited for him to do what he wanted to do. But not now.

"Wait a second, have you found the exit or not?" - I asked him impatiently.

"Yura, let's talk about it later..." - he said wearily, still trying to squeeze past me. Why couldn't he look me in the eye while saying that?

"Yes or no?" - I demanded to know, taking a step to the left to not let him past. I wouldn't be able to wait for even a second. I needed to hear it, no matter what his answer would be.

He let out a heavy sigh. Stood motionless there for a few seconds.

"Yes."

I felt like hugging him. I was ready to kiss him on his filth-covered forehead. Alexei was our brilliant savior. All of our struggles weren't for naught now that he had found the exit. We weren't suffering for nothing. We were just waiting for him to find the way out of that hell.

"Then screw the shower! Let's go right now!" - I said impatiently. "You won't believe the day we've had here. We need to get out now, while the path there is still fresh in your memory!"

"The path won't be a problem. I've charted a map of how to get there," - he slapped the backpack on his back to show where he had it. "It's a pipe leading out of the town into one of the rivers in the forest. It's awfully quiet there. I don't think the military patrols that area, and I haven't heard any beasts there, either."

That sounded like terrific news. It was just what we needed, but we needed to hurry. We needed to get out there before either the military or the anomalous life forms that had been stalking us got there. Why couldn't he see that?

Why was he still refusing to look me in the eye? Why was he so weary?

"Then let's go!" - I told him again, although with less enthusiasm in my voice. I already understood that something was wrong, but I refused to accept such a deduction. Alexei was just too tired from his trip. We all were. I just needed to cheer him up, to let him know how horrible it was while he was away, to show him that we were fucking dying and going crazy in that hellhole and that his goddamn shower could wait!

"Yura… The pipe has a grate on it."

I stood in silence for a few seconds, contemplating what it was that he just said. Then, I laughed.

"What?" - I said through laughter. I wasn't feeling cheerful, but my guts were shaking. The muscles and the diaphragm were quaking on their own, squeezing laughter out of me.

Alexei just nodded to confirm that I'd heard him right. I found that hysterical.

"Wha- What?" - I asked again, laughing so hard I could barely breathe in. I was laughing so hard that tears started streaming down my face. I knew how improper my reaction was, but that only made me laugh harder.

"The- The- The grates? The grates on a pipe? We've been welded shut and grated, but the moment we've found the exit… It has grates on it, too?"

I was laughing harder and harder. I was laughing so hard my sides were starting to hurt. I wanted to stop, but at the same time, I knew that the maniacal laughter was the only thing that was keeping me sane. If I stopped laughing, my mind probably wouldn't be able to take it.

I thought that the building was our prison. But it turned out that the prison extended all the way out there. You could walk up to the very border of freedom, take a peek at it through grates, but you wouldn't be able to grasp it. It would remain just a striped picture.

"I tried dislodging it," - Alexei said as if explaining himself. My laughter wasn't bothering him in the slightest. "I spent six hours there trying to do something about it. I even tried shooting at the bolts that were holding it down. No dice. The metal's too thick, and the bolts are covered in rust. We won't even be able to unscrew them if we had a tool. The grate has been installed there when the town was first built, so the bolts are a part of the whole thing by now."

I just kept on laughing. Every sentence he said was like another nail into my coffin, and I was finding it hilarious. It was like some very dark joke that just wouldn't end. With some killer punchline.

"I'm going to go take a shower" - he told me, walking past me.

"Hey, Alexei!" - I told him through laughter. He stopped and looked at me, waiting for me to say something.

"Don't drink the tap water. It makes..." - I took a deep breath to overcome laughter. "It makes people go crazy," - I finished, reeling from laughter.

"Yes, I see that" - he said, making me laugh even more and walking away. I stayed there, on the stairwell, my laughter echoing across all five floors, and getting quiet just in time as I started sobbing.

That was where Maxim found me later - I wasn't sure how much time I had spent there, ruminating on the state of things around me.

"Hey, Yura. Are you alright?" - I heard him ask me cautiously. When I looked up at him, I saw how tense he was, how ready he was to bring down the pipe in his hands on my head had I hissed at him or showed any signs of being possessed. When he saw the look in my eyes the man eased up, but I could see that he was still cautious.

"Alexei's back" - I told him quietly, burying my face back into my knees. I now understood why Alexei had refused to look me in the eye: it was surprisingly difficult to be a bearer of bad news.

"What? How long ago?" - Maxim asked, alarmed. "Where is he now?"

"I don't know. An hour ago, maybe" - I told him my estimate. It could be an hour, but it could as well have been five minutes. It didn't make a difference to me.

"Why didn't he tell me? Why didn't YOU come to me?" - Maxim inquired. So that was what I looked like when I met Alexei...

I told him what I'd been told. Maxim fell quiet.

"Yeah" - I said, still not looking at him.

"Well, we ought to find something that can cut through those grates! There are eighty apartments here, surely someone has something!" - he shouted at me.

"Sixty apartments," - I reminded him. "The fourth flight of stairs is off- limits, remember?"

"Well, even so, we're bound to find something if we just look for it!" - he wouldn't calm down.

\*\*\*

"Don't worry, Yura" - Maxim said with a heavy sigh. I could tell that he was trying to calm down not only me but himself as well. "We'll get through. We'll find something. We'll go through every apartment and find something that can cut through those grates. We'll earn our freedom, we just need to keep going."

"If you don't mind, I'd like to stay out of it," - I told him quietly. "I feel like I've had enough for today."

"Sure, sure," - he quickly agreed. "No one will hold it against you. You go have some rest."

He helped me get up to my feet and gave me a reassuring pat on the back.

"Don't worry, Yura. We, Russians, have been through worse. Someday, this is all going to end, you know. Just like all the other things," - he told me with a tired smile. I appreciated that he was trying to cheer me up even though he himself was out of fumes, but I couldn't return the gesture.

"Yes. I'm afraid that day will come soon" - I told him with a bitter smile and went upstairs.

I went past my apartment straight to Natasha's place. I didn't want to be alone. If I were to stay alone with my thoughts I'd just be sulking. I wanted my last days to be spent in someone's company.

"Everything alright?" - she asked me when she saw my face.

I smiled and shook my head.

# CHAPTER 16 – Eye-to-eye

I always knew that hope was the vilest, two-faced, hypocritical feeling. It was the thing that was making you look forward to the future, making you want to fight, to see another day… Yet it wasn't as pleasing as people were making it out to be. Hope was filling you with anxiety, with fear of missing out on possibilities. Hope was making you look for a way out. And only once you realized that there was no way out could you let go of the suffering and just enjoy your last few days on Earth.

Which was exactly what me and Natasha had decided to do. To relax. To forget that we were under the worst of sieges. That the enemy could already be inside - perhaps it was even already beneath our skin.

Her apartment was occupied for the evening: she'd let the old man who had lived on the first floor to stay in her apartment. After the morning invasion, no one wanted to live on the first floor anymore - it was too dangerous. And so the refugees spent the rest of the day walking around, asking their neighbors to give them shelter.

"That poor man had nowhere else to go - no one else would have him," - Natasha told me later. "When I opened my door, he had such a pitiful look… I knew, if he was at my door, if he came all the way to the fifth floor from the first, then he truly was out of options. How could I refuse him?" - Natasha was pouring her soul out to me. I was just nodding in agreement, trying to remember where I was when he came to my door. Perhaps I'd just ignored his knock - I knew that if Maxim wanted to find me, he'd do just that.

So, for the evening, we decided to stay at my place. To leave the old man alone and not bother him with the things and talks of the youth. Natasha did ask him if he would be okay to stay alone for the night, to which he smiled and said that he had been doing that for the past twenty years. After that, she left him there with a clear conscience.

Through the walls, we could hear people talking inside Maxim's apartment: he had held a small gathering for the people who had helped him fight back the thugs earlier that day. Maxim hadn't been able to find anything that could help us get through the grates, but at the very least he had found some new compatriots, and just like us, they had decided to have an evening off. The day had been hard for everyone, so it wasn't surprising that they, too, decided to rest a bit just like us.

I didn't have a bar or anything of sorts: the only alcohol that had ever been to my apartment were the cans of beer from the closest store: on my way home, I rarely had the strength to look for anything better - the convenience was the deciding factor. They usually settled in my fridge and rarely stayed there for more than a few days. My fridge had been empty for the past few days: I had been surviving solely on buckwheat.

Natasha and Nikita, on the other hand, had a small stash of exotic alcohol. Not just the usual wine and vodka - but also things I didn't even know existed. Foreign spirits that, judging by their names, must've traveled halfway across the world to end up in our town.

That evening, I tried Limoncello for the first time - vodka made from lemon. At first, we were drinking it "as prescribed" - one part Limoncello, two parts water. But after the first hour, we gave up on that recipe, put aside the glasses, and started drinking it straight from the bottle, passing it to each other as we were sitting on my sofa.

"You know, it's going to sound really messed up, but... I'm glad you're also here," - she laughed. "I think I'd go crazy if I was all alone."

"It was the least I could do" - I joked. I had been feeling the same for the last few days, but I was too ashamed to voice it. Natasha, however, didn't have such problems.

She let out a short laugh - one of those which die mid-breath - and took another sip. Then she handed the bottle to me.

"Listen, while we're on the topic, there was something I always wanted to ask you - it's just that I felt uncomfortable asking you before. But since, you know..." - she twirled her finger in the air, as if trying to point at every part of the building at the same time.

I nodded and took a sip from the bottle. The alcohol burned my guts, but I noted that they were already on fire from anticipation. I was hoping that the fire wouldn't spread to my cheeks.

"Ask away" - I urged her on.

"Why didn't you go to study in that university you applied for? Did you not get in?"

I felt a bit disappointed. I had hoped the question would be different.

"I did" - I nodded and quickly took another sip - to drown that disappointment in the fire. Not to mention that Natasha was bringing up one of the least pleasant moments of my life, and I didn't want to remember it.

"Then why didn't you move out of town?" - Natasha wondered, taking the bottle from my hands. "I mean, I understand that this place is our home, but it doesn't mean we have to stay here forever. I'm sorry if I'm sticking my nose where it doesn't belong, it's just that I've been telling Nikita that we ought to move out of town for ages, and look where him not listening to me had gotten us."

I eyed the bottle in Natasha's hands and bit my lip, desperately trying to suck the alcohol out of it. It didn't help. My admission was still going to hurt, no matter how much alcohol I'd drink.

"I withdrew my application."

"Why?" - I wasn't looking at her face, but I could tell that she was almost disappointed in my answer.

I sighed. While I knew the answer, it still wasn't easy to say it. I rationalized it internally, but the moment we started speaking about it, the moment I dragged it out of myself for everyone to see, I realized how silly it is.

"Because my mother... told me to."

There was no vocal answer, but I knew that there was a reaction. She was just processing the answer, and all the explanations and implications that were coming to her mind were making her uncomfortable.

"She wanted me to stay by her side" - I explained, though it didn't feel like I was talking to Natasha. More like I was trying to rationalize it myself. God, how hard it was. I didn't know whether it was because of the alcohol or because it never made sense in the first place.

"She said that she was scared of letting me go out there... I mean, scared of what would become of her. Said that the children owe it to their parents to stay by their side and take care of them once they become old," - I told Natasha. "And, I mean, I get it, children really are a crutch, in some way," - I added to provide an excuse, either for myself or my mother. "Who else will bring you a glass of water when you're old?" - I finished with a chuckle and a smile, looking at Natasha for the first time.

Natasha wasn't laughing. On the contrary, she was giving me a very serious stare.

"Yura, that's some pizdets[14]."

"Well, maybe in some way, but we still owe it to our parents, don't we?" - I awkwardly explained, wondering why was it so hard to voice it. If it was really an opinion that I was sharing, then why was it so hard to defend it?

"Not like that" - Natasha shook her head. "Parents shouldn't undermine their children and their future for their own sake."

"Well, yeah, but-"

"Tell me you think it's alright" - she suddenly pressured me. "Tell me that you think that it's alright that she made you withdraw that application for her own selfish reasons. Tell me that you want to stay in this town until the end of your days."

"Well, it's not like we have a choice nowadays" - I tried to insert a joke into the conversation to lighten up the mood, but Natasha wasn't swayed. She was adamant to get the answer out of me, and I knew she wouldn't drop the topic. With a sigh, I took a bottle from her hands and took another sip.

"Of course, I've never wanted to stay here," - I said bitterly. "But… I don't know, I guess I'm used to her calling all the shots in my life. I'm not exactly… a decisive type. And here she offered me this apartment," - I waved my hand to

---

[14] Pizdets – a Russian swear word with many applications and meanings, the most popular one is "a very bad situation". In this context, it means "this is so immensely messed up."

encircle all the walls and suddenly realized just how much I hated them. "So, I stayed. I at least have something here. And it's not like anyone's waiting for me there," - I finished with a bitter smile.

"Did she tell you that?" - Natasha asked me. I chose not to answer.

"Yura, whatever your mother has told you, whatever you think about the reasons she might've had, you are not what she says you are. I've seen you these past few days, and you're not that. I saw a strong, confident, decisive man who was doing all he could to help others and find a way out while the majority of your mother's peers were sitting on their asses, waiting to be rescued by someone else. For God's sake, how many times have you risked your life for others just today?" - she asked me, suddenly taking my face into her palms. Her touch burned. "Look at me" - she told me, looking me in the eye. "I won't let you disregard that. You are not just her kid. You are a man of your own. Don't let her tell you otherwise. I know you're hearing her tiny voice in the back of your head right now. I know you're more comfortable with the idea that she's right. Parents… they can be like that, sometimes. But you're not the same person she's made you think you are. When the push came to shove - you've showed that you can call your own shots."

Perhaps it was the alcohol, but her speech moved me deeply. I didn't change my opinion on the subject in a moment, but it made me want it to be true. It made me want to believe that what she was saying was really true.

"I don't know, Natasha," - I told her with a sad smile. "I'm not sure I've changed in just a few days. I was just doing what was necessary, what was expected of me. It wasn't me who's started the militia, after all - I was just following Maxim's lead. That's all."

"That's my point, Yura!" - she exclaimed impatiently. "You can tell yourself whatever you want, rationalize it however you want, think whatever you want about what you are, but it is our actions that determine what we are - not our thoughts. You may think that you're no good, that you're dependent on others, that you're just doing what others expect of you - and yet that's not what I see. I see a man who's rushed into danger to save others on his own accord. I see a man who joined the militia because it was the right thing to do. Maybe before you didn't have a chance to expose that side of you, but in these last few days, you've changed quite a lot, all on your own. You've changed by embracing what's always been inside you. You just need to acknowledge that change, or it will go to waste."

"I don't know. I think if I really changed I'd notice it," - I said, shaking my shoulders.

"That's the trap of human condition, Yuri," - Natasha patiently told me. "We expect things to announce themselves to us. We expect changes to us to be like a job promotion, like a date that comes around. A momentary event. We expect some catharsis as if the change is supposed to be instantaneous. But the change is never like that. It is gradual, and sometimes you don't let it come to you - you have to accept it. Otherwise, if you don't notice the change within you, it may as well not be there at all."

"Wow" - was all I could answer to that. Natasha laughed and teasingly punched my shoulder. Then again. I didn't resist: her soft, playful touches were pleasing. "I am serious, you dolt," - she told me through laughter.

"I know, I know, it's just that… that's a lot to unpack there," - I told her, still smiling.

"I can imagine" - she said, her gaze wandering across the room. She must have been remembering something from her own past. "But please, don't disregard my words, Yuri. We just have to look at ourselves from time to time. That's the only way we can tell that something has changed."

"Do you really think I've changed?" - I asked her innocently. I wanted to hear her say that again. I wanted to hear her tell me what a good job I was doing. To pat me on the head. Some infantile part of me, the part that has yearned for a mother's affection - something it had never received enough of - wanted to hear what a good boy I was.

Luckily, Natasha didn't notice any of that. I didn't want her to pick up on that since it would go contrary to her ode to how much I've grown.

"Of course!" - she exclaimed. "Listen, Yura, whatever has happened today - you've done everything to make it better. And going down to that apartment to close the door while that thing was inside? That was the epitome of masculinity. I feel like I'm behind a stone wall when I'm with you," - she said with laughter. I felt a bit embarrassed, but Natasha just laughed again.

"Don't feel shy!" - she gave me a nudge. "It's true. When I was watching you today, while you were running around, trying to save people, or hearing about what you'd done afterward, I was thinking: 'wow, has Yura always been this manly? Why didn't I see this side of his before, where did that come from?'"

"You're flattering me" - I said, feeling flustered. I never knew I was having such an impression on Natasha, and it was very pleasant to learn it.

"I really don't" - she shook her head, smiling. "No chance, mister. You are brave, and decisive, and smart, and..." - she suddenly stopped and smiled, biting her lower lip. Usually, I wouldn't have the courage to ask her what she wanted to say - it was clear that it was something that would make her uncomfortable. But the alcohol and her speech made me loosen up, so I looked her in the eye: "And what? Come on, out with it."

"I just wanted to say that it's really surprising that you don't have a girlfriend," - she said, suddenly getting shy. "You're quite a catch."

There it was. She said it. I felt myself start to slightly tremble from anticipation. Did she mean it? Did she herself share that opinion, or was she talking in general?

Was I supposed to say something back, other than an awkward "thank you"? Would I ruin the moment, and with it, our friendship? My last friendship in the world, all things considered?

I looked at her. She was sitting there, looking at me with anticipation. Was she waiting for my reply?

*"You are decisive, Yuri,"* - I reminded myself. *"Be decisive till the end, whatever it may be."*

"You're very beautiful, too" - I told her, before realizing that the words came out wrong. Damn it! I wanted to tell her that she was a great person. How did that become 'beautiful'?

But she wasn't taken aback, didn't purse her lips or tell me that I crossed the line, or that she didn't see me that way. Natasha blossomed and let out the most genuine smile I had seen on her face since the beginning of lockdown.

"You really think so?" - she asked me shyly.

I decided to roll with it.

"I've always thought so" - I said, feeling my lungs become hot and my heart beating against my ribs. Some part of me wanted me to stop, to end the situation I ended up in, but I kept on talking, disregarding my nervousness: "I've always been glad to visit you guys because I've always thought that you're very beautiful and cheerful. You were always fun to be around. And..." - I braced before saying the next part.

*"What are you doing? Stop!"* - some part of me panicked at my newfound boldness. It wanted me to get back to my comfort zone, to get back to being just a shy introvert who needed the approval of others to act… But I kept on going

anyway. I've been through way too many things to be concerned about such worries.

"...I've always envied Nikita. In a good way. Because he's found himself a great girlfriend" - I said, looking her in the eye. There it was. My confession. I was drunk, and the world was ending anyway, so why not say it as it was?

One moment passed. Then another. She was silent, and I couldn't read her. Her expression was not blank but at the same time more mysterious than Mona Lisa. Was that gratitude? Discontent? Anger?

I couldn't bear looking at her anymore, so I looked away. A few seconds later, I heard her move closer to me. I felt her breath on me, and then she whispered in a coarse voice: "I'm really glad you're here. And that you've finally said it."

Damn. She knew? Did she suspect something? I threw a quick glance at her, intending to just analyze the situation, to see what she was feeling… But once I looked at her, I couldn't look away. My gaze was glued to her eyes. At that distance, something finally connected, something established between us. Her facial expression wasn't a mystery to me anymore. It was an open book - as I was to her.

"Natasha, we can't..." - I said quietly.

"I know" - she answered.

We sat in silence for a few seconds, communicating with nothing but thoughts and faint expressions.

"Can we keep this a secret?" - I asked her.

"From whom?" - she smiled at my question.

"From the whole world. From us" - I said the last sentence so quietly I myself barely heard it.

"Yes" - she soundlessly mouthed, slightly nodding. It was a secret she wanted to learn. If she had to take it to the grave, she was willing to pay that price. And I knew that, despite me having some resistance to the idea, it would inevitably crumble. My hesitation was nothing more than a play at that point - a play I knew the end of. A boring play. A play I wanted to walk out of.

We both wanted the same. To hide our shame, our improper feelings… But also to indulge in them. I sat closer to her. Our shoulders, hands, and knees touched. Natasha jerked away as if burned by my touch, but then pressed to me even closer than before.

"No one will know," - I whispered.

"Not even us" - she whispered back and leaned closer. I didn't lean back.

"I want it" - I wanted to say, but I didn't. Not a sound escaped my lips. She understood me all the same.

"Just a kiss" - she whispered to me, pushing her forehead against mine and looking me in the eye. Her voice was slightly trembling, and I couldn't tell what was causing that - nervousness or excitement. "I can give you just a kiss now."

"I understand" - I told her. Though I remained composed on the surface on the inside, I winced from how awkward our exchange was. What was I saying? Why was I talking about it as if I was bargaining with her as if I was accepting the terms of her offer in a conference room?

"I won't need more" - I added with passion and mentally patted myself on the back: that was more like it. That sounded smooth. Attaboy.

She leaned closer - so close I felt the warmth of her breath on me. A soft breath of a kitten, and yet I felt like it scorched my insides, made the blood rush. She was just out of reach, just a hair width away - so close that it was hard to tell if we were touching or not. She closed her eyes, and I could feel by the shape of her breath that her lips were slightly open. Waiting. Wanting. Short, sharp breaths. Hesitant to go all the way, but willful to come close enough that I had no choice but to do it.

So close I barely had to move to seal our kiss.

It was passionate, yet at the same time - so simple, so straight-forward. Like two kids who were mimicking the adults from the TV, we pressed our lips against each other.

When she finally leaned back, she looked excited. Scared. Happy. Anxious. She had just kissed her boyfriend's friend… and she seemed to enjoy it. She didn't know how to react, how to proceed. I could feel the storm within her - its magnetic whirlwinds resonating with my own. Just like her, I had crossed the line I never thought I would.

Just like her, I liked it.

I put my palm on her cheek. She sighed from my touch, then nestled her head in my palm like a cat, seeking to be patted.

"Maybe one more" - I told her. I knew she could object to that, to tell me that it was supposed to be just one kiss, that I led her on… It didn't matter. I needed to say that, to voice my desire. Everything else didn't matter. I was living in the moment. I was trying to - no, I *was* being brave.

"Yeah, okay" - she agreed rather simply, breathing heavily as if she just ran a marathon. She leaned in again, and this time, we looked at each other in the eye before we kissed.

Natasha. Natasha. Natali.

Natasha and Yura… No. Those were childish names. She was a woman, and by the time the dawn came around, I was a man.

Natali and Yuri[15]. What a pair.

---

[15] Natali and Yuri – full, semi-official versions of names "Natasha" and "Yura".

# CHAPTER 17 – Gone Girl

For the first time since forever, I woke up with a smile.

So strange: the world had to end for me to want it to keep on being there.

Deep inside, I knew I didn't want it to end. Hope had shown its poisonous fangs once more and pierced me with them right under my heart. I wanted it all to continue. Natasha was making me want to fight to see another day because it would be another day together with her.

But it was only that dire situation that had brought us together. In her previous life, she would have no need to be with me - back there, she had had Nikita. Only the circumstances had made her forget about him. The dead don't cheat - and with how things were going, there was no doubt that we'd soon join their ranks.

All we could do was enjoy our small newfound happiness. Squeeze the most out of our situation.

Last night, we kept on going. We kissed again, and again - until we were sober.

And we kept on going after then.

Natasha was already cooking something in the kitchen - I could hear the rumbling of boiling water coming from there.

"Can you make me some coffee?" - I shouted to her.

"Come and make it yourself" - she told me. I could tell by the tone, by the shape of the voice: she was smiling when she said that. Putting on a smile of my own, I got out of bed and headed for the kitchen, thanking Limoncello for sparing me from the morning hangover.

Natasha was sitting at the table, smiling. The kettle was on the stove, rumbling at us with its belly at the tone that warned us: the water was going to be ready in another thirty seconds or so.

"Hey" - Natasha greeted me, smiling but looking away. I didn't expect anything else: what had happened the night before must have been very awkward for her to think about in the morning. I myself was feeling flustered.

"Hey" - I echoed her call, taking a seat at the table. Funny: just the night before I felt like I could talk to her till the end of the world - which, it seemed, was just around the corner. Now, however, no matter what we'd want to talk about, we would have to discuss what had happened between us - or at the very least acknowledge it first.

We sat in silence. After a while, I'd gotten used to the silence. It became comfortable. We weren't feeling like talking about it - so we just silently enjoyed each other's company.

"I have to go check on the old man" - she told me, getting up from the chair and grabbing the third plate into her hands. I quickly glanced at her face: was there resentment, regret? Was she trying to escape from the uncomfortable situation?

No.

She was just genuinely concerned about him. It was in her character. She allowed him to stay at her place because she alone was concerned with his fate and didn't want him to spend the night in the apartment, which was no longer safe.

"Don't take too long" - I told her with a gentle smile. I tried to make it look confident, smirking - but it came off as gentle anyway. And she seemed to like it because she returned it.

"Sure" - she assured me, before walking out of the kitchen.

I stared at the oatmeal she prepared for us. Under my gaze, it was slowly losing temperature, though it was probably going to do the same even if I didn't observe it. Probably. With how things were going, if the laws of physics suddenly stopped working I wouldn't even raise an eyebrow. There were few things left in the world that could surprise me.

I wanted to take it slow, to finish my breakfast together with Natasha. It would feel nice to share such a moment with her: I'd had way too many lonely breakfasts in the past, so even something so small was important to me.

When I inevitably finished it ten minutes later, I felt disappointed with myself. Sure, I was hungry. But why not wait just a little bit?

Then again, my portion wasn't that big. I stretched it as much as possible. If I ate it any slower, I'd stop eating it altogether. I was sure that her own oatmeal was already so cold she'd struggle to pick it with her spoon.

A tiny voice in the back of my head started saying that she just didn't want to go down to be with me because the last night was a mistake. But it didn't dig deep into my mind: in the last 24 hours, I had become too resilient for it to nestle into me. Natasha was just taking her time there, and for different reasons. And since she was gone for half an hour, it was reasonable to go find out why.

I stood up from the table, put on some clothes, and left the apartment, heading upstairs.

I was mentally preparing myself for a sad sight: Natasha, sitting in the middle of her room, crying over her lost boyfriend. I wasn't disillusioned: I knew that those feelings didn't go away - they'd just gotten weaker.

The change was gradual, I reminded myself. It was not instantaneous. And I was ready to be there for Natasha to help her deal with it - until the very end, no matter what it would be.

When I reached the fourth floor I could already hear the voices of the tenants above. Just as usual, they'd gathered to complain about something.

I didn't make a connection. My first reaction was an annoyance. I didn't think that their gathering had something to do with me.

Only when I saw that they were standing next to Natasha's door did I realize that their gathering and Natasha's disappearance were not a coincidence.

The door to Natasha's apartment was wide open. Most of the people were standing around it, more interested in scratching their tongues, and only a few of them were throwing careful glances inside.

Everything within me suddenly felt hollow. I rushed inside, rudely pushing people out of my way. They protested, someone tried to grab me to make me explain myself, but I pushed their hand aside and continued to rush inside.

The signs of struggle in the hallway: coats and jackets lying on the ground, her and Nikita's shoes, usually propped so carefully against the wall, were scattered across the room. I rushed to her bedroom.

More people: a few women were tending to the old man that Natasha had sheltered. He was lying on Natasha's bed, right on her bedsheets, and staring blankly into the ceiling. Every few seconds he would let out an exasperated sigh, not able to deal with the pain of a fresh wound on his head. No Natasha.

I rushed to the kitchen, to the guest room, swung open the door to the bathroom, startling a woman who occupied it and forgot to close the door - no Natasha. She wasn't there.

The old man was supposed to know, I realized. Someone or something took her away, but if he had a wound on his head, then he was probably around when that happened, he took part in it. And if he was still alive, then she could be as well.

"Where is she?!" - I demanded to know from him, bursting into the room. The women shushed me, tried to push me out of the room, but I paid them no attention. I was solely focused on the old man on the bed.

I felt sorry for him: the blunt trauma to the head meant that he probably tried to stop whatever had taken Natasha away. He did not deserve to face my frustration. He deserved to rest. But he was still conscious, and I couldn't miss even a second. I had to act fast.

"Do you hear me? I said get out of here!" - a chubby woman pushed me again, and I had to grab onto the door to stay inside the room: despite being two heads lower than me, she was both heavier and stronger. Decades of hard work had hardened her enough to be a challenge for me. "Running around here like crazy… He needs rest! Get out!"

"Let go of me! He knows where she is! What has happened here, old man!" - I tried to protest desperately, seeing as I was losing the battle: a few more seconds and she would successfully push me out of the room, and then out of the apartment.

"There was no one else when we came. Go get some sleep, you drunkard! I can smell the reek of vodka on you!" - she ignored my pleas and pushed harder.

"I'm sorry, young man" - his voice was weak, but also so unexpected that everyone stopped what they were doing and listened to him, allowing his quiet words to be heard. "I tried stopping him, but I… I was too weak. This is all my fault. This is all our fault."

"Where is she, grandpa?" - I asked him gently. I wanted to scream, to shout, to let him know that we had no time and ask him to get to the point, but I restrained myself. He barely had any strength to talk, and if I snapped at him at such a time, he could just choose to remain silent.

"Taken. Taken away… I'm sorry, young man. We didn't know what we were doing. The whole world was our enemy, and we… We were looking for allies elsewhere. We thought we had no choice. We opened the door for them, but nobody came. We thought they weren't listening, but… They were just biding their time. Waiting for us to lower our guard, to forget about them," - I could see that his cryptic confession was hard for him, and I was even piecing a few things together from it, but it was not the time for it. I had to focus on the more pressing issue.

"Where is she, gramps?" - I repeated my question softly but sternly.

"Where they all are. They've taken her to their nest" - he said in a disregarding, uncaring voice, staring at the ceiling. It was clear that he didn't think that there was a way to get her back from there. I struggled to remain composed.

"How long ago, gramps?" - I asked in a calm voice.

"Maybe twenty minutes ago," - he answered. "I'm sorry, young man, I tried to do something, but-"

I turned around and left the room in a hurry. Perhaps the old man was correct in his assertion and there was no use trying to save her. But I wanted to run somewhere, do something, scream something. I needed to channel all of that anger and hurt within me into something, and it just so happened that I had a perfect opportunity to do just that. It did not matter if I'd succeed or not - it was better to try, to make that desperate attempt, that to live even for a second knowing that I was powerless to save her.

Twenty minutes. That wasn't too long ago. In fact, it should have happened right after she'd entered her apartment. Were they waiting for her? Did they have an eye on her? I didn't even want to think why she caught their attention and what they planned to do with her. If I hurried, I could put a stop to it.

I didn't know what I was going to do, but I knew the destination. That was all that mattered.

Once on the staircase, surrounded by curious people who already started asking me questions, I hesitated for a moment. Do I go call Maxim? Do I ask these people to help me? Or do I go alone, to save time?

"You're from the militia, right?" - some old woman next to me asked me, getting all up in my face. "Some protectors you are" - she scoffed at me.

"Shove it!" - I snapped at her, and surprisingly no retorts followed. More stress was the last thing I needed, but her words and the anger they sparked helped me decide what to do. I pushed another old man aside, ignored his protests, and started climbing to the roof.

The barricade that Maxim and his friends had spent so much time setting up was broken. Whatever had passed through there had more than enough strength to be stopped by a few nails and dismantled chairs.

Once outside, I rushed toward the furthest door. It must've been raining since early morning since the puddles on the roof had already gotten quite big, but I didn't bother to avoid them and stay quiet. Since I'd decided to go alone, I had already thrown the caution to the wind - there was no use acting carefully now.

I had just found Natasha. Just found a close person outside of my family. A woman who wasn't my mother. Even if the world was crumbling around me, I wanted Natasha to be with me during those final moments. Most of all, I wanted her to feel safe and secure, and I was cursing fate for letting such a thing happen during the first few hours of our relationship.

I rammed the door, wanting to get open as soon as possible, but I felt sudden resistance from it. It barely opened, just wide enough to let me peek inside to see that something was propping it from the other side.

Somehow, the people inside had managed to barricade it from their side. It seemed they took a page from our book.

"Open up!" - I shouted through the crack. "Open up or I swear we're going to burn you all! Give her back!"

"What's the commotion?" - I heard someone asking me from the other side. The metal ladder was still shaking under the stranger's feet, indicating that he was rising from the fifth floor to greet me. "It's very rude to be so loud in the morning. Don't you have any manners where you've come from?"

A curious face with a sly smile showed up in the crack of the door. Perhaps I had seen him before, but it didn't matter at that moment. I was only seeing red.

"Give her back!" - I shouted at him desperately. "Give Natasha back, you filthy, good-for-nothing, worthless..." - the fury toward that carefree face that was smiling at my angst, the face of the one who knew what he'd done and thought he could get away with it, was scrambling my thoughts. I couldn't even pick the right words. I could only emote in the most primitive way.

"Do it, you bastard, or I'll crack your head open as I promised!"

"Oh, it's you again?" - the face lit up with recognition. "Yes, you were here just a few days ago? Came back for more?"

"I almost killed you bastards back then, and I'll do it now for sure if you don't give her back!" - I shouted at him and kicked the door. It didn't budge - not enough to open, at least, but just enough to hit him in the nose he'd been pressing against it to take a better look at me through the crack.

"Oh, you bastard!" - he hissed, grabbing his face. "You want the girl? Don't you worry, once he's done with her, and we take our turns with her, we'll deliver her back in small packages!"

After he's done with her? After he's done doing *what*? I felt like my brain was going to explode from the adrenaline rushing into it. Burst like a leaky pipe.

But before his words fully sunk in, before I could process them and act accordingly, I saw an arm holding a gun appear through the crack. The man wasn't looking where he was aiming - no doubt he was still clutching his wounded nose. Had he done it, I would've been dead after the first shot - the gun's barrel examined most of my body before blindly trailing to the left and firing in the direction of the forest.

Not waiting for the second shot to find me, I turned around and ran, covering the distance toward the door of my stairwell in record time. Funny: was that why they used the guns to start the race? More shots followed, but they all missed their mark - the closest one hitting the wall and dislodging a piece of concrete from it near my head as I was opening the door.

Even though I was running away, I didn't give up. I knew where I was going and what I was going to do. I had received the confirmation that Natasha was still alive. I just needed more people to storm the place.

"Maxim!" - I was battering on his door some thirty seconds later. "Open up, Maxim! They've got Natasha! Maxim!"

"Where's the fire, what's going on, Yura?" - Maxim opened the door, squinting from the light. He could see that I was worked up and was doing his best to focus on what I was saying, but that was clearly a challenge for him: he reeked of alcohol, and seemed to be suffering from a severe hangover.

"They've kidnapped Natasha, Maxim!" - I shouted at him. "Come on, I need your gun! Gather men!"

Why was he so slow at such a time? How could he be drinking so much when at any moment something like that could happen?

"Who are you talking about?" - Maxim shook his head and rubbed his temple. "Who are 'they'? What the hell, Yuri, how early is it?"

"The thugs from the fourth stairwell! They kidnapped Natasha and are doing god knows what to her at the moment!" - I explained as patiently as I could. If he was going to ask me one more question I'd just rush back to save her on my own.

But it seemed that my words finally reached him: the realization of what I'd been telling him broke through the shell of hangover and settled in his mind. His eyes went wide from shock and then squinted from fury he couldn't hold back. Finally, I saw the expression that I wanted to see: he was livid.

"Men!" - he hollered into the depths of the apartment. "Wake up, quick! Those assholes kidnapped a girl! Come on!"

They didn't make us wait for them: one by one, they were walking out of the kitchen and into the living room, where they, judging by how they looked, must've been drinking until the sunrise. All of them hungover, all of them sleepy and drunk. And all of them - angry.

I doubted that all of them could comprehend what Maxim was asking of them, but maybe it was for the best. Their drunken stupor, their liquid courage has transformed them from everyday men into warriors. They were probably waiting for a chance to let loose - and me and Maxim were courteously offering it to them. They heard something about saving a girl, and in their state, that was all the motivation they needed.

Perhaps it was selfish of me, but I wasn't concerned about what would become of them. I knew that in their state they knew neither reason nor fear - and that was just what I needed. An army that was ready to crush the heads without questions, without concern about their own well-being.

"Come on, come on! Hurry up!" - Maxim was urging them to pick up the pace.

"No problem pops" - a man at least a decade older than Maxim assured him. "I've been kicking ass like nobody's business back in the day - we'll show them what's what."

While they were busy putting on clothes, I quickly went to my apartment and grabbed the hatchet from the kitchen sink. By the time I returned, the men seemed to be ready to go.

"Lead the way, Yura" - Maxim told me: in the last thirty seconds he somehow went from helplessly drunk to crystal sober, which showed just how seriously he was taking the situation. I nodded and ran upstairs, hearing the men going after me. Sometimes someone would trip or miss the turn, but the rest would help them up.

"Why weren't you keeping an eye on her?" - Maxim scowled at me, running just a few steps behind me.

"She went away for five minutes. How was I supposed to know this was going to happen?" - I snapped back at him.

"Five minutes..." - Maxim grunted. "Better not let her go now. Don't worry, Yura, we're not going to leave her there," - he assured me. "No one will be left behind this time," - he added under his breath.

I knew what he's been going through, but I didn't have space in my heart to care about that. If he wanted to redeem himself, he'd do well to do it through his actions.

"Open up!" - I shouted at the door a minute later, when we finally reached it. "We give you one chance - give us back Natasha or we're going to slaughter you all in there!"

Maxim put his hand on my shoulder and made a hush sign while looking around, but I threw his hand off of me: I knew about the risks of being on the roof, and it wasn't the time to care about that. If something came at us, we'd just have to fight it back - that was all there was to it.

"You hear me?" - I shouted at them again, opening the door and shouting through the crack. "I have twenty people here with me, and we're not going back empty-handed!"

"You tell 'em!" - somebody behind me slurrily cheered me on.

Of course, that was a blatant lie: there were only five people behind me - Maxim had found some new friends since yesterday. It wasn't a significant force to be reckoned with, but still better than nothing. And since they had no way of checking whether it was true without coming up to the roof to see with their own eyes, a little lie wouldn't hurt.

"You again? Feeling much braver when you have some friends backing you up?" - I heard the familiar voice coming from behind the door: the man was climbing the stairs.

"You're the one to talk," - I scowled at him. "Open this door and you'll see that I don't need them to cut you up!"

"Keep talking - you'll get what's coming for ya" - the man gave me a sinister warning, though I noted that his sentence lacked the former confidence.

Someone touched my shoulder: it was Maxim. He was signaling at me to stand to the side and then nodded behind us, where Alexei was already taking aim at the door. When did he have time to go grab his rifle? Had he been drinking with it? Was he ready to shoot that man through the door? Was I ready to let him do that?

That would be a good question - if I considered that waste of skin on the other side of the door human, that is. I took a step to the right so that the man on the other side of the door could see me and focus only on me.

"Bring us Natasha and we'll let you all live" - I warned him, looking him in the eye. I was doing all I could to resist the temptation to look at Alexei - I couldn't deny that I was worried that he'd miss his shot and hit me instead. But in doing so, I could involuntarily give him away. So, I kept staring that vile creature in the eye, hoping that Alexei's shot would strike true.

I wanted nothing else but to see his brain splattered by the shot. I only hoped that the old door between us wouldn't be strong enough to absorb the bullet's lethal force.

From the corner of my eye, I could see that Alexei stopped moving. He has taken aim and was ready to take a shot at any moment. The moment I'd hear the shot, I'd have to try to pry the door open all the way.

The man on the other side of the door suddenly rolled his eyes and shook his shoulders in a careless gesture: "If you've wanted her so much you should've asked nicely."

"What?" - I asked, taken aback by the man's words. Did it mean that they were ready to let her go?

I quickly raised my hand to signal to Alexei to stop. While confused, the man obeyed, and I eased a little bit. Just a few moments ago, I wanted nothing more than for him to kill that man so that we could start our assault. But now that they were surrendering Natasha, I had to stop and think twice.

"You mean it, that you'll let her go?" - I asked him again just to be sure, still holding my hand up, out of the man's field of vision. If it was some sort of a sick joke I wouldn't hesitate to order the man's execution. But if he was telling the truth...

"Yes, the big guy is done with her. He seems to be disappointed," - he shook his shoulders.

"If this is a joke, I swear..." - I started, but he just raised his hand: "Relax! If you're so eager to throw some hands, you can switch places with her. She's a feisty one, alright" - he put on a dirty smirk, and I had to use all of my willpower to restrain myself from waving my hand and ending his miserable life.

"Oh! Here comes the bride. Step back, boy. If you or any of your pals make a wrong move..." - I heard him cock his gun. "She'll be an easy target."

I didn't need to be told twice. I could already hear someone coming up the ladder, and I recognized those small, weightless steps. Natasha. She really was coming up. They really were letting her go.

"Everyone stand back," - I told the rest of the men. "Kakogo huya[16] are you doing, giving in to his demands?" - somebody said, slurring the words. "Are you always so obedient? What if he asks you to suck his-"

"Stand back!" - I roared at the man, and he fell silent. I could see that he had no intention of obeying me - he was just confused and trying to come up with an appropriate answer. But that suited my needs well.

As much as I was glad that we resolved it without a fight - even though I was ready to fight to the last breath - I was

---

[16] Kakogo huya – "what the f*ck"

still confused. Why kidnap her only to let her go? Did they perhaps do something to her? Is she now one of them?

*"If that substance can infiltrate human bodies then surely they could do something to her?"* - I thought, and the thought filled me with dread. What could they possibly make out of Natasha? A spy? A ticking bomb?

I heard the man fiddle with the lock, and then the rattling of the chain. A few moments later, the door swung open, and he pushed Natasha outside, right into the rain, before quickly closing the door after her. Alexei raised his rifle to try to take a shot, but then put it back down: the risk of hitting Natasha was too high.

"Natasha!" - the moment I saw her I forgot about everything else - the man behind the door, my suspicions of what they'd done to her... We haven't confirmed our relationship status - but it was a poor time to think about things like that. She was clearly distressed and needed comforting, so I rushed toward her and hugged her. She awkwardly returned the gesture.

"Here" - I took off my jacket and wrapped her in it. She made no efforts to keep it on, and I had to hug her with one arm to keep it from slipping off. "Are you alright? What did they do to you?"

"You'll ask her later! Let's go!" - Maxim hollered at us.

The roof was still dangerous. Funny how a few moments before that I didn't care about it in the slightest, but now that she was back by my side I didn't want her to be in danger for even one second. Still hugging her with one arm, I followed the rest of the group, who wasted no time to get back to safety.

"Hurry, hurry!" - Maxim was standing by the door and keeping it open for everyone. The rest of the men were already inside and were hurriedly trying to go down the ladder. Their drunken state, something I considered to be a blessing just a few minutes before, was now turning out to be a curse: they were taking too long to descend the ladder, and the small room could only fit no more than three people at a time.

"Hurry, you in there!" - Maxim was urging them on to move faster. "Come on!"

"You go" - I stuffed Natasha in there despite the protests of men inside. "Let the girl through first! Be gentlemen for once!" - I shouted at them, and their protests subsided.

"Jesus Christ!" - Maxim suddenly cried out. Throwing a quick glance at where he was looking, I felt my blood run cold: something was climbing onto the roof from the building wall.

I didn't get a good look at it: Maxim grabbed me by the collar and practically threw me through the door. I bumped into someone, felt their body suddenly drop down as the impact made them miss the step, and then fell right after them.

By some miracle, I didn't miss the staircase below and didn't break any bones when I landed. The landing was still pretty rough, but I got up as soon as I had a chance. I felt someone's fingers under my boot, heard a yelp of pain and protest, but I didn't mind that. Before I even realized what I was doing, I was already climbing the ladder to the roof. Maxim needed my help.

I only peeked my head through the hatch, but at that point, I already knew that it was too late. The door to the roof was already closed – and it was violently shaking. I doubted that the beast could do that – it must've been Maxim who closed it behind me to make sure it wouldn't get inside. Instead of following us to safety, he decided to make sure we'd be safe from it. Perhaps as it was gaining on him, he realized that it was the only thing he had time left to do.

The door was slightly shaking as Maxim was thrashing against it on the other side. I could hear his grunts of struggle and pain as the creature was tearing into him, and through the cracks in the door I could see their shadows locked in a deadly dance. My first instinct was to get out there, to help him fight it off, to get him inside to safety… Only to realize that the battle was already lost.

Maxim wheezed one last time, struggling to get one last breath. The creature screeched. Maxim's wheeze cut off mid-breath. The shaking stopped.

The shadows receded. In the silence that followed, I heard his body being pulled away from the door. I wanted to jump outside, to fight it off, to make sure that no one was left behind… But I knew that it wasn't a fight I could win. I knew that it was already too late. The only thing I could do was go down the stairs and close the hatch behind me, making as little sound as possible. To honor Maxim's sacrifice in the only way I could – making sure that the rest of us were safe.

I felt angry at myself that just a few days before, I had been contemplating the idea that he could be behind all of this. Maxim, the man who wanted nothing but to keep people safe. The man who took it upon himself to organize the militia, to make sure that we'd be all safe.

"Where's Maxim?" – I heard Alexei ask me when I came down. I just shook my head: "He didn't make it."

"Son of a…" – Alexei sighed. I could tell that he was shaken as well. "Just like that. One moment he's behind us, and the next… So stupid."

"Did he have a family?" – I heard someone ask.

"No, not that I know of," – I answered. "He was a widower. But he was a good man. He wanted nothing but to protect the families who lived here. To the very end," – I said, feeling a strange feeling of loss.

We stood in silence for a few moments. A moment of silence for the man who had gathered all of us and put his life on the line for what he'd believed in.

"I'm sorry" – Natasha quietly whispered. In that moment, I didn't realize what she was apologizing for, and then it dawned on me.

"Oh my god, no. It's not your fault," – I quickly assured her. "You're not to blame, you hear me?"

She just nodded. I could tell that she wasn't convinced.

"Are you alright? Are you hurt?" - I asked her, trying to look her in the eye. The girl seemed distant. From up close, I could see a faint bruise on her cheekbones, as well as the purple spot under her right eye: no doubt she'd have a black eye soon.

"Did they hurt you, Natasha?" - I kept pressuring her for answers despite seeing clear signs of assault. "Did they do anything to you?" - I asked her. That could sound heartless, but if a bruise and a black eye were the only consequences of her kidnapping then she got off easy.

"Hey, ease up, Yura" - I heard Alexei's voice. "The girl may not be comfortable to talk about it, especially right after it happened..."

Remembering my earlier suspicions, I grabbed her face and pulled her eyelids down, exposing pink flesh underneath, before forcefully opening her mouth to take a look inside. Everything looked normal. No signs of exposure. I wanted to think that it meant that my suspicions proved to be false, but I didn't know how long it would take for the signs of contamination to show themselves.

That seemed to snap her out of her dreamlike state: she pushed me back and gave a slap - a hard one at that. I didn't object: I felt like I deserved it for giving her such an intimate inspection right after whatever had happened there.

"Sorry," - I apologized awkwardly, looking away. "I was just too worked up. I'll leave you to it. Come on - your apartment is occupied with people, but you can stay at my place," - I said, gently taking her hand into mine.

"It's Nikita."

Her fingers slipped out of my grasp.

"What?" - I asked, genuinely not understanding what she was talking about. Was she perhaps insinuating that Nikita was on her mind at that moment? That she couldn't forgive herself for betraying his trust in her?

"The welder. It's Nikita."

"What are you saying, Nikita is not even here" - I said on autopilot, putting on a dumb, hollow smile. My mind had already started connecting the dots between her cryptic words and the events of the last few days.

No, it couldn't be...

"He came to me when I was in my apartment. He called me through the door. I heard him and I didn't even take a look through the peephole and opened the door. If I had looked first… I'd see what he'd become," - she said with a thousand-yard stare.

"Wait, are you serious?" - I asked her again. "Nikita? Your boyfriend?" - I stressed that word just to make it clear who exactly I was talking about. "He's the one who's welded us all in here?"

"I am not crazy, Yura" - she told me wearily. "Although some part of me wishes I was. It's… too much to take in."

"I'm not suggesting that" - I hurriedly assured her. "But you might be confused right now. It can't be Nikita, Nikita was at his parents' place when everything started, remember?" - I told her, smiling. I knew it wasn't an appropriate time to do so, but I couldn't help it: the corners of my mouth were stretching upwards on their own, twitching in denial when I tried to make them go down.

Nikita. Natasha's missing boyfriend. The only person in this entire building I could call my friend. He was behind it all?

"Okay, so… Why did he come home now? Where has he been all this time? And why would he weld us shut in here?" - I asked her.

"He's a part of some doomsday cult - always has been, apparently" - she said, letting out a dry laugh. I couldn't even imagine what it was like - to learn that your partner was having another, secret life. "One of the cult members allowed him to stay in his apartment - he said he didn't want to disturb me. That he needed… some time away from me, or else wouldn't be able to go through with it."

"Go through with what? What the hell do they need with us?" - I asked, completely confused.

"He said that they were going to change the world, and that it was going to start in our town. That they needed more people, and that they knew the town would be evacuated, which was why they welded the doors of buildings all over the town. They needed us to stay here until… We'd see their point," - she finished with confusion. She didn't understand what he meant by that - but I did.

I had just seen the people change under the influence of some unknown substance that was in the water. I had seen them become slaves to some outside will, which cared little about their well-being and was more bent on propagating itself. And I had heard the strange transmissions of their cult, which now made much more sense than before.

*"...and those who partake his blood and flesh shall be made of his blood and flesh, too."*

We were no more than a sacrifice. An offering to some strange force that polluted the water, and maybe the ground and the air, too - if the cult's messages were to be interpreted directly. We were just puppets waiting to be taken into their master's hands, and if it weren't for a tried and tested custom of filling the bathtubs with water during the emergency, we'd perhaps be already done with.

The military's strategy of opening fire on anyone emerging from town, while still brutal, suddenly made much more sense. How could you know whom could you trust? How could you know if the family of three that was approaching you was not already an enemy?

And behind all of that was Nikita. The man who we thought had disappeared when the sirens were sounded. The man who we thought had escaped the town by now had been with us the whole time.

"He said he came to me because he couldn't keep it a secret anymore." - Natasha kept talking to no one in particular. "Said he wanted to show me what they were doing. He thought I'd appreciate it. Said that it was finally our chance to break out, to see the world, like I've always wanted. To change our lives," - she said, recounting Nikita's words. Her voice was even. "But he's done something to himself. I don't… I don't understand. He comes home a freak, drags me out of there to his place, and says that he wants us to be together forever. Is he out of his mind? And when I," - her voice broke for a second, before she regained her composure. "When I told him 'no', he got so mad… I've never seen him so mad. It's like, he changed on all levels. I didn't tell him about us, but he guessed that, somehow. He threw me out of his apartment and told me to go back, to wait for their King to come like everyone else… He told me he didn't… He didn't care what would… What would..."

She was breaking down in front of me. Little by little, her emotions were seeping through the lid her shock had put on them, and she couldn't handle them anymore. The truth was too much for her to handle. She started weeping, and any words that she wanted to say got lost in that mess of sounds.

I came closer and hugged her. She tried to resist, but without much enthusiasm. After a few seconds she eased up, and I felt her shoulders shake and tremble. I wanted to look her in the face to see if she was crying, but she pulled me in closer and burrowed her face into my jacket.

"Not like this," - she quietly sobbed. "I don't want you to see me like this. Not because of him."

She kept on quietly shaking, refusing to make even a single sound that would betray that she was shedding tears for him. All I could do was stand there and be there for her.

I wanted to hurt him, and strangely, not because he'd betrayed us or because he was behind our imprisonment. I wanted to hurt him for making Natasha cry. For leaving a bruise on her face. For scaring both of us.

And I planned to give him a piece of my mind personally very soon.

"Natasha" - I asked her quietly, trying to contain my anger. "Do you remember the number of his apartment?"

"Seventy Two" - she whispered. "Why?"

"Because if he's the welder, and he planned to keep us here until we were all converted, then he definitely should have something that can cut those doors open," - I told her. "…once you're ready - lead them outside. Unseal the doors." I should have seen it before, but I hadn't thought about it since. Without knowing the welder's location and identity there was no point in paying those words any attention.

"And if it's good enough for the door, then it should do the trick for those bars in the sewers, too."

# CHAPTER 18 – The Plan

As the evening was descending upon us, I was trying to make sense of what was happening. The revelation Natasha had brought me was finally connecting the dots and making the picture whole.

According to the old man's account, all that had been happening around us for the past few days was somehow the fault of the Soviets. Something that they had been doing in our town yielded the results only decades after the country's collapse. Something he described as "looking for allies in other worlds." I had heard many wild rumors about the reasons for founding our town, heard bizarre theories about what the Soviets had been developing here – but not even the craziest of them claimed that the Soviets were looking into trans-dimensional tech.

And now, those "allies" were roaming the streets of our town. The military was ready for such an event - after all, it seemed like the purpose of "The Cricket" was to notify the higher-ups about the phenomena. It was too good to be a coincidence that it had stopped broadcasting just as those things started invading our town. But the military either underestimated the scope of the threat or dropped the ball completely because so far it seemed that the threat was far from eradicated.

There was also a strange cult, of which the welder - Nikita - seemed to be a part of. They had been biding their time for those creatures to arrive, and when they received a heads-up about an incoming invasion they did what was in their power to sabotage the evacuation - if Leonid's words could be trusted it seemed that we weren't the only ones who had our doors welded shut.

Their goal was still cryptic, but if the previous day was anything to go by, it seemed that they wanted us locked in so that the substance that had found its way into the pipes would be consumed by us. They had anticipated that once we'd be locked down, we would have no choice but to drink it. It wouldn't be a stretch to consider that it was only thanks to them that the water was still running - they had probably occupied the water station and polluted the waters there, where they would find their way to every apartment in town.

But they didn't account for the fact that most people started saving up water as soon as they were locked down. Judging by the fact that the water had acquired a strange taste only a day after the lockdown had started, it seemed that the initial batch was not polluted.

And, of course, the bandits, who had picked the worst time possible to pass through our town. Initially, it seemed that they also were just the victims of the circumstances, same as us. But, as more time had passed, they had become exposed to whatever it was within the pipes. The life in prison seemingly made them less cautious and less prone to thinking about the future. They were living in the present, so I could easily imagine them ignoring the common sense and never stocking up on the water.

Everything seemed horrible. We were an offering to their King In Rags. Nothing more than pawns in some upcoming greater game. An initial batch of followers to give his faith some credibility. It seemed that everyone was working against us – the creatures outside, the military, and even the people we used to call neighbors. We were discarded, abandoned things.

But now, on our eleventh hour, we finally had a shot at success. We knew the exact location of the welder, and we knew that he most likely had the tools to get the doors open - after all, the plan was not to kill us but to make sure we wouldn't be able to escape until it was too late. He had his shot to lead us all out of there the day earlier when the sirens distracted the beasts - but he blew it. Most probably because he had failed to indoctrinate the entire building.

Seizing those tools was our only shot at escape. But there was an obvious problem.

The fourth flight of stairs was occupied by the bandits. They had let it be known before that we were unwelcome there, and they had shown their true colors when they ransacked the third flight, and on top of that, judging by how they looked, they were now under the King's control, too. If they wouldn't have let us through to talk to him before, now they would probably lay their lives on the line defending him.

The direct head-on siege was out of the question: they had more firearms on their side, and besides, we weren't the soldiers. We were ready to risk our lives, but it didn't mean we would succeed. Rallying the rest of the tenants and crushing them with our numbers was an option, but if the elderly agreed to be our meat shield it would only mean more deaths on our side - in the narrow corridors the thugs wouldn't have much problem taking their aim at the crowd heading straight toward them.

We needed to proceed with caution. We needed to use our wits to defeat them.

According to Natasha, they had set up guarding posts right on the staircase. "They set up two guard posts – one on the second floor and one on the fourth. They seem to be really bent on protecting Nikita at all cost, either from us or from the creatures outside should they find their way inside" – she paused for a moment, when the memories seemingly overtook her, but then kept on talking. "I don't know if they stay there around the clock but it seems that way – they have tables, chairs, and even mattresses set up right there, on the staircase. Lots of guns, too. You'll have to get through them, first, and frankly, I don't know if you can," – she finished, looking over everyone in the room.

"It's simple, then" - one of the men offered when we were discussing it in Alexei's apartment. "We start a fire underneath them, in the basement, and have it do the work. I've worked as a firefighter in the past – I'm sure I can keep it localized."

I spent a lot of time trying to talk him out of it. The fire would either subside before doing any damage, only serving to alert them to our plans and making them more cautious, or it would grow so big that we wouldn't be able to contain it. While the man wasn't backing down, the rest started to heed my warnings that it wasn't such a good idea and finally botched it. For the remainder of the meeting, the man gave me cold looks.

"I say we just storm the place" - Alexei suggested. "They're not that good with firearms, and you've managed to push them back yesterday. If we rush them at night, we might catch them off-guard. They don't expect us to put up a good fight, but I'm ready to prove them wrong," – he said with bravado. A few men voiced their approval of his plan.

"Alexei, we're back to square one" – I chimed in, raising my voice so that everyone heard me. I could feel the gazes of men on me, full of disdain for daring to question their martial prowess. The blood had gone to their heads, and boredom was urging them to give in to their instincts. For the first time in days they were given a target and they wanted to tear it to shreds, and my words were nothing but an annoyance to them. But I didn't care. I wasn't going to let them die in vain, even if voluntarily. "You can't fight them head-on. You-"

"That's why I'm saying that we should strike them at night. Have you been listening?" – he questioned me.

"Yeah, kid. You best leave it to the adults" – someone remarked. I did my best to ignore it.

"Suppose you ambush the first guard post. There's still a second one, and there's no way we can ambush them as well. We'll still have to face them head-on, and they'll still have more guns than us. Then what? Are you going to rush the armed men with your hatchets and rolling pins? On a stairwell?" – I questioned them. No one had an answer to that.

Even though that wasn't why I was doing that, it felt damn good to give it to them.

"Alright, then" - Alexei looked at me, throwing daggers at me with his eyes. "What do you suggest? Do you have a better plan?"

I, in fact, did have a plan. A plan so dastardly and dangerous, one that was so overly complicated and hinged on so many assumptions that it was ridiculous to bring to the table. Yet at the same time, it was the only plan that didn't involve having to blindly rush at the danger head-on.

As I was laying it out to the rest of the group, people were letting out smirks and grunts. I expected as much, so the only thing I could do was keep talking with confidence. I had to believe that my plan was feasible, that it was good on its own merit and not based on the opinions of others, because who else was going to believe in it if not me?

Little by little, as I was breaking down my plan and explaining why it was feasible, the men were getting silent, until the room was finally quiet. I could almost hear their thoughts and doubts, I could hear their brains rushing to find some holes in it – and yet no one was saying anything.

"You know, your plan is pretty solid, but it's also pretty stupid" – one of the men finally said. Another man laughed. I wanted to object but instead found that I was laughing, too. The rest joined, too. For the first time since we'd gathered there, we felt the tension between us drop.

"Well, if it fails, we can always go back to the original plan and smoke them out" - Alexei said with a sigh. The rest of the men nodded in agreement, although I could see that not everyone was on board with what I proposed.

"And who's going to execute it? It's also risky, you know" – one of the men wondered. I could see that he didn't want to be the one to do it.

"I will" – I heard myself say. When I was formulating my plan, I hadn't imagined myself as the one who'd be setting it in motion, and that was the main reason why I had agreed so easily. I simply couldn't even picture what I was getting into. But someone had to. Since it was my idea I also had to bear the responsibility.

"And if your plan backfires and the welder is killed?" – Alexei asked.

"Screw him" – I was surprised at how easily I condemned my former friend to death, but it didn't feel right to be concerned about him after everything he'd put everyone through. "We only need his tools. I think they'll be alright."

I looked at Natasha to see how she reacted. She looked away, but a few moments later she nodded her head. That was all I needed to reaffirm my resolve. Two closest people to Nikita had agreed to put him to the knife. There was no going back after such a decision.

"Good" – Alexei nodded. "Just don't get cold feet when push comes to shove. Alright, let's get ready. We start tonight."

\*\*\*

It was in the deep of the night when we started executing my plan.

The first thing we needed was the lure.

It was tough finding a piece of meat – no one had any. The meat was perishable goods, so if anyone had had it then they had eaten it by now, and even if they did have a piece lying in their freezer they wouldn't admit it. We tried explaining to everyone that we needed it for a serious cause, but when they heard why exactly we needed it they'd spin a finger at their temple to show us what they thought about my idea.

Finally, after we almost gave up on our quest, one of the new militia members came from downstairs, bringing a bloodied parcel with him – a piece of meat wrapped in a piece of cloth.

"Don't unwrap it!" – he warned when I tried to take a look at it. "Not yet".

The parcel didn't smell fresh, and when I looked at his face he looked away, wiping bloodstains from his face.

I probed the parcel without opening it. A long, soft tube. On one of its ends, I suddenly felt fingers under the cloth. I resisted an urge to throw up.

"You are welcome" – the man grunted. "You wanted a piece of meat – I got you one. Risked my life, too, going into that apartment alone."

We brought it to the basement with us and headed toward the furthest door - the one that led to the stairwell Alexei wanted to burn down so much. The door must've been locked on the hanging lock from the other side, but it was old and wooden. There was a way to get past it - the trick was to do it completely silently.

They hadn't made any efforts to reinforce the door to the basement. Their logic must have been simple: the door was locked on a hanging lock, the same one as the one we broke on the day we went to the basement, and the key to which had been lost a long time ago. It wasn't meant to be open. As such, the lock would do well enough to keep any intruders out, and if they tried to break through the door they would make enough noise to wake up the entire building and alert those who were left on guard.

We spent a good three hours trying to drill through the wood with a wimble we'd borrowed from an old carpenter, making one crank at a time, listening all the while to the noises on the other side - in the complete silence we could hear the thugs who were on overwatch drinking and talking, and the nauseating hoarse voice of a chanson singer they were listening that rang in my ears. But at any moment the music could stop and their tone could change from cheerful to worried, which would mean only one thing - we were busted.

After two hours, the wimble's drill finally reached the nail which held the locking hinge in place, and we spent the next hour working around it, taking turns, trying to make the hole bigger, until finally the nail was separated from the wood. The hanging lock was just hanging from the doorframe now, and the door could be opened.

I took off my boots and entered the stairwell. From then on, I was on my own. It only made sense for me to be the one to bear all the risks - after all, it was my plan.

The men were just one floor above me. I could now hear them with perfect clarity. One wrong step, one noise - and they would come rushing down toward me.

It was time for the greatest gamble of my life. I reached out toward one of the doors.

Unlocked. Of course. When they were fleeing they didn't care about their belongings. They knew that the first floor was dangerous. That the brutish creature could tear down the grates on their windows.

And so did I.

I headed towards the kitchen, opened the window, and put the piece of meat on the floor. Then, carefully taking a knife out of the drawer, I slit my left palm and drew some blood, raining a few drops onto the piece of meat.

The plan was now set in motion. I didn't know how well the Ape could smell, but I banked on the fact that by sunrise it would be tempted enough to break down the grates and enter the stairwell, where it would quickly deal with all the bandits.

I hoped that the old welder would have enough sense to lock the door before that happened.

Looking over my trap one last time, I headed toward the exit. I made sure to leave the door open - that way, either the creature would find its way out of the apartment on its own or the bandits would hear it breaking in, which would prompt them to come over and take a look at what was going on, thus drawing it out onto the stairwell.

I headed toward the basement door, only to find it wide open. The hammer, nails, and pieces of furniture - improvised wooden planks that we planned to use to barricade the door afterward - were lying right next to it, abandoned.

*"Weird"* - I thought to myself - right before I heard it. The pitter-patter of many legs that was getting closer with each second. Coming straight out of the basement I came from.

"The windows" - was all I could think before I turned around and ran. The windows, the tiny windows that lined the walls of the basement, were an easy way for the creature to get in. We'd never seen it, so we had no clue whether it would be able to sneak in, but I should've anticipated that threat. Pavel was not only killed in the basement - we never even recovered his body.

And now it was in there. Cutting me off from safety and pinning me between a rock and a hard place.

And it was approaching fast.

I didn't have a lot of time to spare. I had two options: run back into the apartment I'd just left, where the bait was waiting for the ape, or run up the stairs, toward the bandits, and hope that their shooting skills weren't great.

I chose the second option. In a crisis, the primates had always sought to gain an elevated position or move toward their peers, and that instinct, buried deep within my psyche, re-emerged in the time of need.

The men were so drunk and so bewildered by my sudden appearance that none of them even reached for their gun. Since I only started running when I was already on the stairs to them it must've looked like I appeared there out of thin air. They just watched me with surprised eyes as I rushed past them, toward the third floor.

Toward apartment Seventy Two.

I was moving at such speeds that I had to grab on to the railings to make a sharp turn. My ligaments screamed in protest, strained to a maximum degree each time I made a turn, but it wasn't important. Death itself was on my heels.

One floor below me, the men's' shouts intended to alarm the rest to the intruder's presence turned to screams of terror - it seemed that even possessed and made to do their master's bidding they still could feel fear. One of the screams was cut short as a pair of mighty jaws, or mandibles perhaps, crushed the man's throat. A second later, I heard gunshots.

The men above - the ones who guarded the fourth floor - started rushing down to see what was going on. I could hear their hurried steps. In a second, they would turn around the corner and see me, trying to reach their most guarded apartment…

I could already see the door in front of me.

His door was unlocked. Just like Natasha had told us. He had no one to fear and no one was above him. Locking the door would be nothing more than a hindrance to him.

I opened the door: the lights were out, so I couldn't see past the threshold. But the threat that was on my heels was far more real and tangible than whatever waited for me beyond that rectangle of darkness, so I quickly jumped through it and closed the door behind me. As I was locking it I just glimpsed the creature rear its ugly, angular head around the corner of the stairwell: I wasn't sure where its eyes were and whether it saw me, but instinctively I felt that whatever senses it employed had felt my presence there.

As I was still listening to the pitter-patter of its many feet, trying to determine if it knew I was inside the apartment, I heard another set of footsteps. Much clearer than the sounds coming through the door.

The steps were coming from the darkness behind me. And they were approaching.

With an unholy howl, the cutlery in the kitchen clanking from its footsteps, the unknown thing that had been hiding within the depths of the apartment was coming straight at me.

I turned around and swung my hatchet at it, but it missed its target: I threw my shot in the dark too early. I couldn't see it, but just from the sounds it was making, from the way I heard it shift its weight as it approached me, I could tell that it wasn't a human.

It hissed and charged at me. Its appendage, faintly resembling a human hand, slammed into my chest, pressing me against the door. The creature outside the apartment immediately reacted to it, starting to scratch the door trying to dig through it. The vibrations of its movements traveled through the surface into my back, and I could feel its claws piercing the foam rubber covering of the door, getting stuck on the layer of metal beneath it as if it was my own skin and bones.

The weight of my assailant was squeezing the air out of my lungs, the initial shock making me lose my grasp on the situation. I couldn't even find the strength to retaliate. The thing had come out a winner from our initial collision, but it wasn't in a rush to secure its victory and finish me while I was powerless.

I was struggling to find the strength to resist him when I heard him talking to me. I spent a few moments trying to determine what it was saying before giving up on that idea altogether. The language it was speaking couldn't be human, for even though there seemed to be some complex structure to it, no vocal cords would be able to replicate those sounds.

In fact, the sounds had nothing to do with it at all. The strange words were not heard, I realized, but felt by me. It was not the thing that was choking me that spoke them - it was something beneath my skin. Something within me was resonating with the creature's presence and was letting me know that it was there.

The words made no sense, yet at the same time I could feel them as if they were written on my skin, or underneath it, the quill they were etched into me with caressing my nerves and letting me know that I should find humility before a piece of him and then I'd find solace in the shadow of his rags and the brilliance of his gaze that he set on our world was more magnificent than our radiant sun and oh how pleasant his flesh would feel against mine and how his blood would run with mine and my soul would sing in unison with trillions of others that had found him across the countless unimaginable worlds and I just needed to breathe and drink and partake and soak in his radiating warmth and I would feel how big his heart is and he would love me more than a mother loves her son-

My hatchet rose up without me even realizing it and clumsily slashed the darkness that was choking me.

Halfway through its arc, its blade got snared on something, and the voice within me got quieter. The creature's hold got weaker, too.

The sounds of the waking world returned: I heard it stumbling back. I took just one deep breath - just one to feel the oxygen saturate my mind and muscles - and, still weak and confused as to where I was, landed another blow.

It let out a grunt of pain that sounded surprisingly human and backed away. Not letting it recover, I landed one blow after another, each strike making the voices subside, each strike reminding me that I was a human - a savage and territorial creature. An individual. Not some speck in a greater trans-dimensional collective.

The thing collapsed to the floor and was crawling away from me in the dark. I couldn't ignore the fact that it sounded more human again - my onslaught seemed to make it shed its vicious side.

A suspicion crawled into my mind. Feeling the walls in the darkness, I found the light switch and made darkness go away.

The thing lying on the floor couldn't be called a human - its build was far too different from what could be considered a human being. But I couldn't deny the fact that it had Nikita's face - or at least what remained of it.

It must've been him - after all, the place was right and he had the resemblance to the man I once knew. I now understood why Natasha didn't describe him in more detail whenever she mentioned that he had changed - I wouldn't have believed her anyway, preferring to think that what she was describing was just a result of stress and trauma.

He had changed alright. His skin had the same dark, spotty texture as the rest of the possessed, but it seemed that it had progressed to a greater degree. Whatever it was that had been growing under his skin, that was giving it that purple hue, had ample time and resources to flourish on Nikita's body, manifesting in bizarre arboreal growths that had changed his appearance and general shape of his body so much it wasn't surprising I didn't recognize a human in him when we had been fighting in the dark.

The growths didn't look like they were a part of his body - they looked foreign, alien. The very texture of that flesh indicated that it was nothing like ours, and thus couldn't be produced by it no matter what manipulations would be done on it. No, it seemed like the flesh burst forth through him like it had grown from within his skin and dissolved its way from beneath it. The black and purple spots I had been seeing on cultists and bandits before were nothing but the beginning. No doubt the next stage would begin only after those people had infiltrated the rest of society.

His right eye was covered by a tumor-like formation – a stubby mushroom on the bark of his skin. It was hard to tell whether it was growing from the eye itself or somewhere else. And yet the face was familiar. The face of a man I used to call a friend.

"Nikita…?" - I asked just to be sure. Even though the evidence was right in front of me, I still couldn't come to terms with it.

He crawled back to the wall, used it to prop himself up and take a seat, and then smiled, letting out a waterfall of black, oozing liquid from his mouth. "Hello, Yura. Long time no see."

# CHAPTER 19 – The Welder

It wasn't real. It was too unreal to believe it.

I had seen Nikita just a week ago. A normal guy a few years older than me. No signs of sickness or anything like that.

Since then he had changed so much that I struggled to think we still belonged to the same species. As he prostrated himself on the floor, the growths on his body reminding me of barky roots of pines, it felt like I was talking to a stump with Nikita's face.

"So, it is you" - I said, finally seeing it with my own eyes. It wasn't that I was doubting Natasha's words, but some things needed to be witnessed first-hand to truly believe in them.

"Yes" - he smiled again, letting out another squirt of inky non-blood. He weakly tried to raise his stumpy hand, covered in deep gashes my hatchet left in barky skin, and then put it back down on the floor. The wounds I had dealt him would've made a normal human die a long time ago from blood loss, but he, despite flooding a quarter of the room with his black fluids, was seemingly stuck in a state between life and death.

"Although I've gone through a slight overhaul. Do you like my new look?"

"You're really the welder?" - I asked him.

"The welder..." - he rolled that word on his tongue as if tasting the title the people had given him for his deeds and then let out a short, condescending laugh. "I welded you all shut, yes. Don't tell me you didn't enjoy the protection I've given you all."

"The protection?" - I asked him in disbelief. Who was that person? The Nikita I knew was a caring, calm person. Who was that arrogant imposter? What kind of creature put on his face and started spewing ridicules?

"We could've escaped the town! We could've evacuated along with the rest!" - I shouted at him. The creature at the stairwell screeched in excitement and renewed its efforts in trying to bring the door down, but I had already figured out that it wasn't up to the task, so I simply ignored it as background noise.

"You could've escaped it a long time ago, Yura" - he said with a tired sigh, rolling his eyes. "Long before all of this even started. Both you and Natasha. I even offered her a chance, but she refused. No use complaining about it now."

"She stayed because she wanted to support you!!" - I said with sudden ferocity. Something about how neglectful he was of her sacrifice struck a chord.

"Yes, I know. But I didn't hold her here. And I told her I had plans here" - he explained with that same tired look as if he'd been through that conversation many times before. At the last moment, his facial expression shifted to that of regret, but only for a moment - he shook his hand and the emotion flew off of his face.

"Plans like what? Joining some crazy cult? Transforming yourself into…this?" - I gestured at his body, pointing at no organ in particular. "Waiting for the end of the world in the middle of nowhere?"

"First of all, it's not the end of the world - quite the opposite" - he said with sudden enthusiasm. "And second, we didn't just wait for a random event - we knew it was coming. We knew He was coming. We knew all along" - he said with a victorious look on his face.

I knew I shouldn't have let my curiosity get the best of me. A hatchet to his head, a quick search through his possessions in search of a tool I needed to escape - and then I'd be gone once the slithering creature outside found itself a new target.

But after everything I'd gone through, I just needed to know - what for? What the hell was going on in his head? What would push someone like him to change like that and get involved in something so vile?

What was the greatest secret of our town? What did "the Cricket" fail to tell me?

"Is your cult behind all of this?" - I inquired. He laughed: "Hardly. Yes. Yes and no. It's hard to explain, it's all started long before I was born."

"Try me" - I suggested in a dry tone.

Nikita licked his lips, trying to clean them up from the sticky black substance, coughed out another puddle of it, and then, giving up on the idea, started talking.

"I don't need to tell you that it all began with the foundation of this town, do I?" - he questioned me. I shook my head: that all of these events were tied to the things the Soviets had been doing in our town, I had figured out long ago. Seeing that, he nodded with satisfaction and continued.

"I am not sure what's been going on here. The Soviets made sure that not a single person had enough clearance to get the full picture of what they'd been working on. You have no idea how much that spoiled our plans," - he said with spite, his eyes lighting up with fervor of a European crusader who had set foot onto the holy land to find it defiled by heretics. "We've been piecing it all together for decades."

"So much for knowing it all along" - I sarcastically said. It felt strange to joke with him as if he was still my friend. My mind still refused to accept that he was something else at this point, and the thought of cracking a joke to that thing almost made me lose it.

Nikita ignored my remark and continued talking: "It is not clear what they'd been doing there. Some say that they had been testing some new science that helped them get through the barrier between dimensions - but the science on that is quite wacky and, in our Order, I hadn't met a single person who could explain how it worked. Others say that the Soviets have found something in the woods - a door of sorts, built by no one and that led nowhere. They were just looking for a key. It doesn't matter," - he shook his head. "What matters is that in those places, beyond the boundaries of our realm, they have found their messiah."

"Your so-called King in Rags?" - I asked him. "Is that what you call a messiah – a rabies pandemic? I thought the Soviets were supposed to be atheists, especially in the case of high-ranking academics."

"Gods come in different shapes - just look at different ancient cultures and you'll see what I'm talking about" - Nikita retorted in a matter-of-fact voice, visibly hurt by my remark. "And it's hard to stay an atheist when a literal deity reaches out to you from the outside. The first explorers who have come into contact with him are mostly dead - they have become the saints of our cause. But they have passed down their knowledge to the rest - only those they could trust. Those who could see him not as a tool for some fleeting political agenda, but as their savior. The infallible leader who had already unified countless worlds and was willing to help the rest. The one who could achieve the utopia that mere humans couldn't. Those brave men could see the signs of their old empire crumbling - it was only a matter of time before the greatest sociological experiment, the Soviet Union, would finally fail from human ineptness. They knew that they needed someone above to take reigns. With that, our Order materialized. We have been secretly growing in this town, waiting for his arrival, all this time," - Nikita finished with pride. "And now that we've upheld our end of the bargain and prepared the groundwork for his arrival, he's going to keep his word and give us what we've wanted."

"And you just believe him?" - I asked in disbelief. "Nikita, he's sent hordes of monsters into our town! Does it look like the actions of someone who gives a damn about people?"

"It's just a vanguard, nothing serious" - he said in a dismissive tone. "The beasts from one of the fringe worlds. Sure, the animals may be too dumb to be controlled by him, so they are a nuisance to us as well, but at the same time they keep the military at bay for the time being, until our Order can finish the rest of the preparations."

"Nikita, your cult has been infecting people with something that makes them mad!" – I cried out.

"Not infecting" - he spat the word out with disdain, showing how much he despised my wording. "It's an act of holy communion. These people partook the blood and flesh of their future savior to become closer to him."

"Don't you think that sounds messed up?" - I wondered. He just smiled and tried to shake his shoulders: "The Christians have been doing that for centuries. The only difference is that our ritual is a real deal."

"It also doesn't make them look like that" - I countered, pointing at his abnormal growths. He glanced at them with confusion, as if not realizing what was wrong about them, and then shook his head: "Don't be making any mistakes. I am not like the rest. The offering I was granted was purer and more refined. As a high-ranking member of our Order, I'm supposed to be closer to him, and I ought to guide the rest of the congregation – even if they are unwilling at first.

Of course, should enough time pass and should they show enough dedication to the cause, they may also feel the warmth of his embrace."

"So, you do control them" - I realized, another piece of the puzzle falling into place. What had been just a hunch before was now a certainty. Why else would those bandits call him the boss and lay their lives on the line for him?

"We have no choice" - I heard him casually say. How could he be so calm when talking about such things? Was he really a monster - not just on the outside, but deep within, too? Had he always been that way?

"We need the troops, we need infiltrators for the initial stage. Someone to get behind the enemy lines and disrupt them from within. We've polluted the water supply – sorry, polluted isn't the right word," – he winced from how awkward his choice of words was, but then decided to continue. "You get the idea. But, there has been a delay. We planned to do it before his arrival, but we didn't get to the water supply in time. So, we had to improvise. We needed to keep people inside their houses for the time being until the process was completed. We came up with this little plan – to weld the doors shut and keep everyone inside so that we would have enough time. It hasn't worked out too well yet - the military had seen through our charade with the refugees, but it's not done yet. When the bulk of his army will come it won't matter. And after his conquest is over, people won't need to accept him into their bodies to seek his guidance. They'll see that he's better than any leader humanity could've produced. He's had millennia of experience of ruling countless worlds. They'll come around."

"More are coming?" – I asked him.

"Oh yes" – he assured me with a smile. "With our savior himself at the helm. Have you looked out your window recently?"

I knew exactly what he was referring to. The wave of death that had been rolling through the forest, drawing closer to our building with each day. I haven't checked on it in a long time, but I wouldn't be surprised if it was at our doorstep by the dawn.

And Nikita was relishing that fact. He was ecstatic that he had played his part in bringing death itself to our house. To the building where his closest people had been living for years. I felt another wave of anger rolling through me. I couldn't fathom such betrayal.

"Nikita, why?" - I asked him.

"Why what?" - he clarified.

"Why did you get involved with this whole thing? This started long before you were born, by some old farts who did it for their own reasons. Why did you get involved?!" - I started screaming at him. "What, don't tell me you believe in this cause?"

"What if I do?" - he challenged me. "Huh? What if I do? You see with your very own eyes that it's not just another crazy cult - it's all real and happening! They've known it was going to happen, and they've prepared! It's not us, it's the world that's crazy! You hear me?" - he shouted at me. "What, are you going to say that you're happy with where you live? That you're happy with how people around you have turned out after living in this world? You've always wanted to leave - but did you ever stop and think whether you should have such desires? Maybe if they didn't mess up the country, the town would be an alright place! They've taken everything - you hear me - everything from us! We're just taking it back!"

"Don't play hero with me" - I scowled at him. "Do you even have a clue how many people have died because of your actions?"

"And how many were shot by the military?" - he countered, not intending to give up. "Huh? The military that's supposed to protect us, the military that is following the orders of a government we supposedly chose! As soon as you're not wanted - you're wasted! What a nice world to live in, right? Fricking great! You're nobody in this country - all of us are! And if you can't do anything about it - don't stand in my way!"

"Again with this..." - I shook my head. "Why do you keep saying that this world is so bad? Haven't you had a great life here? You've had it all: a girlfriend, a place to live, friends..." - my voice suddenly gave out on the last word: I wasn't aware that some part of me still considered the mutated piece of flesh in front of me my friend, but apparently, that was the case.

"I..." - he took a deep, hateful breath and locked eyes with me, but no answer followed. He was struggling to pick the right words - or wasn't sure if he even had them.

"You don't know a thing!" - he finally said. "It could be so much more. Have you ever asked the people around you how their life was back in the day?"

"What does it matter…?" - I started before he interrupted me: "It does matter! It does because if you were paying attention you'd know that. Everyone who had lived there kept talking about that. It was a paradise. Have you ever bothered to ask your mother about that time? I have! My parents have told me all about it, and my grandparents, too! And they've taken it away from us! We've been waiting for three generations for the King in Rags to come, and he didn't abandon us. He'll make things right" - Nikita said with a scowl on his face.

"Wait, so your parents are involved as well?" - I inquired. My head was heavy. Nikita nodded. "Who do you think has initiated me to the Order? Do you think they just walk around the town and invite everyone willing? We've survived for so long because we've kept it personal. We've kept this secret close to home, close to family."

"And you didn't think about leaving it all? Can't you see that they've been using you?" - I asked him. How could he be so oblivious to such a thing?

He sent me a crooked smile as if one of the nails it was hanging on fell off. "Better to be of use to your family than to be used by others like a slave. It was nothing short of fate that I was born into this family and in this town."

"Hindsight is twenty-twenty" - I interrupted him. I felt sick. "You say that it's your fate only because you've decided to roll with your family's plans for you."

"I decided to join them because it was my purpose. I was born with it. To carry their mission forward. Can you say the same?" - he gave me a prideful look.

I looked at his twisted arm. At the growths on his face. At the wound that was bleeding more ooze than blood.

"No" - I said. "I guess I have to think for myself" - I told him.

"That's the problem with people" - Nikita smiled, letting another spurt of black liquid out of his mouth. "They don't want to listen to experience. Don't worry. You'll come around."

"So, what now? You're going to kill me? Kill Natasha? Is that your cause?" - I questioned him.

"I was ready for such things. This new world order has had you all brainwashed. I can't change who you are if you resist it. I can only fight you" - he told me.

He was dead serious. He was ready to tear us all down for the sake of the cause he was born into.

And in a way, by voicing that, he lent me some of his strength and determination. For the first time since I'd seen him like that, he said something we could agree on.

"Yes" - I said, stepping closer and squeezing the hatchet in my hands. "I guess you're right."

"Come on" - he urged me. "Do it. I'm ready to become a martyr for the cause. One day you'll see. You'll be living happily in a world that I've built, remember what you've done here, and then hang yourself in your guest room from guilt. I'll have the final laugh" - he told me, smiling.

"I doubt it, since you won't be around" - I told him. Why did I answer him? Was I trying to postpone the moment I'd have to kill him for good?

"Oh, maybe I won't. But you will be. And you'll see things from my point of view - I guarantee it" - he smirked and winked at me. He wasn't just being coy - he was insinuating something.

"What do you mean?" - I asked him, stopping in my tracks.

"You've felt it, haven't you?" - he asked me. "His message, coursing through your veins?"

I knew what he was referring to. The horrible, head-splitting headache when the sirens were sounded for the second time. The voice deep within me when he was pushing me against the door. I was harboring something - I just didn't know what yet.

"He is in the ground. He is in the water. He is in the air" - Nikita quoted me the words from the very first transmission of his cult, stressing the last word. "And he will be the fire that will burn you down" - he finished with a satisfied smirk on his face.

So, it wasn't just in the water, then. Just as I had suspected, it was indeed in the air, too. The infection – or whatever it was – was not just in the pipes, it was airborne, too. We all have been breathing it in, but judging by the fact that Nikita couldn't control me, the concentration of it within my body hadn't reach the critical point yet.

Of course, it could very well be rising as we spoke. Perhaps Nikita was breathing that filth, the tiny particles of his so-called messiah into the air, and at any moment I'd suddenly find myself a slave to his will.

I could cut him down right there and then. I could make him the martyr for his cause, and he probably wouldn't even object. Now was the time.

But I couldn't bring myself to do it. I hated him for betraying my trust, for betraying the very humanity that nurtured him… And yet, I couldn't go through with it. At that moment, when our eyes met and I saw him ready to die on his cross – or whatever their cult prayed to – I felt a strange sense of pity for him.

For his entire life, he had been groomed for his role. Raised on the stories how he would become a hero, a savior of the neglected. A man who'd carry the torch that his parents had lit. He had been told that he was exactly where he needed to be.

Just like I had been.

He never saw himself as something more than what his parents had intended for him. He had never had the chance. I had spent my entire life punishing myself for that by putting myself down, and now, when I finally saw the truth about the matter, I couldn't find it in myself to punish him for it, either.

I had to go. I had to keep my goal in mind and focus only on it. We were very close to finally leaving the town for good. All I needed was his tools.

"Where are your welding tools? I know you have them here somewhere," – I asked him, looking around the room.

"Why? I've already sealed all of the doors, no need to worry" – I heard Nikita's taunting voice. I ignored the question and kept looking. I looked into every corner. Looked under the table where a small radio rested – no doubt the one Nikita used to receive his instructions from his cult's leaders. Opened the closet.

"Yura, why do you need them?" – he asked me again, this time a little bit more seriously.

I kept on ignoring him. He wasn't answering my questions, so I saw no point in humoring him.

"Yura, why? What are you planning?"

There it was. A heavy duffel bag, behind the bed. I put it on the bed, opened it. Took out all the welding equipment.

It was there. A gas torch, at the very bottom of the bag. When I felt its weight in my hand, felt the gas inside the canister, I couldn't resist but let out a sigh of relief.

"What are you going to do with it?" – I heard Nikita carefully inquire, although at that point I was sure that he had already guessed that.

"I'm leaving" - I told him.

"Leaving?" - he wheezed, trying to laugh. "Leaving where? Do you think anyone waits for you there - outside of this town?"

Such familiar words. Words from the previous life.

"I'm leaving" - I repeated myself. "And I'm taking Natasha with me" - I told him with sudden ferocity. I thought I couldn't feel angry at him anymore, but the thought of her ignited the remains of anger within me, lit a spark in the fumes of adrenaline.

"You're not going to see her ever again. We'll find a way out of here. And you'll just rot in this town" - I promised him. I wanted to believe what I was saying.

For the first time since the beginning of our conversation, his expression changed. The facade of calmness and arrogance that he was trying to maintain finally crumbled and fell away. Not in the face of his own mortality – he had clearly embraced it and was ready for whatever was coming.

But the moment I mentioned Natasha his entire demeanor changed.

"No one waits for you there, Yura!" - he cried out. Was it me or did his voice really sound desperate? "You think they care about the people here? They kill us! They kill us without hesitation, Yura! Our people come with the banner of peace over their heads and they mow them down with machineguns! They kill anyone, just to be sure! Do you think they left us electricity because they cared about the people here? They don't give a damn about you!" - Nikita was getting worked up. I wasn't sure what it was: his religious fervor or genuine disdain for the actions of the military. Perhaps both. "They left us electricity because they heard our transmissions! The only reason they keep feeding us energy is because they're gathering intel from us! That's it! The needs of hundreds of stranded people are less important to them!"

"I know" - I lied to him. It would take too much time to explain to him what I did and didn't know - and I didn't want to be around him for another second.

"You'll get her killed!" - he shouted at me angrily. He tried to get up from the floor but the wound I dealt him was too severe. "Don't leave! You have a home here! We can put this all behind us, and if you see what we stand for you might even come around!" - he kept on trying to convince me.

Home. Such a painful word. Was it really my home? A monster-infested, cultist-ridden spot in the middle of nowhere? Sure, I could get a bullet through my brain without even realizing it on my way out - but did it mean I had to agree to how things were here?

"Goodbye, Nikita" - I told him.

"Don't take her there!" - he begged me as I was leaving. "Please, just…let her stay. I…My people will take care of her."

It finally became clear to me what he was so afraid of. The only thing he feared, even as he was lying on the ground bleeding out. He wasn't scared of his own death. He was scared for her.

"Oh yeah?" - I shook my head but didn't turn around. It was tough to face him again. "Where were you when this all started? Why didn't you come to her?"

There was a pause. For the first time since I had arrived, he was struggling to pick his words.

"I just…Didn't want to scare Natasha with…this" - there was a shuffling sound. I didn't see what he was doing but from the sound of it, he lifted his disfigured arm off the ground before weakly putting it back down.

I silently nodded and leaned on the door. Hearing nothing on the other side, I stepped outside. I knew that the creature could be lying in ambush, but I didn't let that stop me. If I stayed afraid of it I could as well never step outside, and I didn't want to spend another hour together with Nikita.

I didn't want him to see the weakness glittering in the corners of my eyes.

# CHAPTER 20 – Outside

The door closed soundlessly behind me - luckily, the hinges and the lock seemed to be lubricated well, so they didn't announce my presence to anyone willing to know. For the next thirty seconds, I stood there in silence, straining my hearing, and too scared to take a step. In such a perfect silence, it would be easy to forget that it wasn't just an ordinary stairwell of Khruschyovka at night, that things weren't as they had been a week before…if not for the trail of blood leading from the floor below to the upstairs.

I was in a strange state of equilibrium: as long as I didn't move, I stayed near the door, and if I heard anything coming I could quickly hide inside. Yet at the same time, if I stayed where I was, I would inevitably be found. I needed to traverse the unknown to get back to the safety of familiar walls. Damned if I do, damned if I don't.

I made the first step. Then another one. Quickly descended down the flight of stairs and looked down at the second floor.

What used to be a lookout was now a place of massacre. Red and black fluids were mixing together, running down the steps, staining the walls… If I were to touch it, I was sure I would find out that it still retained the warmth of the bodies it used to run through. I knew that the thing that had done it was still around, but to see it with my own eyes, to smell it, to feel it make the floor slippery under my feet was a completely different thing.

The men whom I had passed while escaping the creature were still there – frozen in poses no living thing would rest in. Their deaths had been quick and merciless – when the creature had sunk its teeth or whatever it had into them that was it. It seemed that only Nikita was valuable enough to their deity to be kept on this side indefinitely – the rest died like usual, with their god not even caring about that.

I noticed that one of them still clutching a pistol – it seemed that the man had decided to stand his ground instead of running away. I wasn't thinking about my survival at that moment, but I thought that it could still come in handy in the future.

I grabbed the gun and pulled it, only to realize that the hand holding it was not yet dead.

The man I thought to be dead opened his eyes and looked at me. He was too weak to form words, but he had enough strength to form a scowl.

He recognized me. He knew it was me who let the crawling creature in.

A shot rang, and I tumbled down the flight of stairs, clutching my side.

The pain instantly snapped me back to reality, my survival instincts coming back online. I wanted to live. I wanted to live no matter how bleak my future looked.

"What if that crawling thing heard it? What if something else heard it? I'm losing blood. I need to hurry!" - my brain was producing one rushed thought after another.

I descended into the basement, squeezing my wound. I could barely see in the darkness, but luckily, I was alone in there.

I pulled the handle of the door that led to my stairwell. Nothing.

I pulled at it again. It still didn't budge.

It wasn't that I was too weak to open it. It was locked. They must've locked the door behind them as they were fleeing, or maybe the tenants locked it when they heard the sounds of struggle.

I looked back at the windows lining the wall and knocked on the door. I was too scared to shout for someone to open.

I knocked again and heard some noises. But they weren't coming from the other side of the door.

They were coming from the apartment where I left the bait. It seemed that the ape finally took it.

I heard its roar, heard the noise with which the grates were separated from the wall, and shuddered. I had nowhere to run. I was cornered. If it could smell the blood on me…

I could feel that my palm was full of blood, and there was probably a trail of blood drops behind me. My only hope was that it would be drawn toward the bloodbath on the second floor.

I sat down near the door and closed my eyes. There was no point in staying alert - if anything, I had to make sure I'd make as few sounds as possible. The sounds were starting to get quiet.

The last thing I heard was its footsteps as it entered the stairwell and sniffed the air.

\*\*\*

The first thing I saw when I woke up was Natasha's eyes. I spent a good minute looking into them, seeing tiny wrinkles in their corners form when she smiled at me with relief, before looking around.

I was back in my apartment. It seemed that someone had found me, after all, and dragged me there. The clothes were gone: I was wearing nothing but my underwear, and my midriff was covered in bandages, with a brown spot of dried, soaked up blood on the left. I poked it with my finger and hissed from pain: the wound was like a tiny, irritated creature that wanted to be left alone. Natasha gently held my hand to stop me from causing myself more pain.

"Who found me?" - I asked her.

"I did" - she said. "I was worried sick about you, and when I heard gunshots I didn't know what to do. I wanted to go there, but I didn't know if I'd be a help or a hindrance. When I finally opened the door you just…lay there, right next to it."

I felt grateful to that tiny girl. How hard it must've been to pick me up and carry wounded me all the way up to the third floor! How scared she must've been of something from behind her catching up to us…And yet she had done it. She went in there alone and when she found me like that she didn't abandon me.

There was something she wasn't telling me though, and I could see. A suspicion crawled up into me, rearing its ugly head - a suspicion that something horrible had happened. I didn't want to confirm it, but I knew I had to.

"And what about the rest?" - I wondered. She averted her eyes.

"Everyone else, they were…gone."

Gone. I was the last man in the militia. Everyone had died doing what I had suggested. Could I predict that the creature would show up? Could anyone else see it coming? Was I supposed to shoulder all of that guilt alone?

I was too weak to think about that.

"Did…Did Nikita do this?" - I wasn't looking at her, but I knew what she was referring to. My wound.

"No" - I said. "Although we did have a confrontation. He…I don't know how he is right now" - I told her. It was hard to admit to her that he and I had a fight, that I hit her ex-boyfriend with my hatchet a dozen times, even if in self-defense. Even if he was behind all of this.

"Is he...?" - she didn't finish the sentence, but I knew what she wanted to ask.

"I don't know" - I told her. It was the truth: any other creature would have succumbed to those injuries immediately, yet he remained alive even after that.

"So this..." - I lifted the blanket and looked at the bandages again. "This is your job?"

She nodded: "You got lucky. The wound looked deep, but the bullet just grazed your skin. Came out almost as soon as it went in. You've lost some blood, and you'll have a nasty scar, but apart from that no serious damage."

"And the gas torch?" - I asked quickly. That thing was the reason for our yesterday's trip. If it had been lost, then...

Natasha smiled and nodded at the pile of my clothes lying in the corner: "it's there, don't worry about it. I grabbed it as well. Once you'll get better, we'll be able to finally get out of here."

"No" - I wheezed, trying to get up. The pain in my stomach, which before that moment was dull, suddenly exploded as the muscles started to agitate the wound. It felt like it was full of ants and almost made me collapse back onto the bed, but I ignored it. "We need to get going now. We don't have much time. There's something outside, something traveling through the forest." I got up from the bed and carefully walked over to the curtained window - Natasha must've closed them to keep the sun out and let me get more sleep, but I could see that it was at least past noon. How long was I out?

"It's going to be here any moment now" - I warned her and swung the curtains open. The next moment I backed away from the window, feeling like lying down again.

It was already there. Right beneath my windows. The strange black-and-purple vines, the same color that gave the infected people's skin such an unhealthy tone. The same color as the strange growths on Nikita's flesh. Thin and weak, barely having the strength to hold on to the walls, they were getting thicker and more numerous the closer they were to the ground, where they connected to an impressive network of roots covering the ground. The thickest of the roots lay in the thin shade of trees, which had prematurely shed their leaves.

All the way to the horizon the forest was dead. It had transformed into a sea of dead grasping fingers, desperately reaching for the grey sky in a silent and pointless prayer for the sun. The strange unearthly plant had sucked it dry of its life force as it was rolling through that once yellow ocean of wood and now finally washed up onto my shore.

I knew exactly what I was looking at. The King in Rags had finally made his appearance.

I looked at the smallest of the vines which tried to grab onto my window frame. It had a tiny bud on it, the size of a single rice grain. It seemed that while everything else was getting ready for a winter slumber the King in Rags, in defiance to the local customs, was just getting ready to bloom.

I remembered the voices in my head from when I was fighting Nikita, his ominous warning, and the pain in my gut subsided, washed away by adrenaline and determination.

"We have to get out immediately" - I told Natasha and headed for the closet. "Go gather your things."

"Yura, you can't go through the sewers in such a state" - she protested. "You're too weak, and it's dirty down there. I cleaned your wound, but if you expose it to things down there you might get infected."

I stopped in my tracks: she was right. I was not scared of a common bacteria that dwelled down there though: even though it would be unpleasant, my body would know how to deal with them. I was more concerned with other things that could be in the water, and my wound was currently like a small mouth.

"I'll wrap it in packaging film" - I said, going to the kitchen. I intended to wrap myself like a cooked chicken.

"Yura, you need to rest!" - Natasha insisted. I turned around to face her and it took all of my willpower not to wince when the wound protested again: I didn't want her to see me weak.

"That thing that possessed Nikita and the others is already here" - I pointed at the window. "He warned me about it yesterday. Said it was coming, and that it was in the air."

"It doesn't matter what he said - he could be lying!" - Natasha exclaimed. "What, are you going to believe him now?" - she asked me with sudden hostility in her voice.

"I felt it myself yesterday, when I confronted him" - I told her. "He's not lying. We're all already infected with this thing, it's just a matter of time before those like him will be able to control us like puppets," - I said. She wanted to object but I stopped her with a gesture: "I know what you want to say, but my decision is final. You've saved me yesterday - now let me save you."

"You're still too weak" - she protested quietly. I came closer and hugged her. "I'm strong enough" - I comforted her. "Let's just get out of here. Let's leave this place like we've always wanted to. Alright?"

She pursed her lips and wiped her eyes, and then nodded. She wanted to leave, I knew that. The only thing that was stopping her was a concern for my health, and I simply couldn't such a petty reason get in the way of her safety. I needed to stay strong for both of us. I needed to call that shot.

Smiling, I kissed her on the forehead.

"Then it's settled. Go grab your things."

\*\*\*

It took us a few minutes to gather our things: we were taking only the most important things, like warm clothes, money to use wherever we'd end up after getting out, some papers and documents - just in case. We doubted that in the eyes of the state we even qualified as humans anymore - we were just the witnesses of their colossal mess, and they wouldn't want us around. But they could be of some use if we were asked to be identified by someone who wasn't aware of our status as fugitives.

I did my best to wrap my wound in the protective film - the one used to preserve food from spoiling. At that moment, the only thing that could go bad, the only piece of meat in the apartment was me, so in a way, it still served its purpose. It looked ridiculous and I felt hot underneath it, but it would do the trick.

The pain didn't subside, and every time I made a careless move I wanted to scream from pain. I didn't have any painkillers, but when Natasha came from upstairs, all set to go, she brought me a bottle of vodka - the oldest painkiller in the world. It was dangerous to go outside while drunk - I needed my thoughts to be clear and sober, but one sip wouldn't hurt.

We had almost no food, and we had only one thermos for the two of us to fill with drinking water - the water out there in the forest wasn't of good quality even during the best of days. Now it was probably swarming with millions of microforms waiting to possess us. But we decided that if we used it sparingly we'd manage to reach some town before dying of thirst.

The last things we took were the gas torch and the map that Alexei had drawn - the most vital for our escape things. We spent a few minutes trying to memorize the map before setting out - if it became soaked in the sewers or we lost it we needed to be sure we'd be able to find our way out regardless.

After that, we set out.

A few tenants were outside of their apartments

"Listen everyone!" - I shouted to them. "We've found the way out of here. In the basement, there's a manhole that leads to the sewers. Through there, we can reach the outskirts of the town where we'll be in safety and we'll able to leave. It's dangerous to stay here any longer - those vines outside are the reason why some of the people have been going crazy and attacking others. Go grab the bare essentials and let's leave - we'll show you the way!"

Throughout my speech, I could see that no one was buying it. I could see the faces of scorn and doubt and disbelief - something about me was making me an unreliable narrator in their eyes, and they dismissed everything I was saying without even bothering to think to it.

"Do you know what this is about, Masha?"

"It's that crazy one, the one that's been restless since day one. Must've finally lost it."

"Where do you think you're going looking like that? You're pale as a moon!"

"It must be because he's been drinking non-stop! He smells of vodka right now."

I could hear their murmuring, but I didn't pay it any attention. It didn't matter what they thought of me. What mattered was that I led them out to safety. That I finally complete the mission of our militia, of which I was the sole remaining member.

"Come on! Every minute counts" - I tried to hurry them up, but I didn't sound too confident. I still felt weak from my wounds, and the old habit of putting other's opinion above my own was resurfacing, sabotaging me. And the others picked up on my lack of confidence: to them, it wasn't about getting to the truth, it was about being right above all else.

"Sit your ass down, you crazy drunkard!" - one man shouted at me. "No one's going anywhere, and neither are you. Personally, I saw what happens to those who go outside. We are fine as we are."

"We need to leave now! I'm telling you, if we stay here, we're all going to go crazy" - I told him again. Couldn't they see that? Couldn't they just look out the window to see that those things outside were already starting to grow on the walls?

"A kettle calling the pot black" - someone said sarcastically. "You were told to stay put, kiddo. The military will come and save everyone, so stop playing the hero."

"The youth are always like that" - someone else commented. "They've all got an awl up their asses[17] and they think they know best."

"But you have to just look out the window to see that it's right there! It's sucked all the life out of the forest and if we don't move we're next!" - I shouted with desperation. Natasha came closer and put her hand on my shoulder. I knew what she wanted to say, but I couldn't just accept it. I couldn't just stand there and watch those people throw their lives away. I had to do something. I had been risking my life trying to find the way out for everyone, I had joined the militia, and so many men had died trying to protect them. Pavel, Maxim, Alexei…I couldn't allow their sacrifices to be in vain.

"It's called autumn, boy. Have you not learned it in school?"

"If it's so dangerous out there, why would we go there now?"

"Crawl through the filth on your own, brat."

"Stop with this foolishness, boy!" - a woman stepped forward. I recognized her: she was the one who had suspected me of being the one who had welded us all shut within the building on day one. "I see what's going on! The rest of your crazy pals have kicked the dust because they were sticking their necks out, and now you think you're the one in charge because you're the only one left?"

---

[17] A Russian expression, meant to describe someone restless and agitated.

"Those people were sticking their necks out to protect you" - I said in a low voice, feeling that I was reaching my breaking point. "Don't talk about them like that. They were heroes."

"Yeah? Lot of good their heroics did, didn't it?" - she asked me sarcastically.

"Screw you!" - I shouted at her and everyone behind her. Seeing my reaction, she let out a satisfied smirk - to her, it was just another confirmation that I was an immature prick she thought I was.

I couldn't stay calm: the alcohol was not helping, and when I shouted the wound exploded with pain again, making me lose my cool. I wanted to start smashing their faces, to just wave my fists around like windmills, hoping they would hit someone. "Screw all of you, you rotten lot! I was risking my life for you, all of us were, and you people aren't even worth saving!"

"Look at him - what a hero! What do you want, a medal?" - someone shouted from the back of the crowd. For a moment I wanted to look him in the eye, call him out, ask him what he'd done in those past few days for the good of everyone…But I couldn't find him in the crowd. All I could see was scornful, hateful faces of people who didn't like to be lectured.

"I'm leaving" - I said with sudden calmness. The faceless commenter, whoever he was, was actually right. Why even waste my breath for them? What did I expect from them - an admiration? A pat on the back?

My mother suddenly stepping through the crowd and telling me what a good boy I was?

I turned around and smiled at Natasha. She smiled back at me.

"Good riddance!" - the crowd wouldn't calm down, shouting at my back.

"Where do you think you're going, you dolt? Do you think you're smarter than anyone else? Sit tight and wait for a rescue!"

"Let him go. More food for us."

"Hey, that's right. Hey, you! Hero! What apartment are you from?"

I didn't answer. It was up to them to figure that out.

"If any of you change your mind - just follow us. Just go through the sewers, we'll be leaving waypoints for you" - Natasha told them. Such a hopeless bleeding heart, she was!

"Go, go already. Patronizing bitch. Kids these days..." - someone snapped at her. She pursed her lips, swallowed the insult, and followed me.

No one tried to stop us. No one talked to us. People were giving us the mean eye, but no one tried to start an argument anymore.

We descended to the basement and approached the manhole. I tried to lift it, but the moment I pulled it the wound in my gut protested and made me let go of the manhole, almost pinning my fingers underneath it. Natasha came to my rescue, and together, we finally managed to pull it aside.

"Are you ready?" - I asked her. "We're finally leaving. We're finally going outside" - I told her, trying to cheer her up. The words of my mother turned out to be prophetic: no one waited for us there, there was nothing but terror and misery…and yet I was smiling. I had always imagined leaving the town in some other manner - I expected it to be a moment of triumph, imagined that my mother would be there to shed tears at how much I'd grown, imagined people waving at me and wishing me good luck. Instead, I was escaping it through the sewers like a rat, with no approval from the rest of the people and only curses being uttered under their breath.

And yet, I was smiling. Even if it wasn't what I had imagined, I was leaving that place all the same. On my own accord. And somehow, the disapproval of my mother's peers was only making my decision more valuable to me, because I was sure that it was my own.

Natasha threw one final glance in the direction of the entrance to the basement, as if expecting someone to change their mind and follow us, and then smiled at me, too.

"Yes. Let's go."

The End.

Printed in Great Britain
by Amazon